THE BRIDGE TENDER

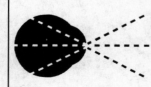

This Large Print Book carries the
Seal of Approval of N.A.V.H.

A SUNSET BEACH NOVEL

THE BRIDGE TENDER

MARYBETH WHALEN

THORNDIKE PRESS
A part of Gale, Cengage Learning

GALE
CENGAGE Learning·

Farmington Hills, Mich • San Francisco • New York • Waterville, Maine
Meriden, Conn • Mason, Ohio • Chicago

GALE
CENGAGE Learning

LIBRARY OF CONGRESS CATALOGING-IN-PUBLICATION DATA

Whalen, Marybeth.
    The bridge tender : a Sunset Beach novel / by Marybeth Whalen. — Large print edition.
        pages ; cm. — (Thorndike Press large print clean reads)
    ISBN 978-1-4104-7188-8 (hardcover) — ISBN 1-4104-7188-8 (hardcover)
    1. Large type books. I. Title.
PS3623.H355B85 2014b
813'.6—dc23   2014019934

Published in 2014 by arrangement with The Zondervan Corporation LLC

Let's be the runners in the mercy rain
Be my bridge when I fear to cross
PETER MURPHY, "MERCY RAIN"

The Sunset Beach Pontoon Swing Bridge was unique too in that it was a pontoon barge with a house on top, called the Tender House. The wooden road built over the pontoons rose and fell with the tide. When the tide was high, cars traveled over a slight incline in the middle of the bridge; when the tide was low, there was a small valley in the middle. All the while, the bridge Tender maintained a watchful eye from the little white house.

— "THE HISTORY OF SUNSET BEACH"
HTTP://WWW.SUNSETBEACHNC.GOV

PROLOGUE

July 19, 2001
Emily Shaw stood on the beach and watched as her husband emerged from the ocean, water beading on his newly tanned skin. He shook his head like a dog, sending droplets in all directions. She smiled at the word. *Husband.* To say the word felt like wearing a sequin cocktail dress when she was used to wearing jeans. The whole scenario didn't quite fit — but she wanted it to. She had longed to be this man's wife, to refer to him as her husband. And as of three days ago, it was official.

The thought sent little zings of excitement up her spine each time she realized it anew. From the moment the church doors opened and she saw him see her in that white dress to this moment, the reality kept lapping at her heart and mind like the waves on the shore of Sunset Beach. *This is my husband. I am his wife.* Even with the warm rays of the

9

sun beaming down on them, Emily shivered, giddy. As Ryan approached, she reached her hand up to take his and pull him toward her spot on the huge multicolored beach towel someone had given them as a wedding present. He laughed when he nearly lost his footing, awkwardly falling beside her and narrowly missing kneeing her in the stomach. He kissed her, and when he did, she tasted the salt of the waves, smelled the scent of his sun-warmed skin. This, she thought, is what happiness feels like.

She tried not to think that their time at Sunset Beach would end in just two days. A five-day honeymoon had seemed like such an extravagant gift when one of her father's church members had offered it to them. Five glorious days in an oceanfront home, time unspooling in front of them like a satin highway. But satin was slippery and the bright ribbon was coming to an end. At least their marriage would go beyond this short week. She tried to focus on how much fun it would be to set up their new apartment, cook Ryan dinner while he studied, maybe get a puppy. Their apartment back in Rockingham wasn't an oceanfront beach home, but it was theirs. She laced her fingers through Ryan's and sighed contentedly as she noticed the position of the sun, sliding down in the sky. Another day was ending.

Reading her thoughts as he often did, Ryan spoke up. "Got any ideas for dinner?"

She giggled. "We already sound like an old married couple."

"I was thinking maybe we cook at the house tonight? Make some pasta? Find some old movie on TV? I saw on the guide that there's that one you said you loved when you were a teenager. I've never seen it so maybe you could introduce me to it?"

She smirked at him. "Are you sure you can handle *Just This Once*? It's a total chick flick." She gave him a coy look. "And besides, I'll have you know I had a serious crush on the lead character." She sighed dramatically for effect. "Ah, Brady Rutledge, what a hottie."

He reached over and tickled her. "I'm secure enough in my masculinity to watch a chick flick. And as for this Brady Rutledge guy, he's no match for me." He paused and eyed her. "Right?"

She laughed. "No match at all." She leaned against him and a quiet moment passed between them, filled with contentment. She watched the waves move closer and closer as the tide moved in, but she made no move to pack up, not wanting another day at the beach to be over.

11

Ryan broke the silence. "I just love hanging out with you, watching TV, taking walks, cooking dinner together. I know we could be doing other stuff, but I'm just as happy being at home, alone, with you."

"Now you're really making us sound like an old married couple!"

She didn't say what else she was thinking about Ryan's suggestion of cooking at the beach house instead of going out. Though he acted like he just wanted to take it easy, Emily knew that money was tight, and eating out wasn't the smart thing to do. With Ryan in law school and them living off her salary as a new teacher, even getting to go on a honeymoon was a miracle, and to Ryan's favorite place in the world, no less. He had been delighted when he discovered that the house they had been offered was at Sunset Beach, the destination of many family vacations in his childhood. He had settled right back into the place the moment they crossed the old pontoon bridge, and she had followed suit. Now she gazed at him with a mixture of admiration and pure bliss on her face — a goofy grin, her best friend Marta called it — knowing that this man would always make good decisions, would always take care of her. He was smart and methodical but he was also romantic and gorgeous. He was right: Brady Rutledge had nothing on him.

Emily wondered how she'd ever gotten so lucky. Blessed, her mother had said on their wedding day, her voice barely more than a whisper as they waited for the ceremony to begin. Three days later, sitting beside her new husband, discussing making pasta and watching old movies, Emily did indeed feel blessed. Short honeymoon in a freebie house with no money to eat out or not, she had hit the jackpot and she knew it. She leaned over and gave Ryan another kiss. "All I ever want to be is an old married couple," she whispered, her voice nearly drowned out by the roar of the waves, the shriek of the seagulls, and the pounding of her own heart.

After dinner they left the dishes and went for a walk around the island they had come to love together. As they walked he shared stories from past vacations, laughing as he recalled family memories associated with the place. There was a magic about this beach, she agreed, a sense that time suspended when you crossed the old swing bridge. Life seemed slower at Sunset, people seemed friendlier, more carefree — and the feeling was contagious. Each evening Emily and Ryan had meandered up and down the numbered streets and around the perimeter of the island, dreaming of their future and scheming about how they could someday afford to buy a house of their own at Sunset.

That evening they ventured down to the opposite end of the island from where they were staying. They'd heard from a shopkeeper that there was a house there that now sat in the ocean due to the erosion of the beach. Ryan had suggested they check it out. Sure enough they found the house, its foundation sinking into the sand as the waves lapped at its edges like a child's abandoned sandcastle.

"We'll be lucky if we can afford this house," she quipped.

He crossed his arms, studying the house for a moment longer before answering. "I've been thinking we could start saving once I'm practicing." He eyed her. "Even if it's just a little bit each month. It'll add up."

She shook her head. "We have to pay off your school loans first. No arguments."

He grinned. "Now how did I know you were going to say that?"

"Someone has to have some discipline around here," she teased. She would change nothing about her husband, except maybe his haphazard approach to life. It went

14

against everything in her to leave the dishes behind in the sink, to ignore the wet beach towels on the floor where he dropped them, to not sweep up the sand they tracked in. It was a wonder the guy made it through law school, and yet when it came to his studies, he was laser focused.

He reached for her, pulled her close, and kissed her as the sea swirled at their ankles, their flip-flops left behind on the sand so they could get closer to the shore. She forgot about the mess back at the house. Looking deep into her eyes, with that look she had come to know meant all kidding aside, he spoke. "I want to give you a house here. A house we can come to all the time, bring our kids to. A place to make our own family memories. I promise you I'm going to give you that someday — college loans or not. It's important to me. I see how happy this place has made you. You should always have access to that."

Her mind searched for a response but there were no words. That word again — *blessed* — darted through her mind like the little minnows darting around their feet. She was even more blessed than she'd realized three days ago standing at the altar making promises about loving for a lifetime. This man was God's gift to her — but this

15

gift was one she'd keep unwrapping for many years to come. Already she was starting to understand this about marriage.

"So what do you say? Should we make that our goal? To own a place here, where our lives together started?"

Emily looked into Ryan's eyes and nodded as tears slipped from her own eyes. "Absolutely."

"No matter how we have to do it? The sacrifices we have to make?" She could see the excitement on his face and found herself getting excited at the prospect too.

"Yes!" He held up his hand and she gave him a high five to seal the deal, then he entwined his fingers with hers and pulled her close again. "Don't forget, you made a promise and I'm going to hold you to it." He winked and started leading her away from the house in the ocean, back to the beach house they were calling home for a few more blissful days. Though she would be sad to leave, she would do so with the hope of returning many, many times in the future. She cast one last backward glance at the house in the ocean, hoping that it didn't let the waves pull it all the way out to sea.

ONE

March 3, 2006

Emily Shaw stood in front of her open closet, her eyes drawn to the black dress hanging there as if someone was shining a spotlight on it. She remembered buying the dress — a wardrobe basic, some fashion article had called it. Every woman needs a basic black dress, she had read, and, being a rule follower, she'd gone out and purchased one almost immediately. But she'd never worn it, preferring to wear colors like red and pink, yellow and blue. Happy colors, she'd always thought. Colors that made people happy to see her. Colors that made her feel happy when she wore them.

But Emily wasn't happy. Not anymore. Might as well dress the part.

She reached for the black dress, tugging it free from the hanger. She held it up to determine whether she could still wear it. She'd lost so much weight in the past weeks

17

as Ryan started to slip away. Her appetite had gone the way of his fight. She pulled the dress over her head and walked over to stand in front of the full-length mirror in their bedroom. When would she stop thinking of it as their bedroom? Now it was her bedroom, hers alone. The bed was made. There was no laundry left on the floor, no folded piles waiting to be put away. There wasn't a collection of discarded, half-drunk coffee cups and soda cans littering the surfaces. She didn't have a thing to clean up, and she missed it. *It's finally clean, Ryan,* she thought.

She looked at herself in the mirror, took in the image of the stranger reflected there. Her hair, once cut in a cute style, had grown ragged in the months after Ryan's diagnosis. The highlights she'd splurged on had grown out, revealing long dark streaks on the crown of her head. She was so thin her head looked too large for her neck. Her eyes no longer held a spark but blinked back at her dully. And the once-flattering black dress looked exactly like a sackcloth on her. She would be a sight at her husband's funeral. And she couldn't care less.

She imagined what her mother would say, the way her mouth would form that grim little line of disapproval even as she bit back her critique of her only daughter. Her mother was the quintessential preacher's wife — used to living in a fishbowl and prone to caring what "the people" thought of them. It just wouldn't do for Emily to have anything less than a positive attitude, a smile on her face, some roses in her cheeks as she bravely faced the untimely death of her young husband. What would the people think? If her mother had her way, Emily would address the mourners today wearing vibrant red or brilliant blue, share an inspiring message of hope for a bright future. She'd quote some pithy verses and rally everyone with talk of God drawing near even in the valley of the shadow of death.

But God, as far as she could tell, was nowhere around.

She turned away from the mirror and went to put her hair in a ponytail instead of styling it. She should probably have washed it but the truth was, she just didn't care how she looked. She had actually considered not attending the funeral; let her parents and Ryan's explain to "the people" that she was just too grief-stricken to drag herself out of bed. The ones who counted would understand. The rest she didn't care about anyway. But a cooler head had prevailed and she'd relented when she looked out the window by her bed that morning and was greeted with a weeping sky. It was as if the world was telling her it was okay to be sad. She'd promised herself she would go and pay tribute to Ryan, but she would not look happy about it when she did. Hence the black dress, the lack of makeup, the unwashed hair.

Marta arrived to drive her to the funeral a few minutes early — more evidence that all was not right with the world. Her best friend had never been early for anything in her life. She frowned when Emily entered the kitchen where Marta was helping herself to the coffee Emily had made but not drunk.

Marta shook her head and blew on the hot coffee. She took a few sips as Emily shifted nervously from foot to foot, watching her. Between sips she saw Marta take in the too-big dress, the way the fabric billowed around her body. She gestured at the dress. "That new?"

Emily narrowed her eyes. "As if," she responded.

Marta ignored her unfunny retort. "When this is over I think you should get rid of it. It doesn't do much for you."

Emily shrugged and looked at the microwave clock.

"You should want to pay your respects,"

her mother had said yesterday when she'd admitted she was seriously considering not going. "This is your time to honor Ryan." Her mother used guilt to guide her like ranchers used cattle prods. Walking out with Marta, she caught her unsightly reflection in the stainless steel oven door. Her mother's guilt maneuver had worked yet again. Maybe she would take one look at her daughter and regret using it. As sad as she was, the thought made Emily smile just the tiniest little bit.

Following the service, her parents opened the church gymnasium for a reception. All the old ladies from the church had made food, plates lining several long tables filled with every kind of food imaginable — fried chicken and deviled eggs, tea sandwiches and ham biscuits. Another table held pies of all kinds — fried pies and apple pie and blueberry pie and a chocolate meringue piled high with a fluffy white topping. Emily surveyed the food as if it were a foreign substance she'd heard of but had no need for. She felt like an alien among earthlings, watching them take part in this ritual known as eating. She was surprised her stomach rumbled in response to Marta's filled plate, the smell of the fried chicken causing this one body part to betray the rest of her. Marta held up the plate. "You sure I can't get you something?" she asked.

Marta's overly attentive attitude was yet another indication that things weren't right. Not that her best friend wasn't kind and helpful sometimes, it just wasn't that often. She looked around them at the collection of men — Ryan's friends from college and his office, many of them single. Normally Marta would've been on a hunt. Even at a funeral. But she seemed not to notice any of them, her eyes focused and intent on her best friend, eyeing her as if she were an armed bomb missing her timer.

"You should eat," Marta intoned, waving the plate under her nose.

Emily nearly remarked that she sounded like her mother, but held her tongue. Marta would take that as an insult when she only meant it as an observation. She just shook her head and ignored the smell of the chicken, her hand resting on her concave stomach to stop the rumbling. She couldn't eat at Ryan's funeral. It just didn't seem right. There were ways to mourn properly, and scarfing fried chicken in the presence of his friends and family wasn't one of them. "Maybe one of the ladies will make me a plate," she mumbled. "For later."

Marta, who was attacking her chicken, stopped midchew. "Great idea! I'll go ask." Obviously relieved to have something to do, she trotted off to find Mrs. Miniver, the grande dame of food at Christ Community Church.

Emily stood still and surveyed the room, grateful for this first moment alone. Her mother and father were occupied with other people and Ryan's parents had ducked out shortly after the reception got underway. Emily had nearly asked to go with them but had taken one look at Mrs. Shaw's face and known that the woman needed to be alone to grieve her son apart from the onlookers. At the very least, Emily understood that. She'd given her in-laws one last hug and watched them go, wondering if they were still her in-laws if their son was dead.

"Excuse me, Emily?" The voice at her elbow startled her and brought her back to the crowded church gymnasium filled with the smell of grandma's cooking. She turned to find a face she recognized but couldn't place, which had happened often that day.

"Yes?" she asked.

"I'm Phil, Phil Griffin?" He watched her face for some sign of recognition and, seeing none, continued. "I worked with Ryan, but not in the same department. I handled

—" His voice faltered. "I handle wills and, um, things of that nature." He finished, straightening his posture and exhaling loudly. "Did Ryan ever mention me?"

She searched the recesses of her mind, thinking back through the months after his diagnosis, the decision not to prolong his life with treatment, the stunning reality that cancer would take his life quickly, and their valiant efforts to enjoy every last minute they'd had together. They'd talked through so much — the gift of time, her father had called it in his eloquent service that day — but had the name Phil Griffin from his office ever come up? No. She shook her head at Phil. "I'm sorry but that doesn't ring a bell."

Phil held up his hands. He wasn't eating either. " 'S'okay. I didn't think he would. Ryan . . ." She was startled to watch the man's eyes fill with tears. He swallowed hard and continued speaking. "Ryan loved you very much. He made me promise I'd wait 'til . . . after to divulge anything to you. He made some plans a long time ago, plans that affect you now." He looked away, scanning the room before looking back at her. "I came today to pay my respects but also to find you and set up a time to have you come to my office. Would you be willing to do that?"

Intrigued, she nodded as the rest of the room fell away — gone was the idle chatter of the collected mourners, the smell of food. All that mattered was this stranger who promised to tell her something she'd not known about her husband. "How soon could we do it?" she asked, waving Marta over so she could introduce her to Phil. She would beg Marta to take her to his office immediately, to this last piece of Ryan she hadn't known existed, whatever it was. Suddenly, even though she was at his funeral, he felt close again. She found herself wanting to wrap her arms around this feeling and hold it forever. But she knew the more she tried to hold on, the more it would slip away.

Two

It didn't take much cajoling to get Marta to bug out of the reception but she elected to wait in the car, furiously tapping at her phone, while Emily followed Phil into his office, her heart hammering away in her chest for reasons she couldn't explain. No matter what this man had to tell her, nothing was going to change. Ryan was still going to be dead, left behind in that cold grave they'd stood beside hours earlier while her father called out the Lord's Prayer and everyone mumbled along. Whatever he'd left for her wasn't powerful enough to bring him back, of that she was sure. And beyond that, what did it matter? She took a deep breath and did her best to compose herself. Phil gestured for her to have a seat across from his desk, first moving some file folders out of the chair so she could do so. He smiled nervously at her before reaching into a drawer and thumbing through more files.

"Sorry I'm not more prepared," he said as he searched. "I had no idea you'd want to come down today."

She shrugged as if she'd come out of convenience and not curiosity, but she knew she was fooling no one. She kept quiet so he could keep looking for the papers he'd promised at the funeral. His desk looked a lot like Ryan's, with piles of papers sloping dangerously. They'd been kindred spirits, she imagined. That was probably why Ryan had chosen him. Two messies in the midst of a sea of buttoned-down type As had found each other. She heard Phil mutter to himself when he found the right one, extracting it with a flourish. "Terribly unprofessional," he said. "My apologies." *There's a method to my madness,* she could hear Ryan tease. She ignored him and focused on Phil.

Without waiting for her to reply, he opened the file he'd placed on the desk. She could see the name "SHAW, R" marked in black ink across the top. He read silently for a moment, then looked up at her, blinking as if he'd just stepped into the light from a dark cave. "How to say this?" he sighed. "I don't usually handle this part, you understand." He waited for her to nod even though she didn't understand anything.

"But because of Ryan's and my professional connection I agreed to do so." He cleared his throat. "For him." His mouth turned up ever so slightly at the corners. She guessed that he was remembering something Ryan had said. "He could be quite . . . persuasive."

She nodded again, willing herself not to cry, even as a memory emerged from the recesses of her brain. Ryan, goading her to strap on their old inline skates and race each other. He'd won, of course, and she'd ended up with a skinned elbow. She'd called him a ringer. He'd broken into a very bad rendition of Abba's "The Winner Takes It All," singing the part about the loser taking a fall especially loud. He'd made it up to her with a big scoop of ice cream on their way home. Now she bit the inside of her cheek and tried to focus on Phil instead, who slid a stack of stapled papers across the desk to her.

"Did you know about the life insurance policy your husband took out early in your marriage?"

She narrowed her eyes at him, thinking through the things like this they'd discussed before he died. She took a guess. "He had one through work? It'll cover his funeral costs and medical bills and leave me a little bit of money?" Somehow she didn't think that was what he was referring to. She was holding her purse in her lap and realized she was squeezing the straps tightly, the leather edges biting into her skin. She made herself loosen her grip.

"Right. I knew about that one. But I helped him with the legalities of another one. One he told me was to be kept secret until the time of his death. I was just making sure he didn't decide to tell you himself at —" His voice cracked. "At the end."

"Tell me himself about what?" Her fingers tightened on the purse again. She twisted the leather around once, twice, until it was nearly cutting off her circulation. What was this guy talking about?

He gestured at the papers in front of her. "He took out a half-a-million-dollar policy on himself and you're the beneficiary." He caught her eye and gave her a small smile. "But he had a condition on what the payout could be used for. He was very specific." From the file in front of him he extracted a photo and slid that across the desk to her. She could've sworn he was blushing as she took it from him.

She looked down at the photo from five years ago, taken by a random woman they'd flagged down and asked to snap the picture.

They'd been walking back from that house in the ocean, holding hands and feeling giddy over the prospect of having their own home at Sunset Beach someday. She studied the two of them as if they were two people she didn't know — a nice young couple with sun-kissed skin and big goofy grins on their faces. They were so unaware of the future she wanted to reach into the picture and shake them. Didn't they know that happiness like that never hung around for long?

She remembered Ryan's promise to her that evening and awareness began to creep in. He had taken that promise seriously. She raised her eyes to meet Phil's, her look telling him she'd figured it out. He nodded and slid an envelope with her name written on it in familiar handwriting. "He explains everything in here." He pointed at the stapled papers. "That's just all the legal mumbo-jumbo. You can look it all over and then let me know how — and when — you'd like to proceed." He chuckled, already visibly lighter now that he'd delivered the news. The poor man had obviously been dreading this part of his job. Used to hiding behind the legal documents, this case had involved getting his hands emotionally dirty. He probably wished he'd never agreed to it, but someone had to keep Ryan's secret for him. Phil rose from his desk. "I'll just be right outside so you can have a moment to read that." He reached over to a box of tissues sitting on a credenza nearby and, without aplomb, handed her a few. She hadn't realized she was crying.

After Phil was gone, she slid her thumb into a small crack in the sealed envelope and tugged it open, trying not to dwell on her name in Ryan's handwriting, trying not to anticipate what he had written to her. She pulled the sheet of folded paper from inside the envelope, smelling his scent on the paper as she did, thinking of his hands smoothing out the folds she was now opening. When he wrote this, he'd done it knowing that the end was near and — even then — thinking of her. She swallowed hard and focused on the words swimming before her eyes, blinking so she could see again. She saw her name at the top and rested her forehead against the page as she gave up and let the tears fall freely. Grief grabbed her by the chest as it had done so many times recently, squeezing the very life out of her as she fought to take in air.

After fighting to gain control for a few minutes, she was finally able to continue reading. She knew Phil was just outside the door, waiting for her to give him the all-clear sign. She should've just taken the letter home and read it there, alone. But she didn't want to wait. She looked down at the words before her, written in the same handwriting that had appeared on grocery lists, notes promising he would return, to-do lists, and the occasional love letter through the years. If she had known she'd lose him so soon she might've saved every one.

With a sigh she began to read her husband's last, unexpected words to her.

Dear Em,

If you're reading this then you know I didn't win this particular fight. And you know how much it kills me to lose. (Pun intended.) But I couldn't go without leaving something behind for you, something you could hold on to even if I wasn't around anymore.

The funny thing is, I started this plan long before I knew I was sick. When we got home from our honeymoon, I took out a life insurance policy with a half-million-dollar payout. Some months it was hard to make that payment without you knowing about it. But I found creative ways to come up with the money that didn't involve dancing in front of screaming women. One month, I will confess, I borrowed the money from my parents, even though we said we'd never do that. Sorry. But hopefully you'll forgive me once you know why.

Remember when we walked out to that house that was sinking into the ocean? It was one of our last days at Sunset Beach and I didn't want our time there to end. Neither did you. All I could think as we walked back to the beach house was that I wanted to give you a place of your own there. I knew that eventually together we'd make it happen, but if something happened to me it never would. And so I did the one thing I could think of doing — I took out that policy. If it was the last thing I did, I would give you a house at Sunset Beach.

And now it looks like it will literally be the last thing I do.

Em, I know you're sad right now. And I know that the thought of going back there and buying a house without me makes you feel like your heart will break even more. I know that because that is how I would feel if it were me. But I need you to promise me that you will do it when you're ready. You will go back there and find a beautiful house at the beach to make a life in, to make new memories, to remember me but to also move forward. You have a whole life still ahead of you and I can't go knowing that your life will be miserable. I have to believe that you have a hope and a future like that plaque my parents gave us for our wedding gift says. And when I think of you without me, I see you at Sunset, walking on the beach. Walking into your future. And when I see you, you are smiling. And you are full of hope.

If I could stay with you, I would. If it could be me walking beside you on that beach, it would be. But I'm starting to understand that was never the plan, for whatever reason. You are supposed to go into a future I'm not a part of. But you don't have to be afraid of that future. I have a feeling it's going to be as bright as that sunshine we walked in, as warm as those days we spent on the beach together, as happy as you've made me. I need you to promise me you'll take this gift and go into the future God has planned for you. I like to think I'll be watching from another shore.

All my love, always, Ryan

Marta put down the letter and stared, open-mouthed, at Emily. "Wow," she said, running a hand through her hair. "Wow," she repeated. She dabbed at her eyes with the cuff of her long-sleeve T-shirt and sniffed loudly.

This was the biggest show of emotion Emily had witnessed from Marta since Ryan's diagnosis. She knew her friend had cried privately but she'd been stoically strong around Emily. She loved her for putting on a brave face on her behalf. Marta had been her rock, intuitively knowing what Emily would need to get through this time. But in that moment tears were unavoidable. This last gesture of Ryan's was so surprising, so selfless, so amazing the only thing anyone could do was cry in response. Marta had summed it up best with her word choice: wow.

Emily plucked the letter from Marta's lap and folded it up, carefully smoothing the folds as she imagined Ryan had once done, feeling connected to him as she did. She looked around the room, wondering if somehow he could see all this — if people in heaven witnessed the ripple effects of their time on earth. Though she couldn't make a case for it biblically, she hoped so. She hoped God had called Ryan over to some special window and let him have a look. The thought made her smile.

Mistaking the reason for her smile, Marta launched into the questions Emily knew were coming. When would she go house hunting at Sunset Beach? Did Emily want her to come too? Did she have any idea what she was looking for? When would the funds be available? Did she want to get out a calendar and look at some dates? Emily put up her hand.

"Please, I can't talk about this yet. It's . . . a lot. To take in." She held up the letter. "You read what he wrote. It's more than that, what he's asking. I can't —" She was silent as her words ran out. She looked at her friend. "I think I might just go lie down. It's been a really long day."

"Of course. I'm sure you're exhausted." Marta pointed to the letter, still gripped a little too tightly in Emily's fist. "We can deal with all that later."

Emily nodded. "Yes. Later." She hugged Marta good-bye.

"Sure you don't need me to stay? I can."

Emily waved her away. "No, it's fine. I'm just going to eat some of that vegetable soup my mom sent over and crawl into bed."

Marta brightened at the promise that Emily would eat. "Good." She poked Emily in the ribs, then turned to gather her purse and umbrella. "You need to eat, girl." Pausing in front of the oven in the kitchen, Marta studied her reflection just as Emily had done that morning. "I, on the other hand, do not need to eat." She sucked her stomach in and turned to study her side profile. Letting her stomach pooch out again, she huffed and added, "At all." She gave a little wave and was gone, the house falling silent after the door closed.

Emily put the letter on the coffee table and went into the kitchen to make good on her promise to eat. But as soon as she opened the container of soup, the smell filled the room, causing her to retch. She quickly replaced the lid and shoved the container back into the fridge. She fled the kitchen, seeking the comfort of her bed, complete with a comforter she could shimmy under and pull over her head. On the way past the coffee table, she snatched up her letter and carried it with her.

She put the letter on Ryan's pillow while she pulled off her black dress and dropped it to the floor, knowing she would never wear it again. In honor of Ryan, she left the dress right where she'd dropped it. She slipped into one of his old T-shirts, inhaling the scent of him as she turned back the covers and dove in. A memory came over her: Ryan already in bed, watching with amusement as she shivered and jumped in after him. "You are not putting those cold feet of yours on me!" he challenged, which only meant she would try harder to do so. She smiled at the memory as she reached for the letter and pulled it to her chest. She stuck her cold feet on his side of the bed, wishing harder than ever that she would encounter the warmth of him. But all that waited for her were cold sheets on the empty side where he should be.

THREE

March 2, 2007

The music was so loud that Emily didn't hear Marta enter the house, didn't realize that she was standing there watching until she turned and shrieked — partially because she was startled to find someone standing in her house and partially because she was embarrassed. With a look that was a mixture of pity and concern, Marta strode over to the stereo and snapped the music off, thrusting the house into an awkward silence that stretched between the two of them.

After a few seconds of staring, Emily turned and went into the kitchen, where she filled a glass with water. She drank it even though she wasn't particularly thirsty. That is what her life had become, a series of actions all motivated by what she *should* be doing. It had gotten her this far — to the one-year mark. One year ago tomorrow she stood dry-eyed at his grave and threw that one single red rose down into the dirt, saving her tears for when she was alone. One year ago tomorrow Ryan pulled his stunt and spoke to her from beyond the grave, getting the last word as only he could.

Pushing the thought aside, she rinsed her glass and put it into the dishwasher, then busied herself with washing the breakfast and lunch dishes she had piled into the sink earlier. Marta came into the kitchen and leaned against the wall, waiting, Emily knew, for her to speak. But what could she say? She missed her husband. She was still grieving no matter how many grief groups and counseling sessions and personal goals and all the other self-help blah-blah that people advised.

Finally Marta spoke, her voice dripping with disdain. "I hate that song, you know."

"I didn't play it for you," she said, wishing there were more dishes to wash so she wouldn't have to look at her friend. For lack of something better to do, she wet a dish-cloth and began wiping down the already clean counter. She was staying on top of her housekeeping, a feat she often congratulated herself for. When Ryan was alive she'd complained about always being the one to clean and tidy. Now she relished the activity, taking comfort in the familiar rhythm that came with scrubbing and washing, enjoying the sight that she could still create order in a world that did not make sense. At least she wasn't one of those widows who let her house fall down around her ears. Widow. The word still caught in her throat like the time she accidentally swallowed a Jolly Rancher.

Marta ignored her. "That song is just so depressing. 'A broken hallelujah'? What is that? And the way he sings it. So hopeless. That can't be good for you, listening to that over and over. Why don't you find a happy song to play? It might help you."

At Marta's unsolicited advice, Emily slapped the dishcloth down on the counter with a loud squishing noise. She spun around to face her, eye to eye. "Help me what, Marta? Help me not miss my husband?" She looked away from Marta, avoiding the concern in her eyes as she continued her tirade. "A happy song isn't going to make that happen. And let me tell you that all songs — all songs — make me think of him anyway. Happy, sad, funny, country, rock, gospel, classical — it doesn't matter. It all reminds me of Ryan."

Tears filled her eyes, which made her angrier. She stalked out of the kitchen, knowing Marta would follow her. She did. She

41

got as far as the den, where she stopped and bent over at the waist, taking deep slow breaths, something she had learned to do when she got overwhelmed, which was often. She felt Marta's hand, tentative on her back.

"I'm sorry," she heard her say.

Emily took a few more breaths before straightening up to a standing position again and facing Marta. "It's okay." She gave her a weak smile. "Sorry I blew up. I just . . ." She searched for words to explain, but quickly settled on her fallback phrase. "No one understands."

Marta turned away slightly, used to the disclaimer. "If it makes you feel better to play that depressing song, then go ahead. Play it 24/7. What do I know? I never lost the love of my life. I'd have to have had one for that to be the case."

She couldn't help but smile at Marta's reference to her nonexistent love life. Feeling insecure about a few extra pounds and still reeling after an unfortunate accident with home hair color this past year had not helped things. The two women had been quite a pair in the year since Ryan's death. Couching it with a huge tub of popcorn and a chick flick had become de rigueur on weekends. Sometimes she was thankful for

Marta and sometimes she felt guilty, knowing that in some ways she was holding her friend back. She should stop being so needy and free up Marta to go and find the great love of her life. She thought of Ryan on the beach on their honeymoon, the way the water beaded on his skin, warm from the sun. Everyone should feel that way about someone at least once. On her best days she felt blessed to have had it at all. On her worst she felt cheated, cheated, cheated that she lost it so soon.

"So," Marta changed the subject. "I stopped by to let you know I can't do a movie with you tonight. I kind of have this thing I said I'd do."

Emily raised her eyebrows, intrigued. "Do tell."

"Did you see that flyer Missy Detwiler put up at school? The one with that seminar for singles at Shining Star Church?" The two both taught at the same Christian school. Randomly seated beside each other for their orientation as first-year teachers, they'd been thick as thieves ever since. Emily had been planning her wedding that year, and Marta had listened to her vent and obsess about wedding details so faithfully she had earned a forever spot as her best friend.

Marta rolled her eyes. "So yeah, the

church kind of has a weird name and Missy Detwiler is a bit annoying, but the seminar sounds good. They're bringing in a speaker who wrote a book about dating and I mean, you know, I might meet a Christian guy there. Or . . . something." Marta paused. "But I also thought maybe you'd need me to be here with you because of it being the anniversary of the funeral and . . ." Marta's voice trailed off. She looked like a child asking permission from a parent.

Emily could take one look at Marta and know that she was uncertain about this departure from their regular Saturday night routine, especially on this particular Saturday night. That was why she'd showed up in person instead of resorting to a quick text or phone call. But whether it was because she was uncertain about bailing on her friend or attending the event, Emily couldn't tell. Either way, she knew it was her turn to encourage Marta. "It sounds really good. You should totally go."

Marta looked at her out of the corner of her eye. "Crazy idea, but would you want to go with me? I know it's probably way too soon but —"

Emily held up her hand and took a step back. "I'm not single, Marta. I'm a widow. That's different."

"But the flyer says it's for people who are single or single again or —"

Emily laughed in spite of herself; the suggestion of attending some event for singles was just that absurd. "I'm not open to having this discussion." She folded her arms across her chest and gave Marta a look that told her the case was closed.

Marta shrugged and gave her a look that said she had thoughts of her own but was smart enough to keep them to herself. "Fine," was all she said.

There was silence for a moment as Emily thought about asking Marta to cancel her plans and stay with her. It would be the selfish, wrong thing to do, but the thought of spending the evening alone filled her with a whole new kind of sadness. She'd already put a movie in her queue for them to watch, one they'd both like. And yet Emily knew that she needed to let her friend go. She watched as Marta began backing toward the door, her eyes on Emily. Emily waved her on and gave her a smile that she hoped looked genuine. "I'll be fine. You should definitely go."

Marta narrowed her eyes. "You sure?"

Emily nodded and added some false enthusiasm for Marta's benefit. "Yes! I might just go visit my parents. They've been asking and you just took away my best excuse." She rolled her eyes, figuring Marta would see right through her, but she didn't. Or she chose not to. She came back to Emily and gave her a big hug, then quickly — before Emily could change her mind, she thought — took her leave.

Before the door could close behind Marta, Emily hollered, "Let me know how it goes! Have fun!"

Marta turned back with a wink. "You know me — I always find a way to have fun!"

Emily watched her friend leave, wondering when she'd stopped finding a way to have fun. A thought flitted through her mind — maybe fun hadn't died for her when Ryan died. Maybe somewhere in the future she would become a girl who knew how to have fun again.

Emily pushed the food around on her plate, feeling like she was twelve again and existing under her parents' watchful eyes. She could actually feel their gazes, evaluating every bite she took, biting back their thoughts about how she was too thin, too sad, too closed off from the rest of the world. Instead of criticizing, her mother made "helpful suggestions."

"Why don't you join the choir? I know how you love music."

"What about taking up a hobby? I hear knitting is very in vogue."

"If you ever do think of dating again, the Gaskell boy has just moved back to town and is quite the catch."

"You really should eat."

And that was just during this meal. Emily either changed the subject or nodded politely, always promising to think over whatever it was her mother thought would help. Internally a phrase ran on repeat play: *She's just trying to help.* In some ways her mother was like Marta. Marta just had a more hip vocabulary and relevant-to-her-age-group suggestions.

By the end of the dinner, she was looking for a way to make a speedy escape, just like Marta had once she had the all clear to go to the singles' event. She wondered how her friend was faring and — for the briefest flicker — wondered what it would feel like to think of dating again, to talk to a man she was interested in. She couldn't imagine ever being interested in anyone. It was like saying she'd suddenly be interested in aliens or zombies. She smiled in spite of herself.

"What's the smile for?" her father asked. He'd been so quiet during dinner, Emily had nearly forgotten he was there. Her mother talked enough for all of them, dominating the conversation with a running commentary on her volunteer efforts, her church involvement, and the occasional tidbit of gossip, which she always managed to look penitent for even as she doled out the news. Emily looked at her father's plate. He'd pushed his share of food around, too, from the looks of things.

Emily knew that seeing her was painful for him. He'd faced his own crisis of faith after Ryan died, loving him like the son he never had and aching over the loss. He'd soldiered through the funeral, delivered a moving eulogy, then collapsed in tears as soon as he was alone, her mother had shared when he wasn't around. He'd been . . . different around Emily ever since. And different in the pulpit too. His sermons, while still challenging on an academic level, lacked the heart they once had. Emily understood, having had her own crisis of faith after Ryan's loss — one that was still going on, if she was honest. She stood in her classroom and faithfully delivered the Bible lesson, taught her students their memory verses, and modeled good character. But inside she was screaming questions at the God who took her husband from her.

"Em?" She heard her father's voice again and realized she'd gotten lost in thoughts. With her mother gone from the table to fetch a dessert Emily wouldn't eat, she could've told her father the truth — maybe even broached the questions she couldn't ask anyone. Her father was her pastor, after all. Instead she just smiled again. "Nothing, Dad. Just thinking about how glad I am that spring break is coming up."

"Spring break?" she heard her mother call out from the kitchen. The same woman who sometimes couldn't hear you when you were talking directly to her could inexplicably hear a conversation in the next room with no problem.

Her mother hustled back in carrying an egg custard pie dusted with a bit of nutmeg. When Emily was little and recovering from an illness, it was always the first dessert her mother made her as soon as she was up to it. "It'll settle your stomach," her mother always said. This fact had never been medically substantiated but her mother believed it so fervently, Emily did too. She caught her eye and gave her a smile. The pie was her mother's way of acknowledging how hard this day was — even if she never said it aloud. Nancy Lawson was not one to dwell on the past or get bogged down in negative thoughts, and she would be the first person to tell you about it.

Her mother set the pie down and began to cut slices that were much too large. "I've got some plans for the three of us for spring break. One of the ladies in my Bible study offered us the use of her home in Pigeon Forge!" Without asking, she hefted a slice of pie onto a dessert plate and slid it in front of Emily. Emily eyed the pie for a moment before picking up her fork and taking a polite bite. But not even custard pie could settle her churning stomach. Her mother's brilliant plans echoed in her brain as she chewed and swallowed, the custard suddenly tasting like glue in her mouth.

"Well?" she heard and looked up from her plate. Her mother had her hands on her hips and was looking down at her, imperious. "Doesn't that sound nice? A little getaway for all of us? And for free!"

"Um, well, it's just that I — I mean, I hadn't thought about making spring break plans. I haven't talked to Marta. She'd mentioned doing something . . ." This was not true and she suspected her mother knew it. She and Marta were close but they'd never planned vacations together. Somehow traveling with Marta just sounded more depressing, a more glaring sign that she had no one else to travel with. She put down her fork. Of course, it was a far better option than the one being presented.

"Well, she could come with us. Beverly said that their cabin is plenty big. You remember Beverly? She made the ham we served at the reception?"

Emily nodded. That ham had been so huge she still had slices in her freezer, waiting for the day her appetite returned.

Undeterred, her mother began collecting the dishes. "Why don't you ask her what she had in mind and get back to me? I'll need to let Beverly know." She looked to Emily's father. "Richard, it's a very nice offer, don't you think?"

Her father, obviously jarred into the present by the sound of his name, nodded his head, an attempt at answering without answering.

Her mother wasn't swayed. "Don't you think we should go?" she pressed.

He made panicked eye contact with Emily before continuing the charade that he'd been actually paying attention to her mother's ramblings. "Um, sure?"

Clueless, her mother looked at Emily before carrying the dishes out of the room. "See? Your father wants to go."

Emily suppressed a grin until she was

gone from the room. She turned to her father. "You just agreed to spend spring break with three women in a cabin in Pigeon Forge. Shopping at antique stores! Dollywood!" She giggled at the look on his face.

"That'll teach me to daydream while she's talking," he deadpanned.

"I'll figure a way to get out of it."

He chuckled. "Maybe for you. But I'm doomed."

"I doubt she'll go if I don't. This is her way of 'getting my mind off things' and we both know it."

He rose from his chair and began gathering dishes. He hadn't eaten his pie. "One can only hope." He didn't comment on her mother's efforts, or address the "things" she was trying to distract Emily from. In the past year, he never had.

After he disappeared into the kitchen and she heard the familiar, comforting sounds of running water and her parents' voices amidst the clatter of silverware and china, she pressed the tines of her fork into the custard, making a print on the surface of the pie. As she did she thought of how she could get out of this trip of her mother's, planning an escape from somewhere she hadn't even gone.

FOUR

March 2, 2007

She woke the next morning to the sound of someone banging on her door. She shook her head and rolled her eyes. Usually Marta just used her own key and barged in. Today she wished she'd done just that — gotten coffee started before she woke her. Pulling a robe over one of Ryan's T-shirts, she extricated herself out of the tangle of sheets and padded through the house to let Marta in, cinching the robe tightly closed as she walked. She tugged the door open with a smile, wanting her friend to know that — in spite of the tension from the day before — everything was fine. She needed Marta too much to let anything simmer under the surface of their friendship. And she also needed her friend to help her come up with a Plan B for spring break.

"So are you here to tell me you met the love of your life last night and are running away to get married?" she joked upon seeing Marta's face.

Marta shook her head and pushed her way into the house, wired and excited. She placed her hands on Emily's shoulders and steered her back into the den, pushing her down to have a seat on the couch. "What are you doing?" Emily asked, half laughing, half nervous. Marta could be odd and dramatic (Emily attributed that to her being a drama and art teacher at the school), but this was over the top even for her.

Marta began pacing back and forth in front of the couch. "I did meet someone last night. Well, I mean I didn't meet him for the first time. But I saw him last night." She stopped pacing and looked at Emily. "We re-met." She waved her hand, impatient with the need to explain. "But it had very little to do with me. He talked to me about you mostly."

"Me?" Emily put her hand against her chest, her eyes widening as she felt her heart pick up its pace beneath her fingers. "But why?" She didn't like the thought of another man talking about her. She didn't like the thought of being anyone's topic of discussion, though she knew she had been lots of times in the past year. She heard snatches of conversations when she passed women in groups of two or three at church or school — the whispered words and grim looks. She knew they used words like *poor* and *sad* and *tragic* when they spoke of her. She also knew none of them wanted to be her.

Marta grinned. "Look at your face. Don't get all worried. It's good." She sat down beside Emily on the couch and put her hand on her knee, covered by the flannel of the robe. "It's Phil." She studied Emily's face for a sign of recognition. "Phil Griffin?" she tried again.

Emily tried to think of a guy from church or school but came up with nothing. She shook her head.

Marta surprised her by hitting her knee a little too hard for emphasis. "You know Phil Griffin! From Ryan's office? I took you there after the funeral last year."

Recognition dawned on Emily's face. "Oh, yes! Phil! Of course!" She tried to act happy upon hearing the man's name, but it was the last one she wanted to hear. Because with the mention of his name she suddenly knew why Marta was there.

"So he was interested to hear that you never did anything with what Ryan left you. He said that he thought you were going to take immediate action. I told him that you've had a hard time and he said he understood. But . . ." Emily could tell Marta was trying to tread lightly, which was almost impossible for her friend.

"Look, this was Ryan's gift to me. There's no timetable on when I have to redeem that gift." Emily couldn't keep the frustration out of her voice. There were many days she wished she'd never shared the letter with Marta, that no one — not even Phil Griffin — had known what Ryan planned. She thought about the letter she had stashed in her lingerie drawer, hidden beneath the lingerie she'd worn on their wedding night. She had memorized the words by now, the paper soft from many handlings, the folds starting to fray.

"I told him that I would talk to you about it. That I'd be bossy if I had to."

Emily gave her a half smile. "And that would be different from usual . . . how?"

Marta cocked her head and bugged her eyes out at her. "Hey. Don't shoot the messenger."

"Look, I appreciate that you and Phil both think I need to cash in on Ryan's last wish. And I intend to — someday. I promise." She held her hand up as if taking an oath, pleased she'd kept calm and they'd put the issue to rest for now. She stood up and started to the kitchen for coffee, but Marta's voice halted her.

"Wellll," Marta replied. "I kinda promised him something a little more . . . definite than that."

She spun around and faced Marta. "What did you promise?"

Marta had a panicked look on her face. "Look, there was this really creepy guy who was trying to talk to me and the longer I kept talking to Phil, the more that guy had to wait. I figured if I kept him waiting long enough, he'd give up. So, really, when you think about it, this conversation I'm about to relay to you just might've saved my life. So that should actually make you feel good about my promise."

Emily couldn't keep from smiling. "Well, when you put it that way, maybe I won't kill you right away."

"Trust me, I think creepy guy might've." Marta shuddered.

"So what did you promise?" Emily just wanted to get it over with.

"I promised Phil that I would make you go there for spring break. That I'd help you find a house."

Emily thought of her mother's announcement about spring break and the dread that had filled her at the thought of a week trapped in a cabin in Pigeon Forge with her

57

parents and Marta. But this new suggestion wasn't much better. In fact, in some ways it was worse. Emily hadn't returned to Sunset Beach since her honeymoon with Ryan. There'd never been enough money, enough time. They'd just started planning a return trip when Ryan was diagnosed. And the thought of going back — of crossing that bridge — just seemed too huge to even contemplate. What could Ryan have been thinking?

Marta pulled her phone from her pocket and responded to a text while Emily was thinking.

"What are you doing?"

"That was Phil, checking to see if I'd talked to you yet. He's excited about our plan."

Our plan. Who was "our" exactly? Marta and Emily or Marta and Phil? She tried to remember what Phil looked like, but all she could recall from those hazy days after Ryan's death were shadowy figures ducking in and out of her line of sight. Phil was — as far as she could recall — a pleasant enough person, rather nondescript. Had he been wearing a wedding ring? Were there pictures of a family on his desk? She raised her eyebrows. "Why do I feel like all of this is just some scheme to keep you and Phil talking?"

Marta gave her a smirk, then turned around and went to the kitchen ahead of her. Over the sound of the cupboards opening and water running, she called out, "Well, I mean, he *is* a lawyer." With a sigh that was dramatic enough to rival one of Marta's, Emily followed her friend into the kitchen. She'd never needed coffee more.

After Marta finally drained the last of the coffee in the pot and left, Emily slid the chain lock on her door into place. She found herself tiptoeing back to her bedroom, as if she were trying to sneak up on herself. She chuckled at her actions, admitting that she was acting crazy. And why not? Her parents were trying to whisk her away to Pigeon Forge and Marta was forcing her to go to the one place in the world she didn't want to go. To be honest, she didn't know which of the two scenarios was the worse option.

She sat down in front of her dresser and pulled open the drawer containing Ryan's letter. She took it from its hiding place and held it to her, just as she always did, imagining he was hugging her. "Hi," she said to the ceiling. "I sure wish you were here to help me decide." She laughed at herself. " 'Course, if you were here none of this would be happening. We'd be spending spring break finally planting that garden in the backyard." She wondered if there was some sort of gardening camp she could enroll herself in for the week of spring break, an ironclad excuse to stay home, one that required a nonrefundable hefty deposit. She opened the letter and read the words she could almost recite from memory, her eyes running over the swirl and tilt of the familiar handwriting. She only allowed herself to take out the letter once in a while, focusing as much as she could on staying busy and not wallowing in her grief. And yet with the trip on her mind, her grief was catching up to her, her thoughts of Ryan unavoidable.

Tears streamed freely down her face as she finished reading, dripping from her chin and hitting the carpet. She sniffed loudly and swiped at her nose. The letter had that effect on her every time. She slumped over on her side and stared at the letter through watery vision, the letters swimming in front of her. She blinked them away and saw the words, "Promise me." He used to always make her pinky swear whenever she promised him something. It was a goofy thing to do and it never failed to make her laugh, but she always went along with it. Well, this was one promise he hadn't gotten her to pinky swear to. So maybe that meant he couldn't hold her to it?

She could hear his response: *Nice try, Em. That's weak.*

She thought of another time she wanted to get away. It was the first time he had to be admitted to the hospital, the first time she'd seen him truly sick, staying beside him yet helpless to stop his misery. She'd never felt more useless in her whole life, more incapacitated. When his mother came to relieve her so she could shower and get a nap, she fled the hospital, raced home, and crawled into their bed, burrowing under the covers to block out the light of day. From her cocoon she tried to stop the memories of the past few days from replaying in her head, the worries about what was going to happen and doubts that Ryan would ever get better. She had to be strong for him, she told herself, falling asleep mid-thought.

For a split second when she woke, she forgot why she was there and what was happening. She wriggled and stretched and inhaled the smell of home — her laundry, her sheets, her nice cozy bed. Then she realized it had grown dark outside as she slept, a large yellow moon outside their window replacing the sun that had shone brightly before. 7:18 p.m. She'd slept for hours, released into the sweet oblivion of sleep. But consciousness brought reality with it.

She remembered where she was, and where she was supposed to be, leaping from bed and racing around so she could get back to the hospital, her heart in her throat as she dialed her mother-in-law to check on him. "Take your time, honey. He's just sleeping. Get a shower. Get something to eat. You won't do him any good if you wear yourself out," Ryan's mother said. Emily forced herself to slow down and do what she'd been told. Her mother-in-law was right. She showered and dressed, and even made a peanut butter and jelly sandwich, eating it over the sink as she surveyed her quiet, empty house. He would come home again. She tried to keep her thoughts positive. He had to get better.

On the way back to the hospital, she felt her heart rate begin to pick up the closer she got to the parking deck. The place had become far too familiar, a place she both hated to leave and longed to get away from. At the stoplight just before the turnoff to the hospital she saw the building, looming large and white against the black sky. She could see the helicopter used for emergencies sleeping on the roof. She could see the hundreds of windows, some lit from within, some dark, all containing stories of birth and death, illness and healing. She looked away from the place, focusing instead on the red light ahead of her. And for those few minutes before the light turned green, she wished as hard as she could that that light would just stay red so that she didn't have to return to her sick husband.

She was ashamed of that wish, bright spots of color coming to her cheeks whenever she recalled her cowardice. As Ryan suffered she'd been the weak one. She had pretended to be there for him when all she really wanted to do was hide. When push came to shove, she'd wished for a way to abandon him. She'd never told anyone about that moment at the stoplight, how fervently she'd wanted to stay right where she was, even if that meant she wasn't with him. He had needed her, and she had betrayed him. People had called her "brave" and "strong" but they had it all wrong. They didn't know what she was really thinking and feeling all along. And here she was, essentially doing the same thing again — desiring to stay in one place so she didn't have to do the hard thing.

With a sigh she got up and walked into the den where the plaque he mentioned in his letter held its place of honor on their mantel. His parents had had Jeremiah 29:11

etched into glass and presented it to them at their rehearsal dinner. Now when she read the familiar verses, the words bounced around in her head but never made it to her heart. She wasn't sure she believed in hope and future anymore. She hugged the plaque to her and thought of the image Ryan had painted in his letter. She was walking down the beach and she was smiling. Maybe she should give his vision a chance. Maybe Ryan had known more than she did. Maybe she hadn't found her hope and future because it was waiting at Sunset Beach. It was worth a try because she certainly hadn't found it here. She couldn't stay at the stoplight forever. She put the plaque down and went to find the phone so she could call the one person who would make her follow through with the search.

FIVE

April 7, 2007

The scent of eucalyptus enveloped her as she settled her face into the padded hole in the headrest and squeezed her eyes shut tight. Sounds of nature floated through the speaker just above her — birds calling and wind blowing. She felt herself begin to relax and let go. She was both thankful to her parents for the gift certificate they'd given her for her birthday the month before, and to herself for having the foresight to schedule this massage just before the trip she was dreading.

The masseuse kneaded her knotted muscles, expelling the tension and luring her into a relaxation she couldn't seem to achieve in day-to-day life. Her guard was always up, the walls around her heart fortified lest it all come crumbling down. She was in control at all times, safe within the limits of emotion she put on herself. But there under the warm and prodding hands of the woman with the Eastern European accent, she felt that control begin to slip away along with the stress and worries. She let her mind wander as the sounds from the speaker changed to the sound of a babbling brook. Caught up in the moment, she didn't push away the memory of a day trip she and Ryan had taken together to the mountains the fall just before he got sick. They had hiked beside a stream holding hands, stopped for apples on the way home. She'd made her first apple pie that night and they'd had pie for dinner. Just pie.

The masseuse pressed harder and something about the combination of memory and muscle release triggered an overflow of emotions. She could taste that apple pie, feel the swell of her heart as she lifted it out of the oven. She could smell the perfect blend of cinnamon and apples and the tiniest bit of nutmeg wrapped in a store-bought crust that Ryan swore tasted as good as homemade. She could feel his lips on hers as he kissed her, hear his voice as he said, "It's perfect." She opened her eyes and stared into the darkness as tears dripped from her face to the floor. It was perfect. And it was gone. She began to sob, embarrassed, yet unable to stop what was happening. The masseuse never stilled, just kept working away, her strong, capable hands continuing to coax out what Emily had kept locked away.

When she was finished the masseuse waited until Emily was composed again before she spoke. "You carry much sadness inside you," she said simply.

Emily, clutching the big white towel around herself, nodded, certain her eyes were rimmed with red and her nose was glowing. She was more than a little embarrassed over falling apart and thankful that this woman she would most likely never see again had been the only witness.

"Is good to let sadness out," the masseuse said. She folded her hands in front of her and cocked her head. "You let sadness out, you have room for joy." She nodded once and hurried out of the room, leaving Emily to dress and ponder just how she could accomplish that away from the massage table.

Emily tugged her suitcase from under the bed and coughed as a cloud of dust emerged with it, trying to forget her odd experience during the massage and get back to something that felt normal. She waved her hand in front of her face to disperse the dust and pulled the suitcase up onto her bed, flinging the top back to reveal the empty space designed to hold clothes, shoes, and the like. She glanced at the packing list she'd made and frowned. There were only a few things on the list — not enough to get her through a week at the beach. She reached for the phone to call Marta and complain again. Just as she did, the phone rang. Assuming it was Marta calling to give her a pep talk, she reached for it without looking at the caller ID and answered, "I'm packing, don't worry."

"I'm sorry?" a nervous male voice replied.

"Oh, goodness! *I'm* sorry. I thought you were someone else." She rolled her eyes at herself and crumpled her useless packing list.

"This is Arthur Groves, the real estate agent from Sunset Properties. I was just calling to confirm our appointment for this coming Tuesday."

"Oh yes, Arthur. I've got it down." She didn't say she was looking forward to it, because that just wouldn't be true.

The truth was she was dreading the appointment with the Realtor like other people dreaded a trip to the dentist. The other night Marta had called her on her bad attitude. "Oh poor, poor me. I have half a million dollars to spend on a beach house. Everyone please feel sorry for me."

She'd narrowed her eyes at Marta but had no good comeback. Mostly because Marta was right. For all the things that were wrong with her life, buying a beach house could hardly be counted among them. And yet when she thought of crossing that old bridge her stomach clenched in dread.

"I'll just meet you at the real estate office at ten o'clock if that's still okay?" Arthur asked.

"Sure, I'll be there." She tried to make her voice sound enthusiastic for Arthur's sake. She doubted he'd ever had a client who had the money but didn't want to buy a beach house.

She hung up with Arthur and dialed Marta's number but there was no answer. This had happened several times lately and Emily had tried not to be put off by Marta's recent absence in her life. Things had escalated between her and Phil. As a result of their scheming, a relationship had blossomed, just in time for spring. Emily wanted to be happy for her friend, but she also missed having Marta accessible to her anytime she needed her. She tossed the crumpled paper into the wastebasket and gave herself three points for an outside shot. If Ryan were there he'd have only allowed her two.

If Ryan were there . . . The phrase populated her thoughts and resounded in her heart a hundred times a day. If Ryan were there she'd have plans for the weekend. If Ryan were there she wouldn't need Marta so much. If Ryan were there she'd take more interest in decorating the house. If Ryan were there she'd have someone to see that new romantic comedy with. If Ryan were there she'd be happier. She eyed her empty suitcase. If Ryan were there she wouldn't be going to the beach in two days to buy a house.

With a huff, she opened her closet to see if anything in there was worth packing. What did one wear to buy a beach house? Her eyes fell to the black dress, eventually hung there after the funeral and never touched again. Without thinking too much about it, she yanked it from the hanger and balled it up. She stared down at the wad of fabric in her hands, telling herself it was just a dress, nothing more. But the dress symbolized one of the worst days of her life, running neck and neck with the day Ryan got diagnosed and the day he died. Impulsively she tossed the dress toward the trash. She didn't give herself any points when it made it in. She thought about plucking it out of the trash and folding it up for Goodwill but turned away. Some things shouldn't have a second life.

Her phone buzzed and she reached for it, happy to have a distraction. Not that she was getting any packing done. Marta's smiling face showed up on the screen, the ringtone belting out an old Hall and Oates song Marta had chosen from a random list. She answered. "I tried calling you earlier," an accusing tone crept into her voice that she didn't like. She sounded like a nagging wife.

"Sorry, Phil and I were having brunch." Marta hardly sounded sorry. She sounded happy.

Brunch? Marta was hardly the brunch type. "Oh, that sounds nice."

"Yeah. It's going really well with him, thanks for asking."

She grimaced. "Sorry. I'm self-involved, but at least I recognize it. Isn't that the first step?"

She could hear Marta's smile through the phone. At least she'd broken the ice. Lately their friendship had been . . . off. She knew that she was primarily responsible for that — who would want to listen to another person whine for over a year? But she also knew that Marta's developing relationship with Phil was pulling her friend away. She was

71

glad they were going to the beach, just the two of them. Marta's sense of humor would help her cross that bridge, meet that realtor, find that house Ryan wanted her to have. "I'm packing right now, you'll be glad to know."

"Yeah . . . um, about that."

It wasn't so much the words Marta said, it was the way she said them. Laced with guilt and heavy in the delivery, Emily knew Marta was about to deliver a death knell to their trip. "Phil's parents are coming to town for Easter and staying the week. He's asked me to stay in town to spend time with them and I —"

"Said you would."

There was silence on the other end. "I have to do this, Em. It's my chance at happiness." Marta always did tend toward the dramatic.

"But you were the one who made me go through with this. You said you'd be with me. That I wouldn't have to do this alone."

Marta sighed, a real sigh this time, not one just for effect. "I know I did. And I want to be with you. I do. But . . . he's asking and I can't shake the feeling that with the way things are going, it's really important to be here, to meet his folks, if you know what I mean."

Emily sank down onto her bed, resting her arm on her empty suitcase. She wanted to crawl inside it at that moment, tuck herself into the fetal position and suck her thumb, zip the lid closed around her and shut out the world. "I understand," she managed.

She expected Marta to argue a little bit, put up a fight or keep her talking about her feelings the way Marta always did. Instead she let out a little whoop and exclaimed, "You're the best friend ever. Thanks!" Marta threw out a few other closing remarks — platitudes all — and Emily was left with a dial tone buzzing in her ear. She had thought that perhaps she'd tell Marta about what had happened during her massage that afternoon. Marta was always bugging her about keeping everything so together, always pushing her to fall apart more often. It sounded odd but Marta would be thrilled to hear she'd done just that. But that wasn't going to happen now.

She looked at the closed drawer where the letter resided and said to the ceiling, "Happy now? This is all your fault." With a heavy heart she rose from the bed and resumed her halfhearted packing attempt, feeling less like braving the beach than ever before.

■ ■ ■ ■

She arrived at Sunset Beach on Monday afternoon, leaving just enough daylight to get checked into her motel and get something to eat before getting a good night's sleep, maybe watch a movie on TV before she dozed off. Lately the TV had become her constant companion, her white noise, her evidence that there was life on this planet without actually having to interact with that life. She found it easier to view other people's crises than to think about her own.

She managed to cross the old swing bridge without having to wait for boats to cross the intracoastal waterway. Her car made the same sound she remembered from before as she came off the bridge railings, *da-dum, da-dum.* She kept her eyes peeled to the road and tried not to think too much. Before she knew it she pulled into the motel parking lot without fanfare. She sat in the car and took a deep breath. First bridge crossed. *No pun intended,* she heard Ryan say. A little smile flitted across her face.

Ha, ha, ha, she thought. *You're funny for a dead guy.*

She took in her surroundings, gazing across the motel parking lot at the parking lot for the pier, the gazebo that sat off to the left of it, and the ocean beyond. She turned to check out the motel she had reserved sight unseen. Though not fancy by any means, the place looked clean and in good working order. Since it wasn't the high season and still pretty chilly, there weren't many people milling around. The deserted feel of the place matched the way she felt inside. Nothing like a ghost town when you're dealing with ghosts of your own.

She got out of the car and collected her suitcase, now bulging with an assortment of clothes she ended up tossing in without much rhyme or reason. She half dragged, half carried it across the parking lot and ducked into a small front office, only to find it empty. "Hello?" she called out, feeling ridiculous.

When no one came, she called out again, louder this time. "Um, hello?"

She heard a rustling from behind a closed door and stood a bit straighter. After a few seconds, the door opened and a young girl emerged, wiping her mouth with a bright yellow fast-food napkin. "Sorry," the girl said sheepishly and tossed the napkin into the trash. "I was eating dinner." She went over to the computer on the desk and started pushing buttons. She looked at

Emily for the first time, and as she did, Emily noticed her startling green eyes. "And you are?" the girl asked.

"Emily," she responded. "Shaw," she added. "Emily Shaw."

The girl began typing, her fingers flying expertly across the keys. Emily studied her as she did, deciding she couldn't be much older than Emily's students. She took in the girl's clothing — jeans and a long-sleeve T-shirt with the motel's logo. Her thick red hair was pulled back and she had no makeup on. She probably looked younger than she actually was.

"Is this your after-school job?" Emily ventured, just to fill the silence in the room.

The girl didn't look up. "Nah, this is our family business." The girl let out a grim little laugh. "I mean it's just me and my dad, if you want to call that a family."

"Well, sure, it's a family," Emily rushed to say, her words tumbling over each other. She felt and sounded like an idiot. The girl gave her a look that told her she didn't need some stranger validating her family life. You could take the teacher out of the school . . . If Ryan were there that's what he would say. He was always teasing her about her love of kids, especially teenagers. But Emily couldn't help it. She remembered how hard it was to be a teen — not a kid but not an adult, everyone acting like they knew what was going on when no one really did. She'd had an even more difficult time as a preacher's kid. Her lingering memories of the awkwardness and uncertainty of that time gave her a heart for that age when most people ignored or avoided them.

She tried giving the girl a smile, but the girl looked away, her emerald gaze directed back at the computer screen. She was forgetting that to her she wasn't Mrs. Shaw, the popular teacher students clamored to have at school. She was just some strange woman in need of a room for a few nights in her father's motel. She would have to tone down her enthusiasm.

The girl passed her an old-fashioned key attached to a green plastic disk bearing her room number, 202. She pointed toward the door, reciting in a monotone the directions to get to the room. "Let us know if you need anything. Checkout's at eleven," she finished.

"Sure. Thanks." Emily dropped the key into her purse and lugged the unwieldy suitcase back across the room. She wrestled with the door while managing to keep hold of her purse and suitcase, a feat that she thought deserved recognition, but the girl kept on pecking at the computer, oblivious.

Once she was outside on the sidewalk she began reciting in a snippy voice what the girl should've said. "Thank you so much for choosing to stay with us. We know you could've stayed any number of places and we appreciate your business." She got up the stairs and into her room with only a few bruises on her shins from the suitcase knocking up against her legs, balancing it against the wall as she used the key to let herself in.

Once inside she found a large clean room, if not decorated in the loveliest — or even matching — décor. It was good enough for a few days at Sunset. Using her heavy suitcase to prop open the door, she stood out on the open-air breezeway and gazed across the parking lot at the ocean. For a moment she focused solely on the lovely view. She breathed in the salt air, letting it fill her lungs and fuel her with something she wasn't used to feeling. Something she faintly remembered was called hope.

Six

April 10, 2007

Arthur Groves pulled into the parking lot of the motel and shifted the car into park with a barely audible tired sigh. He looked at her with a sheepish expression and turned the car off. "You sure you don't want to go over to Ocean Isle Beach to look? It's just one beach over." His voice was low and without hope. This wasn't the first time he'd mentioned this option. Somewhere around the fifteenth house they'd looked at, he'd started suggesting other options. Emily couldn't tell if he was impatient with her or sympathetic. It didn't matter. She'd been unable to find the house she pictured in her mind, the house she would know Ryan wanted for her.

Her mind had wandered many times in the past two days as she and Arthur had traipsed around Sunset Beach, their hopes dimming with each "no." She'd thought of the many times she and Ryan had mused

79

over the perfect beach house — a blend of shabby yet nice, not a designer model home but not a dive. It seemed all the houses were either one or the other. She'd looked at some very nice homes that were out of her price range, and tried not to be a snob at some of the ones she could afford. Some of them looked like a group of high school students partying over spring break had just left . . . and the maid service hadn't ever showed up. Some of them simply lacked personality. None of them touched her heart. None of them said "home" when she walked in the front door.

"I'm sorry, Mr. Groves," she said for what seemed the hundredth time. "I mean, Arthur," she corrected herself, recalling his request to call him by his first name.

The older gentleman patted her hand and put his own hand back on the wheel. She figured he was anxious to get her out of his car. She couldn't blame him. He'd been hospitable and accommodating for two days — and now it looked as though he wouldn't even make a commission.

He cleared his throat and turned to look at her once more. "Maybe it would help if you spent some time thinking about what you want."

She gave him a polite smile and tried to

keep from sighing aloud. "Mr. Groves — Arthur," she amended herself again. "I want to fulfill my husband's last wish and buy a house here at Sunset. I want to get through this summer so I can say that I did what he asked. I want to shut up my best friend once and for all so she'll stop harping on me to do this. I want . . ." The sigh escaped her lips anyway. "I want to figure out why he wanted me to do this in the first place. Why he ever thought I'd want to do this without him."

Arthur Groves shifted uncomfortably and nodded. "I, um, can certainly understand wanting all those things, Emily. But what I actually meant was what you wanted in a house. Make a list of what you'd really like and what you can't live with. It might make the process easier and bring some things into focus." He gave her a kind smile she was sure was meant to encourage her. "I find it helps clients sometimes."

Embarrassed by her unnecessary outburst, she nodded obediently, just wanting to get out of the car and slink up to her room. "Okay, I'll work on that."

He turned the key in the ignition and the engine responded with a rumble. "I'll head into the office first thing tomorrow morning and make some calls. Maybe we can come up with something that hasn't hit the listings yet. Let's not give up," he said.

"Okay," she said. She pulled on the door handle and felt a rush of warm air fill the car as the door opened. She inhaled the salt air, wondering if she'd ever take that smell for granted. She and Ryan had talked about that — how their children would grow strong and healthy breathing in that sea air. She quickly blinked away tears. Maybe she and Ryan had just been entirely wrong. Maybe she should donate the money he left her to cancer research so someone else could live the dreams she and Ryan never fulfilled and let this crazy scheme of his die with him.

She said a quick good-bye to Arthur and got out of his car, crossing the dusty parking lot as she made her way to her room, her pride still smarting over the way she'd blurted out the wrong answer to his question. At that moment all she wanted was to throttle Marta for bailing on her. They'd talked of driving down to Myrtle Beach to go shopping, heading over to Calabash to dine on fried seafood and wander through the tourist shops, maybe even making a day trip up to Southport or Wilmington. What could've been a moderately fun spring break was just one long disappointment. If she didn't find something tomorrow, she decided as she climbed the stairs to her little room, she was going home. Maybe she really would take a gardening class. Anything was better than this.

She sank down into the couch in her room and clicked on the TV for lack of something better to do. At some point she'd have to venture out for dinner, maybe head up to the sub sandwich shop just over the bridge and bring something back to eat in front of the TV. She wasn't up to dining in public alone. Looking at happy couples laughing, talking, and gazing into each other's eyes was more than she could take. She clicked through the channels mindlessly, hoping to magically land on something worth watching.

When the image of Brady Rutledge filled the screen, she groaned out loud. Too late, the memory of watching this movie with Ryan, teasing him about his competition, filled her mind. She could see Ryan stripping off his T-shirt and bowing up his arms. "Oh yeah?" he'd asked, flexing his pecs, tanned and slick with oil. "Can he compete with this?" She'd fallen over on the couch laughing. She'd known then she had something special with this funny, handsome, charming man. She'd just never thought she could lose it so fast.

She studied Brady Rutledge's image for a moment, taking in his handsome features, the sound of his captivating voice. "Okay," she said to the ceiling. "I still say he's good looking. But he's no you. Happy?" She clicked off the TV and looked around the silent room. She couldn't spend all evening closed up in there. It would make her crazier. Remembering a sign tacked up in the office that said they would loan out bikes to guests, she walked back downstairs to ask if she could take out a bike. Maybe a ride around the island would clear her head. At the very least it would get her out of there.

She walked into the office, expecting to find it empty again. Instead she found a good-looking twentysomething guy leaning across the desk where the girl who'd checked her in sat. When he saw Emily he jumped back like he'd been jolted with electricity. She looked from the guy to the girl as she came to stand behind him to wait her turn. They were all silent as the girl stared at her computer and the guy shifted his weight from foot to foot. "Okay, well," he finally said to the girl, "I guess I'll just come by later to pick up those extra towels." Emily couldn't be sure but she thought she saw him wink at the girl before he left.

When he was gone the girl turned her emerald gaze in Emily's direction. Emily could see why the guy was acting foolish around her. It wasn't just that the girl was beautiful, it was that she had no idea she was. There was something attractive about that. Her red hair was down, brushed into silky scarlet waves that flowed around her shoulders. She seemed to be trying harder with her appearance today. Emily glanced at the door the guy had exited through and wondered if she'd made an effort for him. She wrinkled her nose at the thought. That guy was too old for her. She resisted the urge to say something teacherish and decided it was none of her business. Better just to get the bike and leave the parenting up to the girl's father.

She turned back to find the girl staring at her. "Can I help you?" the girl asked.

"Yes, I'd like to get one of your bikes to use," Emily responded, then gave her her best smile.

The girl hitched her thumb backward, indicating an area behind her. "Just go back out that door you came in, turn left, and you'll see the storage room." She held out another key with a green disk attached. This one said "Storage" on it. "That'll get you in, then you can take whatever bike in there looks like it'll work." The girl made a face that told Emily there wasn't much chance of that.

Emily took the key from her outstretched hand, noting that her nails were painted a very pretty red, a grown-up color. She thought of the guy from earlier and again decided not to say anything. "What's your name?" she asked instead.

"Amber," the girl said flatly. She pointed at the top of her head. "For obvious reasons."

"It's lovely," Emily said. "I mean, your name. And your hair."

Amber blushed. "Thanks." The hot pink coloring in her skin traveled up her neck and across her cheeks. She waved at the key. "Just bring it back after you're done with the bike. Or you can just turn it in when you check out. We don't get many requests for bikes these days."

"Oh, okay. Thanks." The two blinked at each other awkwardly for a moment, Emily thinking of all the things she'd want to say to this girl if only she had license to do so. Realizing how stupid she looked to this teenager, she gave a little wave. "See you later." She started for the door, then turned back to catch the girl's eye one last time, saying the one thing she could think to say.

"Be careful."

She turned and fled the room, hoping the girl took her inferred meaning and sent that guy away the next time he came sniffing round.

She pedaled up and down the streets of Sunset aimlessly, traveling past the houses she'd spent the past two days peeking inside, a running commentary playing inside her head of why each one hadn't been "the one." She took to saying the names of the houses aloud as she whizzed past: Time in a Bottle, Sea La Vie, Marsh Madness, Pier Pleasures. She wondered what she would name her house when she got one, if she got one. She wondered if just going to look at Ocean Isle would be cheating since Ryan had intended for her to buy a place at Sunset Beach. Arthur seemed to think that she'd find a house there.

But it was Sunset that held their memories, Sunset that captured their hearts, Sunset that Ryan had mentioned in his letter. She thought of their trip, how they'd always meant to come back but never made the time or had the money. She wished they had. Maybe a return trip would've seemed less magical, would've made Sunset seem like any other place. Maybe then Ryan would've changed his mind, canceled the policy and used the money to take her out to dinner more often or buy her a piece of jewelry. If he had, she wouldn't be here right now. She'd be at home, listening to Marta's blow by blow of her new relationship with Phil.

But of course that didn't sound a whole lot better.

She pedaled away from the house that was sinking into the ocean, putting distance between her and the memory. The opposite direction took her toward 40th Street, the end of the island. She pedaled until she ran out of road, staring at the miles of undeveloped coastline known as Bird Island. She'd heard there was a mailbox there known as the Kindred Spirit. She and Ryan had said they'd go there, but they ran out of time before he had to be back for school. She'd heard that people left notes in that mailbox addressed to soldiers overseas, lost loves, and God. Maybe she would leave a note to Ryan there, if not on this trip then the next. If she was going to buy a house there, there would surely be more trips. She didn't plan to ever live there full-time, but perhaps she would spend summers there.

She straddled the bike and stared out at the windswept beach, her hand making a visor for her eyes. She scanned the horizon, wondering if just beyond it heaven awaited, if in that intersection of sky and water there was a place called eternity. She'd believed that as a little girl, imagining the great cloud of witnesses her daddy preached about waiting there for the souls who crossed from this life to that. Though she didn't subscribe to such simple beliefs anymore, she liked thinking those little-girl thoughts, believing that Ryan waited there, far away yet closer than she realized.

She and Ryan used to talk about things like that all the time. It was how their relationship formed, in a religion class at their small Christian college. The professor had initiated discussions that sparked debate, sometimes passionate, sometimes lasting more than one class. He hadn't been afraid to broach the subjects some of the "good Christian kids" were afraid to touch. He'd insisted they think beyond just regurgitating what they'd been taught, challenge themselves to look deeper, probe into the things they'd always accepted at face value. Oftentimes a group of the more passionate kids would reconvene after class at the local coffee shop to continue the debate or talk more freely. Though at first the questions scared Emily, she felt drawn to them. And to the cute pre-law student who always seemed up for a good fight, if truth be told.

They'd been discussing the concept of grace the day he asked if he could walk her back to her dorm when everyone stood to leave. Talkative, bright, and quick-witted, he'd grown suddenly quiet and even shy as they crossed the quad toward her dorm. She'd found herself to be the one initiating the conversation and, by the time they got back to the dorm, she'd been convinced she'd turned him off somehow, that he'd rethought any interest he'd had. Later that night she'd been reading an assignment for her English class when the phone rang. Thinking it was her mom calling to check in like she always did, she answered with a lazy, barely understandable "Hello?"

His voice was a voice she didn't recognize with her ears. As strange as it sounded, her heart knew it before any other part of her did. When he said her name, it echoed through her whole body. She could never have explained it to anyone — though eventually she did fess up to him — but she knew then and there that she was, somehow, some way, talking to her future husband.

Usually one to enjoy the thrill of the chase, the buildup that came with making small talk and discovering compatibility with Ryan was infuriating. She found herself wanting to just shout it out: "Oh, come on already. We love each other. We were meant to be." As cheesy and trite as it sounded, she was that certain, that fast. But she played along and, though it seemed like the days dragged by, eventually he kissed her. And eventually he proclaimed his love for her. And eventually he met her parents, asked for her dad's blessing, gave her a ring. In some ways it dragged by — that year they spent together before becoming engaged.

But looking back now she realized it had gone by in a flash, an instant. How she longed to go back and do it all again. To sneak glances at him in that coffee shop. To wait for his phone call. To wonder if tonight was the night he'd kiss her. But the question was, if she'd known she would lose him in the end, would she have even accepted that invitation to walk with him? Sometimes she thought that perhaps a safer love — one less consuming — would've been the better route. People who said it was better to have loved and lost than never to have loved at all must not have gone through what she had.

She hiked herself back up onto the bike seat and turned the rusty contraption around. There was a small kink in the chain that caused an annoying hitch in the rotation of the tires, making for a bumpy ride. It was clear no one used these "courtesy bikes" at the motel. No wonder the girl had been more than glad to hand off the key.

She turned up 40th Street, reasoning that she would ride to the end of the street and then head back to the motel and find something to eat for dinner. Her stomach was starting to rumble and the sun would soon start its descent. The bike sometimes seemed more like an untamed horse with its tendency to sputter and shake. She was nearing the end of 40th when she noticed there were some short side roads. Curious, she ventured down one, then another, idly noting the houses. Closer to the intracoastal waterway than the ocean, some of the houses had a good view of the bridge. It might be nice to sit and watch the boats coming and going, watch the cars wait in line to cross over. She'd heard there were rumors they were going to replace the bridge but she didn't want to believe it. The bridge added to the personality of Sunset Beach. Remove that and — as far as she was concerned — you were removing its heart.

When she saw a small For Sale sign tacked

to the porch of one of the smaller, older houses, she started pedaling slower.

She turned around at the end of the street and made another slow pass by the house, her eyes taking in the details as fast as she could without seeming too obvious. There were lights on inside and she didn't want whoever was in there to see her stalking the place. Just as she was about to make a clean getaway, the front door of the house opened and an old woman peeked out. "Can I help you?" she asked, stopping Emily in her tracks. Half of her was still hidden behind the door but Emily could see most of her face through the crack. She looked frightened by Emily's presence, her eyes wide and darting, her mouth void of anything close to a smile.

"I'm sorry. I was just looking at your house." She pointed at the small, nondescript sign tacked to the railing. "I saw your sign and I'm, um, actually looking for a house." She slid down off the bike seat. "Here. At Sunset." She gave the woman a smile and hoped she looked nonthreatening.

"Not used to strangers milling around this time of year." The woman still sounded hesitant, but Emily noticed the door opened a bit wider as she spoke. "In summer, sure.

But it's pretty deserted right now." The woman scanned the street as the door opened fully. Emily noticed the floral print housedress she wore, the moccasins on her feet. She took a step forward, her white calves flashing, laced with enlarged blue veins.

The woman motioned to the porch she was now standing on. "The house, it's not much," she said. "But it's been my home for thirty years." She walked over to the railing, running her hand lovingly along the peeling paint, a caress.

Emily shifted her weight, feeling as if she was observing something intimate, something she didn't have the right to see. Her nosiness had landed her in an odd situation. That would teach her to be a stalker. She searched for the right thing to say but remained silent as her eyes took in the house and the houses on either side of it. A child's tricycle was turned upside down in the yard on the left, one pedal missing.

The woman looked up suddenly, her reverie interrupted for no apparent reason. "You want to see inside?" she asked.

The sun was rapidly descending in the sky and Emily didn't want to bike back to the motel in the dark. And yet, she felt a sense of urgency as she took in the house, the porch with the peeling paint and the small, overlooked sign. She met the woman's eyes, saw something recognizable there as she did. Emily's head began to nod almost reflexively. Before she knew it she was agreeing to come inside, following the old woman past empty flower boxes affixed to the porch railing, the soil gone dry and cracked inside. She kept her eyes on the doorway that led into a house she almost missed completely.

SEVEN

The backyard led to a small dock, the last thing she saw on her tour of the house, although the land was mostly hidden in shadow as the sun disappeared, the last amber rays slipping below the horizon. The house was perfectly positioned for viewing the breathtaking sunsets the island was named for, and Emily found herself drawn to it for the view alone. It was true the inside of the house wasn't much to look at — nice enough, but certainly lacking designer touches. Those were found outside and not made by human hands. She took in the sweeping view of the marsh and Blaine Creek, which fed into Mad Inlet on her left.

To her right she could make out the lights of the bridge twinkling in the distance like a beacon. While touring homes that day Arthur Groves had been chatty, filling her in on the battle over the bridge that waged in the community. Divided almost neatly down the middle, some thought that it should be replaced by a bridge that wouldn't break often or stop traffic every hour on the hour. Others — the romantics, Emily thought — didn't want a large bridge to take the place of the old one. They didn't like the thought of how accessible it would make the island, didn't want more people to find the place. They thought part of the island's charm was the quirky bridge, a good indicator of what waited on the other side.

At the moment all Emily could think of was that the view was perfect just as it was, bridge and all. She inhaled deeply and closed her eyes for a moment as if to seal it in her mind. It was clear that the old woman had left this part for last on purpose; it was the house's best (only?) selling point. Emily stole a glance at her host, whose name she had learned was Ada, to gauge whether she was appreciating the view as much as Emily was. The look on Ada's face was pure reverence, but it was mixed with that pain she had recognized before, on the porch.

The evidence of pain had told Emily they shared something and, as Ada walked her through the house, she had come to learn just how similar their circumstances were. Ada's husband had died a few months earlier after a battle with emphysema and a stroke that weakened and crippled him. Left alone, Ada had made the hard decision to leave this place she loved so that she could go and live with her sister in Florence, South Carolina. "My sister, Ida" — she winked, presumably at the cutesy similarity between her and her sister's names — "she says we'll have a good time, and I like to think that's true," Ada said. Then her voice grew wistful. "But sometimes I can't bear the thought of leaving all this behind."

Emily nodded. "It would be very hard," she agreed, but her words sounded empty and useless even as she said them.

Ada sighed. "But he made me promise, when he knew he didn't have long. He said, 'Promise me you'll go be with Ida, that you won't try to keep this place alone.' " Emily thought about the irony: this woman was giving up a house at Sunset Beach because her husband made her promise, and Emily was buying a house at Sunset Beach because her husband had made her promise.

Ada shrugged, her next words almost as if she'd read Emily's mind. "And we have to keep our promises, don't we? Especially to the dead." She turned to her. "I put that sign out there thinking it was so small no one would see it for a while, it being the off season and all. It was my little test to see if this was meant to be."

Emily thought about Gideon's fleece, one of her father's favorite topics to preach on. He liked to debate whether it was right or wrong for him to lay it out, what it said about Gideon's faith. And yet, it seemed we all laid out fleeces of our own at times. This trip, if she was honest, was her own version of a fleece, telling herself that if she found the perfect house, she would know she was supposed to do what Ryan wanted. Had she not stumbled upon that tiny sign, what would've happened?

Ada spoke again, smiling in earnest for the first time, her words again a reflection of Emily's own thoughts. "I was trying to get out of it, I guess."

Emily smiled back, thinking about being with Arthur Groves that afternoon, the way part of her had felt relieved when none of the houses were right. She could say she tried, but she could also avoid Ryan's wishes with a clear conscience. She chuckled at the thought of the two of them, widows both, trying to get out of what their departed husbands wanted for them and finding each other in the process.

She shivered a little. The temperature had dropped now that the sun had set. She took one last good look at the view from the dock, thinking of how she'd sit out there at night and think, and pray. How she'd feel closer to Ryan on this dock than in the bed they shared in some ways. It was as if he'd arranged a place for them to meet, there by the water. He would've loved this place, of that she was sure. She wondered if he and Ada's husband had finagled this deal from the great beyond. That would be just like him, scheming to get his way. A smile crept over her face. Even now she could feel him nodding and pushing her to say the next words. She followed Ada back into the house and accepted her offer of tea, waiting until the cup was in her hand to speak.

"Thank you for showing me your house," she said. "I like it very much."

Ada nodded and took a sip of her own tea. "I suspected you would." A few seconds of silence passed before Ada spoke again. "You like it enough to take it off my hands?"

Emily nodded, her eyes meeting the older woman's as something passed between them, a look that acknowledged the pain that comes with letting go, and starting over. "I promise to take good care of it," she said.

"It's a special place. You'll see," Ada said.

Emily couldn't say that the place already felt special to her. That she suspected it was the place Ryan had somehow led her to. Instead she finished her tea and carried her cup to the sink, rinsing it as she looked out the kitchen windows into the dark spring night, trying to make out all that would be hers.

EIGHT

June 4, 2007

She'd waited until school was out to close on the house, giving Ada time to make the huge transition of leaving the home where she'd spent thirty years. What would it feel like to lose someone you'd loved all your life? It had been hard enough to lose Ryan and they'd had less than a decade together. What if you'd been with someone for multiple decades? Her heart clenched at the thought. She'd never know that now.

She had arranged to meet with Ada and Arthur to do one last walk-through of the house before she took possession at the closing. She found herself pausing to give Ada the space to say good-bye, her heart breaking a little each time the old woman's voice quivered. Just before they left the house to head to the closing, she put her hand on the old woman's shoulder. "I want you to know I'll take good care of this house," she said.

There were tears in Ada's eyes that she didn't bother to hide. "I know you will. I prayed about who should have this house and I know you're it." She pointed at Emily with a commanding finger. "But I also know this is no place to be alone. This is a house for a family." She gestured at the expanse of the great room/kitchen area behind them, filled with the old furniture she'd thrown in with the house simply because she didn't know what else to do with it. "Lots of room for kids to play here, memories to be made. When our kids were little this place used to be full of wet bathing suits and shell collections, and this floor" — she gestured at the dark hardwood beneath their feet with a laugh — "used to always have sandy footprints tracked across it."

Together they walked out of the house, Ada linking her arm through Emily's for both emotional and physical support. They were about to tackle the few steps from the front porch when Ada turned to take in the house one last time. She looked back at Emily, her eyes widening as if she had remembered something, but then seemed to think better of it.

"Yes?" Emily asked, wondering what it was the woman was not saying.

Ada waved her hand through the air, dispelling whatever thought she'd had. "Nothing, nothing. I'll take care of it," she said. As they made their way slowly down the stairs, she heard the old woman say under her breath, "If I can remember, that is." But Emily didn't press. She didn't want any more advice from Ada, or anyone else for that matter, about what this next chapter of life was supposed to look like.

Emily returned from her day of unpacking for one last night in her second stay at the motel, wanting a bed that was made, a television that was already set up and working. The first thing she'd done was to put the plaque with Jeremiah 29:11 in a prominent space in the house, to remind herself of that hope and future Ryan had said was coming for her, though it seemed out of reach at that moment. All she could see right now was work, work, and more work in her future. She was looking forward to Marta's arrival the next day, both for her best friend's moral support but also for her help with the physical labor of unpacking boxes. Her mom and dad had offered to come down, but Emily had asked them to wait until she was settled. The last thing she needed was her mother's brand of help, which was synonymous, in Emily's world, with critique.

That afternoon standing in her new (old) house, she'd thought better of having them come anytime soon. There was still a lot of updating the house needed and she wondered if her parents would question her sanity at having picked this particular house. Indeed, at that moment she questioned her own sanity. Her emotional reaction to Ada's story, the connection they felt as widows both trying to honor their husbands' last requests, and the way the view of the backyard at sunset all seemed trivial months later in the light of day. She had a panicked thought: What if she'd made a mistake? She shrugged. It was buyer's remorse, and everyone got it. Even she and Ryan had felt it when they'd bought their little starter home — not much but all they could afford at the time. She'd worried about the neighborhood being safe enough. He'd worried whether he could keep up with the responsibilities of home ownership like yard maintenance and household repairs. And it had all turned out okay then.

Trying to block her erratic thoughts, she went to switch on the TV and veg out properly. But when she hit the remote, nothing happened. She began pressing random buttons, watching the blank screen to see if anything happened. But the screen remained black. There were moments when she missed Ryan more acutely than others, and this was one. She wanted him there to help her figure out why the remote wasn't working. In their marriage he handled all the "technical difficulties," as he called them, which basically meant he dealt with anything that ran on electrical current. She looked around the empty room, then, frustrated, called down to the front desk to ask what to do.

The young girl answered, which didn't surprise Emily. She'd yet to see the father. She wondered if he was even around and if the girl was covering for him somehow. Could a girl that young maintain a motel all on her own? More important, could she fix a broken remote? "Hi, this is Emily. Shaw. I'm in the studio room upstairs?"

"Unh-hunh," the girl replied dully.

"My remote control isn't working and I was wondering if you could fix it?"

"I can bring you a new one," the girl said.

Emily thought about asking the girl to leave the office, felt bad for pulling her away from her desk. She was all alone, manning the phone. Then she thought of the last time she'd been there, how she'd seen the girl leaving another room. She obviously expected to have to visit rooms from time to time. "That would be great. I was hoping to watch something mindless, unwind a bit. I bought a house here and —"

"I'll be right up," the girl said and hung up.

She looked down at the dead phone in her hand and shook her head. Teenagers could be so rude. But usually she could find a way past the bravado and posturing and get to their heart. She liked to think that most of her students liked her at school. But none of them unnerved her like this girl, got her rambling in an attempt to create a conversation. She sounded like an idiot and she knew it. She'd have to play it cooler around her. Not act like she cared. And why did she care, anyway? Chances were she'd never see this girl again unless she made an effort. And yet there was something about the girl — the guy she'd seen flirting with her, the way she seemed alone all the time, the flat way she answered questions that told Emily the girl was quietly longing. But for what, Emily couldn't say.

Emily wandered around the room, her eyes straying to the black screen and the door, alternating between the two as the minutes went by. She walked over to the window and peered out, looking for the girl, but saw nothing but the parking lot and the pier beyond. Though it was the beginning of summer, the motel didn't have that many guests, most people visiting Sunset preferring to rent a house and all that came with it. She smiled. A house. Her house. Hers.

She sat down on the loveseat that came with the studio, taking the quiet moment to think of all she should do to set up the house. A list formed in her mind, one that got long quickly. She needed to buy new linens and get groceries — staples — and she wanted some new dishes for the kitchen, beach dishes, she'd come to think of them as. Happy dishes to eat fresh-caught shrimp from, forks to twirl pasta around the tines, glasses to fill with water, yellow rounds of sliced lemon floating on top. Her mother had offered to buy her something as a housewarming gift, perhaps she would ask for those things. And then she would pray about what faces would gather around her table to eat. Beyond the usual suspects, she hoped she'd find some new faces too, that Sunset Beach would offer her some new relationships with people who didn't know her as Ryan's widow first.

She heard heavy footsteps lumbering up the stairs. She waited for the knock to tug open the swollen door, the girl's green gaze meeting her own as she did.

"Hi," she said. She opened the door widely and gestured for her to come in. She watched the girl pass by, noting that she seemed a bit heavier than the last time she saw her. Too much sitting, not enough exercise, too much junk food. Emily remembered a large fast-food cup sitting on the motel desk, filled with soda. She would bet that there'd been fries and a burger with that soda. Maybe she'd start making healthy meals and invite the girl over. With no mother to tend to her, she was unsure whether the girl got many home-cooked meals.

She retrieved the remote from the coffee table and handed it off. Amber pressed buttons just like Emily had done, also watching the TV to no avail. Finally she sighed and put the remote down, crossing over to the TV set itself. She bent down and looked at the set, then crawled around behind it. After a moment she came back out, then walked over and pushed one button on the remote, the set blinking to life with too loud voices. Emily wondered why she'd even wanted it on once the canned laughter and grating voices of a sitcom filled the room. "What did you do?" she asked, impressed.

"Plugged it in," she said. Then she gave Emily a look that told her all she needed to know as to her opinion of Emily's intellect.

Amber gave a little wave and headed for the door, Emily casting about for something to say but reasoning it was best to let her get back to work. The girl was almost at the door when she stopped short and bent over at the waist, her hand covering her mouth. Emily rushed to Amber's side, put her hand on her back. "You okay?" Her voice was barely a whisper in spite of the loud TV.

The girl straightened up, her back stiff and proud as she did, her momentary weakness gone. She looked at Emily and nodded. "I'm fine," she said, then she hurried out of the room, leaving Emily alone with just the TV for company. She stared at the open doorway, wishing Amber had stayed, had told her what accounted for the depths of sadness she kept behind those startling green eyes of hers.

She stepped outside into the breezeway, wanting to smell the salt air and wondering if it would've been better just to stay the night in her new house than to come back to this place. As she did she could hear a sound below. Someone retching into the bushes by the parking lot. She couldn't see the face, but she knew who it was. She listened for the sounds to stop and then she heard footsteps walk away and the door to the office open and shut again. "Okay," she said to the air. "I'll help her."

She went back into the room, thinking of another sermon her father preached as often as he could, the gist of which was that we are all connected, we are all here to help each other, and the most random encounters are all part of a bigger plan.

NINE

When Emily checked out of the motel the next morning, she found Amber behind the desk, business as usual, no reference to what had happened. Even when Emily made a joke about being so dense about the TV, Amber only gave her a brief, polite smile in response. "You here alone again?" she tried.

"Yep," Amber said flatly.

"Haven't ever seen your dad around," Emily ventured.

Amber looked up at her, her green eyes as flat as her voice. "You won't," she said, then turned back to the computer. She didn't even wave good-bye when Emily left.

If she was supposed to help this girl she had a hard row to hoe, to borrow one of her mother's phrases. She longed to cut through the pleasantries, look into those beautiful green eyes, grab the girl's hands, and beg her to tell her what was going on. But that would scare the poor thing to death, not to

112

mention be decidedly uncool. She would make up a plan to keep in contact with Amber, and somehow she would wear her down.

When Marta arrived, she brought up Amber right away without even offering to take her on the "grand tour" of the house. Marta refused to offer her two cents until she did. So Emily did exactly what Ada had done that day in April when she'd gone on her tour, taking her through the main living area, then each of the four bedrooms — two on either side of the great room — before parading her out to the screen porch off the back of the house with the view of the yard and dock and water beyond. Emily had already carried two plastic chairs out to the dock and had even allowed herself a precious few moments to sit out there first thing this morning.

Now Marta flopped down into one of the chairs and tilted her chin up to the sun. She waved Emily away. "You get back to work. I'm hanging here all day."

Emily grinned. "How did I know that's what you were going to say?"

Marta squinted up at her. "Because you know me so well. Surely you didn't think I was going to come down here and *work*?"

"If we both work hard, I think we'll get

the place set up in no time. Then we can go to the beach and sit out here as much as we want." Her eyes flickered over to the bridge and back to Marta. She'd seen a sign on the town bulletin board when she took a walk announcing a meeting about the proposal for the new bridge and wondered if she should go. "How long are you staying anyway?" Emily asked. She'd envisioned Marta being a summer roommate, taking advantage of her friend's unexpected inheritance by staying at the beach most of the summer. They were both off from teaching anyway.

Marta didn't answer, instead she abruptly stood up and began trudging to the house. "You're such a slave driver!" she called out teasingly over her shoulder. "Work, work, work."

Emily followed, a premonition nagging at her as to why she'd avoided the question. But she didn't want to know if Marta didn't want to tell her. She knew she'd get around to answering the question eventually. "So getting back to my story about the girl at the motel," she said, allowing the conversation to be the subject change they needed.

She caught Marta up on her few encounters with the girl, adding up all the things she'd both witnessed and guessed at, creating a justifiable case for her immediate involvement, she thought. She waited for Marta to concur. What she couldn't explain was why she was drawn to this particular girl. It wasn't like she didn't have her fill of teenagers at school.

Marta and Emily worked side by side in silence, wiping down counters and shelves, before they added dishware and food items to them. Marta looked thoughtful but in no rush to render a verdict. Emily stole a few glances at her, trying to figure out what she was thinking.

"I can see why you'd want to help this girl. And I agree it sounds like something's going on with her. But I just hope you're being safe — not looking for a cause just because you're without one currently." Marta put down the rag and spray bottle in her hands. "I think for a long time saving Ryan was your cause. And then for the past year just keeping your head above water was enough to think about. Now you've done this" — she gestured to the house — "really brave thing and maybe you're kind of looking for a purpose in this new . . . chapter in your life."

She sighed, flustered. "I don't know what I'm saying. I guess I mean just be careful. You don't know anyone here. You don't know anything about this girl's father. Or . . . anything. I just don't want you to get yourself in a mess here."

"Well, if I do, you'll be here to bail me out," Emily replied, giving Marta her best "it's all right" smile.

Marta closed her eyes for a moment, then opened them again. "Well, that's the other thing." She met Emily's eyes.

"You're not staying," Emily said, the dull, flat tone of her voice sounding close to Amber's from this morning.

"I can't, Em." Marta's face revealed how torn she was. She didn't want to ditch Emily, but she didn't want to leave a burgeoning relationship while it was still . . . burgeoning. Emily understood, but that didn't make it any easier to hear.

"He wants to take me to a baseball game. He wants to see that new summer blockbuster movie about aliens invading the White House. He wants to drive to a peach stand and come back and show me how to make his mother's famous cobbler. He . . ." Marta stopped talking but the eager, happy look she'd gotten when she described the coming summer with Phil stayed on her face.

Emily held her hand up. "I get it. I totally do. I'd do the exact same thing. It's okay."

She thought of that first summer with Ryan with a pang. They'd had such a good time together, each experience as if they were the first people to ever have it. Falling in love was irreplaceable and she wouldn't deny Marta the chance to savor every moment. But she hated the thought of being alone at sunset in the meantime.

"I'll still come down some. I can come during the week when Phil is working and stuff. You know you can't get rid of me that easy."

Emily shrugged and put on her best brave face. The same one she'd used to convince her parents she didn't need to move in with them after Ryan died. The same one she'd used the day she went back to work after the funeral. The same one she'd worn in front of Phil when he told her that Ryan had arranged for the house she now stood in. "I'll have plenty to keep me busy here, I'm sure."

"You'll see," Marta agreed. "This summer will fly by." She winked. "You'll have your little project to keep you busy. Maybe you'll change that poor girl's life."

Emily pondered that for a moment. She didn't feel qualified to change anyone's life. But she couldn't deny the pull she felt toward Amber, and the suspicion that there might be a reason for it.

The next morning she awoke to the smell of something sweet and rich baking in the oven. Marta wasn't one to cook much, but when she did, her delicacies made people sit up and take notice. She wondered if Marta had baked anything for Phil. That would probably seal the deal if it wasn't sealed already. She smiled at the thought — taking joy in being able to feel nothing but happiness for her best friend.

She entered the kitchen and watched silently as Marta bounced around, pulling a tray of muffins from the oven and resting them on the counter. She looked up to see Emily and grinned. "Thought I'd give you an excuse to talk to that girl." She gestured to the muffins. "Chocolate chip," she explained. "No teenager can resist them. Just ask my students. Even the most anorexic-inclined can't say no."

Emily thought about Amber throwing up in the bushes and wondered, not liking the conclusion she came to.

Marta waved her hand in Emily's direction, dismissing her words. "You're an adult. Any interest you take in her will scare her initially. You just have to get past that part."

Emily had to smile. This was not the first

time Marta and she had tried to invest in people. Ryan used to call it their "meddling schemes." He would say, "You two are like a steamroller and a jackhammer had a love child."

"We just want to help people," Emily would retort.

He would raise his eyebrows and nod. "Yeah, whether they want to be helped or not."

He'd never gotten over the time she and Marta set up Ryan's sister Susan with Marta's brother Rob. For the record, that scheme had actually worked — for a while. Unfortunately, it had ended with Susan camping out on their couch for several days eating multiple cartons of ice cream and blubbering over sad romantic movies. Ryan thought she'd never leave and completely blamed Marta and Emily. After that he'd forbidden any more matchmaking of family members. Not long after that he got sick and all of Emily's energy went toward getting him better anyway. Come to think of it, she and Marta hadn't hatched a meddling scheme since then.

Marta picked up a muffin, plated it, and handed it to Emily. "No time like the present, I say. But try one first."

She thanked Marta and accepted the

plate, slathering the muffin with butter Marta had set out. She poured a cup of coffee and carried the plate and mug to a seat at the kitchen table, admiring her view as she did. She could see the water from where she sat and thought that this wasn't a bad way to start the day. She looked around the room and wondered when the furnishings that had come with the house would stop feeling like someone else's, when the house would come to feel like home. She took a bite of the muffin, the rich taste of warm, melted chocolate chips mixing with the sweet bread. Paired with her cup of coffee, it was the perfect breakfast. "I hope you made plenty of those," she said to Marta, who was starting to clean up. She tried not to think about her leaving, how much she liked having her around.

Marta held up a freezer bag. "I even made enough to freeze for later," she said and winked. She was trying to take care of her, she knew, to leave something behind for when she was no longer there. Emily appreciated the effort even if it made her miss her friend while she was still standing right in front of her.

"Now I want you to get dressed and take a basket of muffins to the girl to thank her for her hospitality," Marta ordered. "I'm going to sit on the dock and enjoy the view for a bit."

Emily almost argued with Marta about the "hospitality" Amber had showed her, but instead she mock-saluted her. "Yes, ma'am." Emily finished her breakfast and carried her plate to the sink. Last night they'd gotten the kitchen all set up and made a big grocery run that made the place feel more habitable. The smell of coffee and baked goods helped even more. Marta shooed her away and she obediently went to her room to dress and throw her hair into a ponytail. It had gotten long in the last year and Emily liked the way it looked. Sometimes she caught herself wondering what Ryan would think of it before she realized that Ryan didn't have an opinion anymore. At least, not one she could ask him about. She thought about the horizon, the place where the water met the sky, and wondered again if Ryan waited there.

She shook her head, her ponytail swaying as she did, and put on some lip gloss and mascara — her bare minimum makeup for the summer. Once she had some sun on her cheeks the look would be complete. Maybe she and Marta would head to the beach for the afternoon, tilt their chins toward the sun, and take their chances with the harmful rays. Cancer didn't scare her nearly as much as it once did. She'd already fought that particular villain, already accepted its defeat. If it came gunning for her, well, at least she'd be with Ryan. In some ways, Emily didn't care what happened to her anymore. Her life was, in some very important ways, over. No one had to understand or accept that but her.

In the kitchen she found the basket prepared as Marta had promised. She'd found a small one in Ada's things she'd left behind and tucked the muffins into a hand-embroidered tea towel. Emily fingered the tea towel, tracing the outline of a flower done in pink and green. It was simple and pretty and Emily found that part of her wanted to keep it. She could hang it on a towel bar in the kitchen, a little memorial to the woman who once loved this house. But Amber might enjoy having something pretty, something special. Without a mother around, she probably didn't have little feminine touches in her life. Emily picked up the basket and called out to Marta that she was leaving.

"Good luck!" Marta called out from her room, the door closing between them. Emily guessed that she was talking to Phil. She remembered those early days of a relationship, the excitement that came each time you heard the other person's voice, the revelations that came with each conversation, the connection that grew with every phone call. She remembered how she used to get that goofy grin on her face whenever Ryan would call, how she hated to hang up the phone, how each time they talked it seemed she gained some new insight to who he was — and why she wanted to be with him more than ever. She suspected every married couple looked back fondly, and wistfully, at those early, exhilarating days. The memories became even more substantial when there was only the past to look back at, with no prospect for a future.

As she walked to the motel carrying the basket, she thought about all the nevers of her marriage. She would never share a positive pregnancy test with him, never drive to the hospital to give birth, both nervous and scared and giddy. She would never stare down at their child and see if he or she got his eyes or her ears, his smile or her coloring. She would never celebrate another anniversary, another birthday, another holiday with her husband. She would never know what he looked like as an old man, never see each other as mom and dad, then grandma and grandpa. She looked around her as cars drove past and happy families milled around the shopping area in the center of town. She would never spend a single night with him in the very house he made possible for her.

She arrived at the motel feeling more than a little sad, and a bit upset with herself for entertaining the thoughts she'd allowed to roll around her mind as she walked. She should be happier, she reasoned. She should work harder to appreciate what she'd been given. She was smack-dab in the middle of paradise and acting like she was anywhere but. She glanced down at the muffins. Marta had the right idea. She would focus on others and maybe it would help her have a better attitude.

She entered the office to find it empty. She crossed the small room and set the muffins on the desk, glancing around as she did. There was no sign of Amber and, to make matters worse, Amber had left her purse in plain sight on the desk. There probably wasn't much of value in it, but she didn't want it to get stolen by someone who saw an opportunity, and there could be any number of opportunities with all the tourists milling around this area, especially other bored teens looking for something to do, a bit of daring.

Even though it wasn't her business — not really — she went around behind the desk to hide the purse and write a note to Amber explaining that she'd left the muffins as a thank-you and she was sorry she'd missed her. As she lifted the purse it fell open. Lying right on top of the other contents was a telltale white stick, similar to the one Emily had bought just before Ryan got diagnosed. That one had been negative, something she'd spent many sleepless nights wondering about. Was that good or bad? Would it have been too hard for her to have a baby during his battle with cancer? What would it have been like to raise that child without him? And yet, she would have some part of him, living on. Her hand went to the test, almost before her mind realized what she was doing. Another thing that was none of her business, not really.

But that didn't stop her as she held the stick up to the light, studying the control window with its definitive pink line. The window beside it almost looked empty until Emily looked closer. She could just make out a faint line there too. She tilted the test and peered closer, uncertain as to whether her eyes were playing tricks on her. But then she remembered how Amber had thrown up in the bushes, running from the room in

125

an effort to hide the telltale signs from another person. And she knew that what she was seeing was real. She dropped the stick as if it had burned her but it missed the open purse and fell to the floor.

She dropped to her knees to feel around underneath the desk where it had fallen. She was crawling around down there when she heard the door to the office open and Amber's giggle. She froze, wishing she could hide but there was "nowhere to run, nowhere to hide," just like the old song said. She froze, listening as Amber's giggle was echoed by a deeper laugh. Then there was silence and the sounds of lips meeting, the smacking sound she knew from distant experience. She closed her eyes and prayed for them to leave, to give her just a moment to get out of there.

And then, amazingly, she thought her prayers were answered. "Want to go to my room?" she heard the deep voice ask.

Her heart sank as she thought of the young man she'd seen leaning across the desk that time, his body language too familiar, too entitled to be just another customer. She looked down at the pregnancy test she held in her hands, made a mental note to wash her hands as soon as she got out of there, and held her breath waiting for Amber to answer him. A better person would've willed the girl to say no. But Emily wanted a chance to escape the awkward position she'd found herself in. She thought about that second line and reasoned that one more trip to this man's room wouldn't make things any worse. At least she didn't think it could.

She waited until they were gone to let out the breath she'd been holding since they entered the room, deposited the test back into the purse, and breathed a second sigh of relief that Amber had been too wrapped up in that guy to notice her muffins, walk over to the desk, and find her hidden underneath it. She left the muffins without the note she'd intended to write and fled the office, but not before scanning the front of the motel to determine which room could possibly be his. Part of her wanted to go door to door until she found them and yank Amber out of there. But a cooler head prevailed and she turned away, feeling worse about the situation than when she'd come, holding up those silly muffins as if they could fix anything. She walked home trying to decide what her next move would be, grateful Marta would be there to help her figure it out, and worried about when she'd be left to do life at Sunset alone.

TEN

Marta left three days later — days spent finishing the unpacking and settling in, cooking and eating delicious food, watching old movies on the small television Ada had left behind, and walking the beach talking about Phil and debating Emily's options for reaching out to Amber. By the time Marta left, she was certain of two things: Marta was smitten, and Emily shouldn't give up on helping this girl. How she would do that still remained a mystery. A few times she and Marta "happened by" the motel, hoping to spot the young man going in or out of his room or steal a glance of Amber entering or exiting one of the rooms looking guilty, or happy, or whatever the girl was feeling at this point. No matter how Amber felt, she had to be confused and lonely. This wasn't exactly the type of thing girls discussed with their fathers and Amber had been pretty clear he was the only family she had.

Before she left, Marta had put her hand on Emily's shoulder. "Be careful," she had warned. "You don't know anything about this kid."

Emily had nodded obediently. "I will," she promised. But she wasn't so sure.

Marta's return glance told her she knew what Emily was thinking but blessedly left it alone.

That night after Marta left, she went and sat on the front porch, feeling sad and more than a little lonely without her friend's presence. She understood Marta had to go. Phil had an important work event he wanted her at — a cocktail party where she would be meeting his coworkers and boss. It said a lot that Phil wanted her there, and she was excited about the direction things were headed. Emily felt a bit of pride that she — and Ryan, come to think of it — had a part in Phil and Marta pairing off. She shook her head at the mystery of it all, the way things worked out, coming together even as they were coming apart, woven by an expert weaver. One thing was for sure, she wasn't going to understand His design this side of heaven.

She was about to go inside when she saw a man walking down the quiet street. Off the beaten path, this wasn't a road you typically saw people walking along. Most people didn't venture this far down 40th Street, she'd come to realize, not knowing that these houses were even down here. The effect was private but also isolating at times. Sometimes she liked the quiet, the time for reflection, but sometimes she wondered if she'd been better off in the center of town where all the action was. The merry widow instead of the reclusive hermit.

For lack of anything better to focus on, she watched the man walk, figuring he was just out for a stroll, a tourist exploring the island. From a distance he looked to be about her age, trim and nicely built, the kind of man Marta would point out if she were still there. "Now what about him?" she would say. "If he lives here you should find out where." Emily would object, of course, tell her how ridiculous she was being. And yet, as the man got closer, even she had to admit he was a nice-looking guy. Nothing like Ryan though. She always had to add that.

Her heart picked up its pace when he slowed as he got to her house. She watched as his eyes narrowed when he saw her sitting there. He looked as confused as she did as he turned and made his way up her walk.

"C-Can I help you?" she asked, feeling not at all brave. She scanned the length of the street, wondering if there was anyone around to hear her scream. She'd watched one too many true crime documentaries, she told herself. This was Sunset Beach, North Carolina, not the mean streets of New York.

He looked past her, at the door of the house behind her. "Is Ada here?" he asked.

That explained it. He didn't realize Ada had moved. "No, I, um, bought her house. She moved in with her sister. I just moved in a few days ago." She put her hands on her knees to steady herself. There was something familiar about this man, something that set her on edge and made her heart beat even faster. She didn't need Marta to point out his looks. Tall, dark, and handsome described him to a T. She swallowed and forced herself to hold his gaze.

He gave a little laugh and shook his head. "Well, that explains it. She's gotten so forgetful lately and I couldn't get her on the phone, and I finally just decided to head over here and check on the old bird."

"Well, I assume she's just fine, living in Florence, South Carolina, now. I can give

131

you her new address if you like." She rose from her seat on the porch just for something to do. From her place at the top of the stairs she found herself looking down on him and she rather liked the height advantage. Even though he seemed like a perfectly nice guy, she was also upright in case she needed to run.

"Did she happen to mention I might be coming by, to get something?"

Emily shook her head. "No . . ." She thought through her few conversations with Ada, trying to remember anything like that. "Sorry." She shrugged and — she couldn't help it — wondered what she looked like to him in her denim cutoffs and Ryan's old T-shirt that no longer smelled like him, her hair wind-blown and her face makeup-less. Her cheeks, at least, had picked up some sun so she didn't look like a gaunt ghost. She broke his gaze as her cheeks grew warmer, her eyes focused on the plank floor of the porch and her bare feet. She should've painted her toenails like Marta suggested.

"Are you sure?" he pressed. "She might've mentioned something about the bridge tender's log? That doesn't sound familiar at all?"

She shook her head again. But then a memory from the day of the closing surfaced, Ada nearing the porch railing close to where she stood now, her steps slow and deliberate as she took one last look at the place. She'd started to say something to Emily, but then said she would take care of it . . . if she could just remember. "Wait!" Emily said. "She did start to tell me something but then she said she'd do it. She might've meant to get in touch with you and make arrangements. I guess." She shrugged.

He let out a relieved sigh and nodded. "That sounds like the last few conversations I had with her. I was a friend of her husband's and when he died, he left me something. She promised when she sold the house she'd get it to me but I never heard from her." He looked around, seeming to notice the empty street for the first time. He grinned and when he did, the feeling of familiarity struck her even more, her mind scrambling for the name that was on the tip of her tongue. "Sorry if I scared you," he apologized. He climbed the few steps between them so he was close enough to extend his hand to shake. "I'm —"

She interrupted. "Brady Rutledge," she breathed aloud, mortified even as the name slipped from her lips, her breath catching as her hand was enfolded by his for the briefest of moments. He let go, his momentary shocked expression quickly replaced by a laugh. He threw his head back and looked up at the sky, that wide trademark grin she'd memorized in film filling his very real-life face. "No one's called me that for years," he said and looked back at her. The grin was gone and a smirk remained. He nodded. "My name's actually Kyle Baker."

As he said it she remembered reading an article while waiting for her hair to be cut in one of those celeb magazines about "The Disappearance of Brady Rutledge." He had left the film business shortly after the success of his one and only film, *Just This Once.* The article had said that he'd gone into acting hesitantly, persuaded by those close to him because of his good looks and love for acting. He'd given no interviews as to why he left acting, just declined subsequent roles and slipped away when no one was looking. The interview had speculated on where the talented young man had landed. And where in the world someone with his recognizable face could hide. She thought of how desolate Sunset had been in the off season. With the exception of the summer season, this wouldn't be a bad place to fall off the radar.

"Sorry," she apologized. "I just recognized you from . . ." She searched for the right words to finish her sentence. *From my favorite movie? From your pictures I stared at a little too long? From the ongoing joke I had with my now-dead husband about my crush on you?* She settled for, "From before."

"It's fine." He smiled at her. "I just don't meet new folks all that often. I tend to stay behind the scenes or hang out with people who already know me so this kind of thing doesn't happen too much." From the way he looked at her, she could tell he knew she was mortified by the whole exchange, and more than a little thrown off by his presence. The look on his face wasn't that of a confident, cocky movie star. He looked like just another guy trying to say the right thing. A guy who, as it were, just happened to be far better looking than any other guy she'd seen in a long time. Later she would apologize to Ryan for thinking that. But for now she tried to take in the changes in him, gauging whether he looked older or better. She decided on both. She had to laugh and shake her head. She'd had a strange couple of days but this took the cake.

"I'm sorry," he said. "I should've thought about what I was doing. I didn't even think about the movie thing. Those days were so long ago, I figure most folks have forgotten all that by now."

She shook her head. "No, not really. I mean, I haven't." Nice. She sounded like an idiot.

He nodded, chewed on that for a moment. "Well, they have here. And that's what counts most. You'll find things are different here. In a good way. If you're looking to start over, or change your life, this is about as good a place as any."

She looked away, her eyes filling with those pesky involuntary tears that were as much a part of her life as hangnails and hiccups. "That's good to know," was all she could say in return.

"Maybe you have a number where I could reach her?" he asked. "I'd like to come back when you're more . . . settled and pick up what Ada's husband left for me. But I'll call and make sure she left it like she said. And if you want, you can call her and check out my story. Just ask her about the bridge tender's log and she'll explain what it is, and why I want it."

"Sure. I'll get that for you," she said. She walked inside quickly and over to the number she'd placed under a magnet on the fridge, scribbled it on the back of a grocery receipt, returned to the porch, and handed it to him. "Nice to meet you," she managed to add, even though just being around him made her tongue-tied.

"You too," he said. "Although I never got your name."

"Emily. Shaw." She fumbled, feeling more and more stupid the longer they stood there. "And that's the only name I have." She tried to recover with an even stupider joke.

"Good to know." He smiled. "Well, nice to meet you, Emily Shaw." He winked and, when he did, all those heart-fluttering, long-ago crush feelings came swelling to the surface. "See ya later."

He turned and ambled away as she lowered herself back down on the porch chair, watching until he disappeared from sight and thinking about how his hand felt in hers, warm and weathered, not like a movie star's hand at all.

ELEVEN

Emily eased into a life at Sunset that was quiet, simple, and, if she was honest, lonely. She found a small bookstore on the mainland that kept her beach bag filled with new novels for reading on the beach, thanks to the consistently good recommendations of the book mavens who staffed the store. But brief encounters with salespeople hardly counted as real relationships. And the books she took home, while filling her time, didn't fill her heart. As each story ended, she couldn't help closing the novels with a renewed sense of loss and pain at the thought of never again having a great love like the ones she'd read about. And yet, she was resigned to this hand she'd been dealt, this end she'd come to. She looked around from her dock as the sun began to set on another Wednesday night and reasoned that it could be worse. Alone as she was, Ryan had certainly arranged for an amazing place to spend her widowhood.

Laughter perked her ears, rising over the sound of the water lapping and the birds calling. She looked in the direction it was coming from, knowing it was the children in the house next door. She'd caught sight of them and their mother from time to time, always offering a polite smile before darting inside. The last thing she wanted was to be around a happy family. It was hard enough to see their cartoon-print wet towels and bright bathing suits hanging over the deck railing, reminders of the things she should have by now.

She looked away from the sight, focusing back on the water. She debated going inside. Maybe there'd be something good on TV. She needed to replace Ada's old set soon. Perhaps tomorrow she would venture to the big box store in Shallotte and splurge. There was a bit of money left in the account from Ryan's life insurance policy for home improvements. And a flat screen, top-quality television would be a definite home improvement.

Sometimes she thought about going back home, living there full-time and arranging visits to Sunset for a few days at a time. But something made her stay, a child digging in her heels out of sheer stubbornness. Ryan had wanted her here, had intended to give her this and — even if she hadn't exactly wanted it for herself — she had to trust that somewhere in this summer was a new beginning for her. She just had to keep waiting. And the truth was there wasn't much to go home to. Her mother would only pester her about dating again, arranging contrived meetings with her version of appropriate men. And Marta was still head over heels over Phil, though she had promised another visit soon the last time they'd talked.

"Hey!" A little voice cut through her evening reverie, startling her.

She looked over at the house next door, toward where the voice was coming from, and spotted the child in the strip of grass between their yards. "Yes?" she asked, her voice tentative and hoarse. She wondered how long it had been since she last spoke to another person. She had to change that. Get a job or volunteer or something. Maybe the little bookstore was hiring.

"You want a popsicle?" the child called. He walked closer, waving a red popsicle in the air that was melting down his arm. Emily would be willing to bet that he had already licked it before his offer to "share" it with her.

She gave him a polite smile, her heart hurting a little at the sight of him. He was barefooted and wore plaid pajama pants but no shirt, his chest streaked with additional red stains. His blond hair was damp, sticking to his forehead, and his mouth was also ringed in red. "No thank you," she said, hoping he'd get bored and go away quickly.

"My name's Noah," he said. He looked from her to the popsicle and back again. Then with a shrug he ran his tongue up the side of it, sucking the juice with a loud slurp. He swallowed, grinned, and held out the popsicle. "If you change your mind, we've got more inside. My mom got them today. She said I couldn't have one, but since you don't want it, I figure I better eat it."

She nodded. "Good thinking," she agreed. Hey, she wasn't the kid's mother.

On cue a woman's voice hollered from the porch next door, "Noah!" Next to her a blond-headed little girl stood, her hands on her hips, just like her mother's. She also called Noah's name, with the same amount of insistence.

"I think your mom wants you," Emily said to Noah, who seemed not to have heard. He was intent on watching a boat traveling down the intracoastal waterway. He bit into the popsicle, oblivious as he happily crunched away.

Emily waved her hand in the air in the direction of the mother and daughter. "He's over here!" she called. "He's with me."

The woman started down the steps and crossed the yard toward the dock, her daughter struggling to keep up. Emily rose to greet them, feeling a bit nervous at the thought of meeting her neighbors this way. She hadn't bothered to shower and was still wearing the cut-off sweats and T-shirt that she'd slept in the night before. She ran a hand through her hair, as if that could help.

"I'm so sorry he came over here uninvited," the woman said. She strode forward and snatched the popsicle from Noah's hand. He began to holler at the indignity. "I specifically told you you couldn't have this," the woman said to him. She shook her head at the popsicle, now dripping onto her hand. She pointed at their house. "Go," she instructed.

Noah gave her a little wave, still sniffling. "It's not fair," she heard him mumble as he walked away.

The woman turned to the little girl standing beside her with a matching scowl. "Sara, will you please go with your brother and help him wash off?"

The girl rolled her eyes skyward and with a huff, expressed her displeasure. "Now he's going to be all sticky and he just had his bath." She stalked after Noah, catching up to him in a few strides. Emily and her neighbor watched them go in silence.

"Sorry again," the woman said. "Nothing like a little family drama on an otherwise quiet summer evening." She gave Emily a little smile. "I'm Claire Connolly." She started to extend her hand but looked at the dripping popsicle in it and changed her mind. "I'll save you from the formalities."

"I'm Emily Shaw," she replied and smiled, feeling more at ease around her neighbor now that she was in front of her. Though beautiful in a careless way, with the blonde, sun-kissed good looks of a Hollywood starlet, there was something disarming about her, something genuine and unassuming. Emily felt badly about avoiding her for the past few days and wished she had words to explain her rudeness.

"I'm so sorry we haven't been over here before. We got down here later this summer than usual and it seems I've been playing catch-up ever since, trying to open the house and do all the things the kids want to do. I feel like a cruise director." She glanced down at the red trails the popsicle was starting to leave down her arm and sighed. "Mind if I take this up to the house to throw it away? It's going to start dripping off my elbow soon."

"Oh, sure." Emily gave a little wave and took a step back toward her chair. "It was nice to meet you."

Claire gave her a confused look and shook her head as she made a waving motion for Emily to get up. "No, you come with me. I want to know all about how you talked old Ada into finally giving up her house." She started walking away, waving her arm again to indicate that Emily was supposed to follow. She continued talking as they made their way across the yard to her house. Emily glanced back at the dock, her lone chair, her drink perched on the weathered boards beside it, ice melting in the glass. Maybe she wouldn't be spending a lonely evening watching the sun go down and staring at the lights on the bridge in the distance as cars came and went across it. She listened to Claire's running monologue as she ushered them into the back door of her house. She deposited the popsicle in the trash and washed her hands without so much as a stutter.

"We never thought she'd actually sell that house. She talked a good game but she loved this place so much. In fact, when we first got here I didn't even realize someone else was living over there. I kept meaning to get over and see if Ada needed anything, and I wondered why we hadn't heard a peep out of her. She was usually on our doorstep before we could get the car unloaded." She grabbed a towel from a hook and wiped her hands dry. "Do you happen to know where she went? I'd love to send her a card."

"Oh, sure," Emily replied. "I have the address of her sister, Ida. She went to live with her."

"Well, good for her. I know that's what Frank wanted. But of course once he was gone I had no idea whether she'd keep her promise." She laughed. "He used to tease her about that. Tell us we were to 'report her to the authorities' if she didn't comply. As if we knew what authorities to report her to!"

Emily thought of that evening, her conversation with Ada and how seriously she'd taken her promise. Even if it meant giving up something she loved to do so. "She was happy, I think," Emily said. "In the end. With her decision. She seemed . . . excited about spending time with her sister. This place gets kinda . . . lonely. At times." Emily thought of the empty chair beside her on the dock, another long, lonely night stretching out ahead of her before Noah showed up with his red popsicle.

"Ha!" Claire said. "Lonely is not a word in my vocabulary. I never get a second to myself. Even in the bathroom. They find me, I swear!" She looked around, as if suddenly realizing the kids were unaccounted for. "Noah! Sara!" she called.

From the loft above she heard Sara's answer. "We're up here. I'm reading Noah a bedtime story."

"Okay!" Claire called back. She looked back at Emily. "That girl is God's gift to me. I'd have lost it years ago without her around. She's such a big help with her little brother. If he'd have been born first he'd have been an only child, I can tell you that." Claire started scrounging around in a cupboard and produced a bottle of red wine. "Can I interest you in a glass?" she asked. "This is Mommy Juice, I tell the kids." She winked at Emily.

Before Emily could answer, she poured two glasses and handed her one. Emily thanked her and took a tentative sip. As the daughter of a Baptist preacher she'd never been one to drink. But she had to admit it felt nice to share a glass of wine with this energetic woman who could possibly be a friend, or at least another human being to trade bits of conversation with from time to time. It certainly beat another lonely night contemplating running back home. Emily followed Claire into the adjoining living area and waited for her to move toys and books out of her way so she could sit. All around them was the detritus of family life — laundry piles, cast off sippy cups, a stray red flip-flop, the sole printed with ladybugs.

"Sorry about the mess," Claire said, noticing her noticing. "I'd tell you to come back on the weekend when my husband gets here and it'll be cleaner but that wouldn't be true." She shrugged her shoulders and took another sip of wine. "I keep promising myself that one weekend I'll actually clean up before he gets here on Friday, but it never happens."

"I could help you sometime," Emily blurted before she knew what she was saying.

"Oh no! Did you think I was fishing for help? I'm sorry!" Claire exclaimed. "I'm just trying to be honest. I mean, if you're going to be my neighbor you might as well know the deal."

"I didn't think you were asking. I just thought I could help. I mean, I'm not married and I don't have any kids, and I have a lot of time on my hands this summer and . . . I wouldn't mind having something to do. That's all," Emily said. She saw Claire's eyes flicker over the plain gold band on Emily's left ring finger, then dart away. Someday, if they truly got to be friends, she'd explain.

"Well, that's awfully nice of you." Claire set her wine glass down on the coffee table and reached for the pile of laundry, her hands folding the clothing without even looking, robot-like. "I will never turn down help. These two little monkeys wear me out." She set down a small folded T-shirt and looked around the house as if she was seeing it anew. "Every spring I tell my husband I'm not coming down here alone again." She sighed. "And every June I'm right back here." She grabbed another item of clothing, a miniature pair of khakis like the ones Ryan used to wear. He would've loved to see a son of his in those.

"Where's your husband?" Emily asked.

"He stays home and works." Claire gestured to the house. "Someone has to pay for all of this." She laughed, gave up on folding the laundry, and leaned back against the couch. "This house has been in my family a long time. My grandfather and Frank were friends, actually. So when Rick — that's my

husband — and I were planning our life together, we decided that once we had kids
this is how we'd do it. My kids would get to
grow up like I did."

"So you spent summers here?"

"Oh yeah. Worked at the Island Market,
hung out with the summer kids up at the
pier." A small smile crossed her face. She
held her hands up. "Summer romances,
constant pranks, sneaking around our parents. The whole shooting match. It was a
great way to grow up." She sighed, folded
her hands across her stomach. "It's a sacri-
fice though. I miss my husband. My friends
back home. And while life in paradise is
wonderful, it can get kinda dull sometimes."

Emily laughed. "Yeah, I'm finding that
out."

Claire's eyes lit up. "You should come
with me tomorrow night! I'm going to a
community meeting. We're fighting to save
the bridge." She pointed in the direction of
where the bridge was, as if Emily didn't
know which bridge she was referring to.

"You want to save it?" she asked.

"Oh yeah, it's part of my childhood. I
can't imagine my kids getting to Sunset on
some big sophisticated high-rise bridge like
the state wants to put in. Our little pontoon
bridge is part of the charm of this place."

149

She grinned and lifted her chin. "And I'm not going down without a fight."

Emily nodded. "Sometimes at night I sit and watch the bridge open and close and, in the distance, I can hear the cars rumbling over it. I watch the lights of the boats that line up to get through. It is kind of quaint and appealing."

Claire leaned forward, eager. "Exactly. Can you imagine them just doing away with that?"

She shook her head. "I really can't."

"Then you'll come? To the meeting?" Claire's excitement over the cause shone in her eyes.

"Sure . . . I mean, I guess," Emily agreed. How did she explain to her neighbor that she literally had nothing else to do and that any offer was better than another lonely night? Even if her heart wasn't in the bridge fight, she would welcome the opportunity to be around other people. And maybe some of their passion would seep into her, carried on the summer breeze.

TWELVE

She was ready to go with Claire and the children to the meeting hours before it was time to leave. She sat in her living area and stared at the clock hands making another laborious loop around the face, still feeling like a guest in her house. "Why would you have ever thought it would be good for me to come here without you?" she asked aloud in the empty room.

Speaking to Ryan was a habit she'd developed, one she kept to herself. But somehow she felt he was listening no matter how weird that might be.

A knock at her door startled her. No one ever came over to her house. Then she remembered Noah and his dripping popsicle and smiled. Maybe this time he'd be bearing chocolate chip cookies, something she couldn't help but say yes to. She tugged open the door to find Brady Rutledge — Kyle Baker, she remembered — standing there again. She'd done a good job at convincing herself that whole encounter was just a dream, some imagined encounter her grieving mind had latched onto. It was too crazy to believe. And yet as she blinked at him with the afternoon sun streaming behind him, he looked as real as she was. Certainly more real than the ghost she was attempting to communicate with moments ago. "Yes?" she managed, but her voice was shaky.

"I'm Kyle? If you remember I came by a few weeks ago?" He gave her that smile that she once knew only onscreen and her heart sped up. "I'm sorry it took me so long to get back here but Ada was hard to catch up with. It's safe to say she's enjoying her time with her sister."

"Oh, that's good," Emily said. She felt as stupid as she sounded. When the movie came out she had felt a kinship with the slightly nerdy girl who fell for his character, the one he rescued at the end. Standing there with him, she had no doubt the kinship was real. She felt as nerdy as the character was — and yet *she* wasn't acting.

He gestured at the room behind her. "I hope I'm not being too forward but if you don't mind, Ada told me where she left the log I was telling you about. I kind of need it for tonight. For this meeting I'm going to."

She knit her eyebrows together at the mention of the meeting. "The meeting about saving the bridge?"

"Yes, that one. How do you know about that?"

"I'm going." She hitched her thumb in the direction of Claire's house. "My neighbor invited me."

A smirk came over his face. "So Claire's told you how she feels about the bridge?"

"Yeah, she's for it. She's really passionate about saving it. You know Claire?"

The smirk stayed. "Sunset's a small place. Everyone knows everyone. You'll see."

"Oh, well. I mean, I guess if you want to come in and get the book, that would be fine." She widened the door opening and stepped out of the way to allow him in. As he passed she waved her hands in the air and mouthed to the back of his head, "Brady Rutledge is in my house!"

She dropped her hands to her side and tried to compose herself just as he turned back to look at her. "She said it's in the guest bedroom closet." He gestured to one of the side bedrooms she hadn't ventured into much. Marta had said there was some old stuff back there that Ada had left behind but she'd brushed it aside, intending

153

to just get rid of the stuff later. Now she was glad she had put that particular chore off. Sometimes procrastination did pay.

"Okay if I just go and get it?" he asked.

She did her best to act cool. "Yes. Sure." He disappeared into the bedroom and she took a seat on the couch where she'd been sitting before he knocked. She debated turning on the TV so she could look absorbed in a program and feign nonchalance when he came back. But before she could retrieve the remote he was back, his hands full with some old papers and books.

"I just grabbed it all if that's okay. I'll sort through it unless, I mean, you'd like to first?"

"No, no. It's yours. Take it. Ada obviously wanted you to have it."

He smiled. "Thanks. I'm sentimental about this stuff. History and all." He held the bundle of musty-smelling papers up.

She nodded. "It definitely looks . . . old."

"Old things are worth saving, right?"

"Yes. I guess they are." She knew he thought that those papers would help save the bridge somehow. For his and Claire's sake, she hoped he was right.

"Well, I better get cracking. I've got a lot to look through before the meeting. Thanks again!" He strode to the door and opened it before she could get to it for him.

"Okay, well, I guess I'll see you tonight."

He turned back and gave her that grin again, the one that, in spite of herself, made her breathless. "You bet," he said, and was gone, toting relics from the house she'd bought, a house that none other than Brady Rutledge himself had a tie to.

She couldn't help but think of the joke she and Ryan had made on their honeymoon, that Brady Rutledge was "no match" for Ryan. But if Ryan could set her up with anyone, Kyle would be the obvious and comical choice. "Well played," she said to Ryan in the silence, ignoring, as always, that no one answered back.

Emily stuck close to Claire as they waited for the meeting to begin. She hadn't seen Brady yet — ugh, Kyle, she corrected herself — and couldn't admit to herself that she was keeping a close watch on the door for him to walk through. Instead she busied herself with giving Sara and Noah gum from her purse, then plying them with some old church bulletins and pens that she found there as well, relying on her mother's old tricks for keeping her quiet in church all those years. "Thanks," Claire mouthed as the meeting got underway.

The Sunset Taxpayers Association (or STPA as they referred to themselves) began by weighing the financial costs of continuing to operate the old bridge versus the substantial expense the state would spend to replace it. The owner of the restaurant where they were meeting stood up and spoke about how her restaurant would be affected by the removal of the bridge. According to the state's plan for the new bridge, cars would never come far enough to even see her restaurant, which could mean a loss of business for them. Other longtime residents shared sentimental stories about the history of the bridge.

Then the state representatives presented their concerns about continuing to operate the existing bridge. The biggest of which, Emily noted, was the safety factor. The bridge was notorious for breaking down and causing no way to get on or off the island for hours. Also, at low tide and high tide fire trucks couldn't cross because the bridge was either sitting too low in the water or too high. It was a floating bridge dependent on water levels and the trucks were just too heavy. Emily thought of her father's heart attack years ago and how the quick response of the EMTs was the only reason he was still alive. How would she have felt if it had happened here, on the island, and rescue crews couldn't get to him? She studied Claire's face to see if she was swayed by this relevant argument.

Sara tapped her on the shoulder and shyly handed her a picture she'd drawn on the back of the church bulletin. Noah, she'd noticed, was drawing bombs hitting the photo of the church on the front of the bulletin with flames coming out the windows. But Sara had drawn a woman and a little girl holding hands. Their hands, she noticed with a smile, were huge in proportion to their bodies. "Is that you and your mommy?" she whispered to the little girl.

Sara shook her head. "No," she stage-whispered back. "It's me and you." Emily couldn't explain why tears unwittingly filled her eyes. She glanced back at Claire, guessing that she had received hundreds of these type of drawings, so many she hardly even registered when one was placed in her hands. Her neighbor was overwhelmed, but in Emily's opinion, in the best possible way. She squeezed Sara's shoulder and whispered to her, "I'll treasure it." Sara gave her a shy smile in return, tucking her chin into her chest.

When Kyle, who had slipped in late, began to speak, Emily looked quickly back to

157

the front, her eyes trained on him, hoping that Claire couldn't hear her heart pounding, grateful she couldn't see the way it had risen in her chest at the sound of his voice. She was taking this schoolgirl crush a bit too far, clearly. Perhaps because it was safe since there was no way Kyle knew she was alive beyond the fact that she lived in Ada's house now. She guessed that if she passed him on the beach he'd blink at her without a trace of recognition.

Either way as soon as she got home she was calling Marta to tell her about it. If nothing else they'd have a good laugh at the absurdity of it all. And maybe it would incite a visit from Marta that much faster. If she knew her friend, she'd show up just for the possibility of a glimpse of him.

She shook her head and made herself focus on Kyle's words. They'd saved him for last — probably because he had acting experience or maybe because he'd just been late. He commented on the cons of the bridge, acknowledging the trouble it caused when the bridge broke. He shared how the restaurant they were meeting in had installed a special freezer just for people who got stuck with perishable groceries in their cars so no one would lose their meat or ice cream to the heat. At the mention of ice cream, Noah piped up, "I want some ice cream, Mommy," a bit too loud and everyone laughed as Claire shushed him, embarrassed. Emily made a mental note to offer to take them for ice cream after the meeting if Claire said it was okay.

But after Kyle acknowledged the cons of the bridge, he went on to tell about his father and grandfather before him who had been bridge tenders. How he'd "pursued another profession" for a while, but ultimately returned to the bridge, the pull of the place too strong for any amount of distance to be enough. "It's in my blood, this bridge," he said to the state representatives. "It's part of my history." He looked around the room.

"But it's not just my history. It's our history." He held up the dusty old books he'd carried out of her house earlier. "These are logs from one of our first bridge tenders. They're filled with more than just documentation about an old bridge opening and closing. They're filled with slices of North Carolina history: The barges that carried pipes to develop this area of the country. The pleasure boats that carried young people headed down to Ocean Drive to shag. The shrimping boats that carry the meals we've eaten here for many years." He held his hands out to indicate the room they were using. "These logs carry my history and yours. Another bridge — the big fancy one you're talking about building — might be more efficient, but it won't have the heart and the history of this one." He turned to face the state representatives and continued speaking as if there was no one else in the room.

"I ask you to consider that as you decide what is best for this island. We're a little place where people come to forget the world on the other side. Crossing this old bridge means they're crossing over to a sanctuary for their souls. I just can't help feeling that a new bridge like you're proposing won't mean the same to all of us." He thanked the men for hearing him out, then took a seat at the front of the room. Emily wondered if everyone else was as moved by his speech as she was. She stared at the back of his head, her mind recreating the scene in the movie when the heroine did the same thing.

After Kyle was finished speaking, the owner of the restaurant, a woman named Ruth, thanked everyone for coming and adjourned the meeting. People broke off into clusters, clearly familiar with each other. Claire hugged Ruth and bantered back and forth with her for a moment, allowing Ruth to introduce her to the state reps. Emily watched as Claire poured on the charm, her laughter carrying across the room. Emily stayed seated with the children, hoping Claire hurried up before they got restless. She had a hunch that Claire had invited her because she would have help with the kids. Emily didn't mind so much, she liked Sara and Noah and felt bad for Claire, being a single parent much of the week. Like Kyle, she seemed intent on preserving history for the sake of history, even when some of the arguments for moving forward sounded more rational. Emily didn't intend to ever voice that to Claire though. Let her have her history. She certainly knew what it was like to want to hang on to what was.

She looked around the restaurant, remembering as she did how she'd pouted to Ryan about not being able to afford to eat here when they were on their honeymoon. "When we buy a house here someday we're going there and taking our kids," she'd said emphatically. Now as she looked around she realized she had finally gotten to the restaurant; she did own a beach house. In a way she had everything she needed and much of what she'd ever wanted. And yet none of it was what she'd dreamed.

"Deep in thought?" she heard the unmistakable voice ask. She looked over and realized he'd sidled up to her while she was thinking. While she was lost in thought Noah had ventured over to his mother and was pulling on her arm to get her to leave. Sara, quiet, sweet Sara, had stayed seated beside her, thankfully. She was clearly not the best babysitter.

"Just remembering. Your talk on the history of this place got me thinking," she said, turning to face Kyle and being shocked again at the reality of him. He was Brady Rutledge, and yet, here in this place, he wasn't.

"Good memories, I hope?" he asked.

Ryan's face filled her mind, the way he'd promised her when they came back one day they'd bring their children to this restaurant. He'd be a successful attorney by then. She'd go back to teaching when the kids were in school, which would provide the money they'd need to afford two homes and fancy dinners out. They had it all figured out, they'd thought.

"Bittersweet ones," she admitted.

He gave her a half smile. "I get that." Something about the look on his face told her he wasn't just making small talk. His smile widened and he seemed to want to lighten the conversation. "Thanks for coming out tonight. It helped just to have people show up so the state knows that it's more than a handful of people who want to save the old bridge."

"So you're the bridge tender?" she asked, stating the obvious and wishing she'd thought of something better as an opener.

"Yeah, I gave up Hollywood because this was so much more glamorous," he joked.

She laughed. "I'm sure it's nice. Quiet. Private. Maybe that's what you wanted."

He nodded, thinking it over. "Yeah. Hidden in that tender house no one can see who you are, and no one cares as long as you open and close that bridge on time. It's much simpler, I can tell you that."

She was about to say something inane when Claire came over and pulled on her arm. "Sorry, gotta go. Natives are restless." She regarded Kyle for a moment and gave him a dismissive wave.

"Hello, Claire," he responded dully. Emily sensed a tension between the two of them. She would have to ask Claire about it later. He gave Emily a smile and gestured for her to follow Claire, who was headed toward the door with both kids' hands firmly grasped in hers. "Wouldn't want to keep Her Highness waiting. Nice talking to you. Thanks again for letting me bust in on you

163

this afternoon." He gestured at the state reps, who were now paging through the logs he'd held up as he spoke. "I think they were a nice touch."

"I do too. Hope they made a difference," she said.

"Me too," he echoed. But his voice didn't sound hopeful, and Emily didn't blame him. As she followed Claire out of the restaurant she couldn't help but think of the cons they had listed. If she was keeping score, she would have to admit one side outweighed the other. History and heart, she was finding, had little place in the real world. Everyone seemed intent on forward motion. There weren't enough people who thought like she and Kyle did. At the thought of lumping herself in the same category with Kyle a smile filled her face. She smiled all the way to the ice-cream store.

They drove all the way to Ocean Isle Beach for ice cream, where Emily learned a bit more about her young neighbors. Noah liked sprinkles and cared very little about what flavor ice cream held the sprinkles up. The ice cream only served as a vehicle to get the sprinkles into his mouth. Emily sympathized: she felt the same way about fries and ketchup. Sara liked bubblegum, mainly because it was pink.

Emily watched as Claire patiently waited for them to make up their minds, then placed the order, surprising her with an ice-cream cookie — two large soft-baked chocolate chip cookies with a thick slab of vanilla ice cream between them — that she insisted they split. Claire groaned as she took a bite. "Oh man, are my thighs going to pay for this. But it's so good!"

Emily agreed, finding that that smile remained on her face, this time for a different reason than the attention of a lost movie star. She recognized that she was having fun. She took a big bite of the ice-cream sandwich, giggling over how wide she had to stretch her mouth to actually get her teeth into it. Marta had recently commented that she was glad to see Emily's appetite returning, and that she could stand to gain some weight back from all those months she barely ate while Ryan was sick, and after. Food was starting to taste good again and she even enjoyed the occasional indulgence. It felt like progress, and she suspected the long days in the sun and the briny beach air were helping things along.

She looked around them at the store filled with customers milling around, enjoying a summer evening. And while she still wished more than anything that Ryan was here splitting that ice-cream sandwich with her, she had to admit that she was still grateful to be here at all. She had the feeling this is what her mother had meant when she intoned before she left that she hoped Emily would start living again. "I hope you find a life there," she'd said, her voice wistful and hopeful. It must've been hard for her mother to watch her mourn Ryan and not be able to do anything to take away the pain. Almost as hard as it was to bear it, in a different way. She knew her mother wasn't used to feeling helpless, to not have the answers. And yet, though they had both searched the scriptures that had always brought comfort, it wasn't as easy this time. The easy answers eluded them all.

They moved out of the way so the folks in line could have more room and Claire motioned for them to take a seat outside on one of the benches. She nodded and followed, shepherding the children in the right direction, her eyes scanning the crowd automatically, used to picking out familiar faces. Ever the preacher's daughter, she rarely went anywhere without running into someone she knew back home. Old habits died hard. She smiled at herself, searching strangers' faces, forgetting that here she was

166

a stranger herself. She wondered if, though she was a homeowner now, this place would ever feel like home. She hoped so, hoped that she would find friends, put down roots, feel a sense of homecoming when she crossed the Sunset Beach bridge.

She turned to face Claire and the kids, who were giddy over being out past bed-time indulging in a sweet treat with their mother and a new friend. But as her eyes swept over the crowd she thought she saw a familiar face after all and looked back. They were sitting off at a picnic table to the side of the building, folded into each other. She could see the amber-colored hair falling over a bare shoulder onto milky white skin that probably never did anything but burn. Though it was night, there was enough light on the porch and surrounding lampposts to illuminate Amber and her mystery man as she fed him ice cream and giggled. Emily stared a moment too long, prompting Claire to ask what she was looking at.

She turned back and shook her head. "No one, just thought I saw someone from back home. A student. But it wasn't her." She tamped down the guilt that rose up over her little white lie. Maybe later she'd tell Claire all about Amber. But now, with the kids lis-tening to every word, wasn't the time.

"That's right!" Claire smacked herself in the forehead. "You said you're a teacher. No wonder you're so good with kids!"

"What grade do you teach, Miss Emily?" Sara asked. She had a pink ring around her mouth and Emily wished that Ryan could see her. Happy as she was at that moment, there was always his absence there, a gaping hole that opened up no matter where she seemed to go.

"I teach eighth grade." She looked at Sara and widened her eyes, making her eyebrows fly up. "The big kids." Though they weren't high school students yet, she knew to Sara that age seemed like giants.

Sara widened her eyes to make her expression match Emily's. "That is big. I'm going into first grade next year."

She held up her hand so Sara could give her a high five. Then Noah, for no reason in particular, wanted to slap her hand too. "I'm going to preschool," he informed her after he slapped her hand. He looked over at his mother, then back at Emily. "But I don't want to."

Claire laughed and patted her son on his head. "Mommy wants you to, Noah, and that's all that matters." She looked meaningfully at Emily. "I have a countdown going until the first day after Labor Day." She winked and kissed Noah, coming away with a few sprinkles around her own mouth. Emily grimaced when she licked them off and Sara yelled, "Ew! Gross!" as Claire laughed. "You'll love preschool, Noah. Sara did."

Emily noticed some motion over where Amber and the young man were sitting. She watched them get up. He pulled Amber to him and kissed her, then smiled. Emily stared at Amber's middle and wondered if she was showing yet. She wondered if he knew. She wondered if Amber had told her father. She hoped the girl hadn't gone to some clinic and "taken care of things" as she'd heard a girl at school describe it in an anonymous journal entry that broke her heart. She'd felt helpless and heartbroken as she read it — typed so she couldn't analyze the handwriting. And no one had ever given any indication beyond that one lone assignment. And yet she'd always felt responsible somehow, that she should've tried harder to find the girl and help her.

She watched Amber leave with the man from the motel — a man too old for her, a man most likely hiding a whole other life from her and using her for a good time when he was in town. She hoped she was wrong but knew that likely she was exactly right. The smile slipped from Emily's face, replaced by a look of concern and a string of ideas about how maybe she could help this one.

THIRTEEN

Marta answered the phone on the first ring the next morning. Emily had called her best friend when she got in from the ice-cream store, anxious to sort through her ideas to reach out to Amber. She got no answer, something that was happening more and more. Emily tried not to feel hurt when her friend didn't answer, picturing her laughing and flirting with Phil, then looking down when her phone rang and pressing the Ignore button, Emily's face instantly disappearing from her phone's screen. Instead she tried to remember that glorious feeling of falling in love. She'd once been the same way and now it was Marta's turn. But in the meantime she'd been anxious to tell her about Amber . . . and about Kyle.

But before she could go into it, Marta asked if she'd gone back to see Amber. Emily sheepishly admitted that she'd been too chicken to go back to the motel, hoping that things would just work out for the girl and all would be well. "That's a great attitude, Em," Marta said. "That's just WWJD all the way."

Emily smiled and filled her in on seeing her at the ice-cream place. "I've been thinking about how I can worm my way into her life without looking like a total stalker; i.e., not end up hiding under her desk afraid she's going to find me there."

"Well, as long as you don't go sneaking around in her purse and snooping, you should be fine this time. Just take her lunch this afternoon or something. Make that chicken salad you used to make — that kind like your mom makes. The one with the pecans and red grapes."

Emily grimaced. That would mean a trip across the bridge to get the stuff to make it, then a morning of cooking, then a trip over to the motel on the chance that Amber would actually be there and would not have already had lunch. Marta's idea sounded like a lot of work. And yet . . . what else did she have to do? She eyed her beach bag with yet another book peeking out of the top. There would be time to read later — like after the lunch was delivered. "Okay," she sighed. "I'll do it."

"Then you have to tell me how it works

out. Text me," Marta said. Emily knew that was her way of saying she wouldn't be able to talk after lunch.

"Okay," she said, thinking how easy Marta made things sound. She hoped her friend was right. "So things are going well with you and Phil?"

"Yeah," Marta said, a dreamy quality to her voice the minute Phil's name came up. "We're so compatible. We like the same movies, the same food, the same music. Except he likes country, which you know I can't stand, but he's agreed not to listen to it when I'm in the car. I figure if that's the worst thing we have to deal with then we're good. Right?"

"Absolutely," she agreed. "So are we talking marriage yet?"

"Well, neither of us are getting any younger and if we want kids — Sorry. I shouldn't be going into this with you. I know romance isn't exactly your favorite subject." She took a deep breath and started again. "To answer your question, he hasn't taken me to pick out rings or anything so no bells are ringing yet."

"You don't have to apologize for thinking about your future," Emily said, keeping her tone bright. "I'm happy for you."

"Thanks," Marta said. "What about you?

173

I guess there's no chance you've met some handsome surfer dude who wants to share a towel with you?"

"Well, actually . . . ," Emily said.

"What?" Marta shrieked so loud Emily had to pull the phone away from her ear. "I was just kidding! There really is someone?"

Emily laughed. "No. There isn't. There's just this guy who came over yesterday."

"Came over?" Marta shrieked again. "That sounds very promising. You're inviting guys over now?"

"No, no. It wasn't like that." Emily giggled. "And honestly it's so insignificant I wouldn't even mention it if it wasn't for who the guy is." She paused, hearing Marta's bated breath on the other end of the line, savoring the suspense.

"Who? Who is it? I know him?" She laughed. "Just please tell me it's not Perry Jones." Perry Jones was a guy Emily's mother had tried to fix her up with before and after Ryan, a devoted church member who "never could quite find a woman who appreciated him," as her mother always said.

"You know there's a reason for that, don't you, Mother?" Emily always replied.

"I can just see your mother sending Perry Jones down there to stalk you at Sunset," Marta continued.

"That does actually sound like something she would try. But no. It's not Perry. Poor Perry." Emily actually felt sorry for the guy. With his multiple allergies, feminine voice, and tall, Ichabod Crane–like appearance, he was hardly appealing, much as her mother tried to sell Emily on his potential to be the perfect husband.

"He's a good man and he loves Jesus," her mother always said in Perry's defense. "You girls care too much about appearance." This from the woman who still dressed to the nines just to go to the grocery store, applying lipstick each night before her father got home from the church to greet him "with her lips on."

"Can you imagine Perry in a bathing suit?" Marta went on, enjoying the roll she was on. She shuddered into the phone. "My eyes! My eyes!"

Emily couldn't help but crack up laughing. She missed her daily conversations with Marta, how she never failed to make her laugh. But she wouldn't make Marta feel guilty for being busy and distracted. "Do you want to hear about this guy or not?" She attempted to get the conversation back on track and stop being mean about poor Perry, who was a nice guy and who, she was sure, would someday find someone to love.

It just wasn't going to be her.

"Yes, please tell me about this other guy so I can get that mental image of Perry Jones in a bathing suit out of my brain."

"Okay, remember the movie *Just This Once*?"

Marta gave a dreamy sigh into the phone. "Ah, Brady Rutledge. How could any girl our age not know that movie? He practically ruined all other guys for us. Who could live up to that standard?" Marta couldn't resist one last dig. "Certainly not Perry Jones." She laughed at her own joke. Emily ignored her, her heart thrilling at the news she was about to drop on her friend. Anticipating Marta's reaction was half the fun. "Please tell me that the guy who came over to your house looks like him. Please give me that image."

"I'll do you one better," Emily said. "The guy who came over yesterday *is* Brady Rutledge." She braced herself for an ear-piercing scream but was met with silence.

"Ha, ha, ha, very funny. That's a good one, Em."

"I'm totally serious. Brady Rutledge is really a guy named Kyle Baker. Brady Rutledge was his screen name and now he lives here. He left Hollywood and came here to work as the bridge tender because his father

176

and grandfather were bridge tenders before him. I just heard him speak about it last night."

Marta was silent, deciding, Emily guessed, on whether she was being duped. She could hear Marta typing on the other end. "I'm Googling this," she said.

"Go ahead. I couldn't make this up."

"I will admit that this is all too far-fetched to not be true." She heard more typing, then waited while Marta read whatever she'd found. "Okay," Marta said after a minute of silence. "This article says that Brady Rutledge did disappear from Hollywood after the success of *Just This Once.* Says he went home to — well, whadda ya know? — North Carolina because of a tragedy. Says he never returned and has fallen off the face of the earth."

"That's because he's not really Brady Rutledge. I'm telling you. He has another name. But it's him. If you saw him you would know it was him in an instant. He hasn't changed much at all. Except —" Emily stopped. That was enough.

But Marta was smarter than that. "Except what?" she prodded.

"Nothing. He's just a little older looking I guess is all. More mature."

"Annnnd?" Marta kept on, knowing Emily

well enough to know when she was holding back.

Emily shook her head. "And, well, the age looks good on him. That's all."

"Oh man!" Marta shouted. "You're totally into him!"

"Marta, he's a movie star. He looks like a movie star. Any female within fifty paces" — except Claire, Emily thought — "Would think he was handsome. It's a fact of life."

"No. No. This isn't just a Brad Pitt thing. I sense there's more. I think you like him as an actual person."

"He's a nice person," she sighed, feigning disinterest. "That's all. He gave a very nice speech about the bridge last night — what losing it would mean to the community — and everyone was moved by it. Not just me. He's passionate about something, and that's always admirable. That's it."

"You just keep telling yourself that, Miss Thang. Let me know how it works out for ya." Marta laughed. "Listen, I hate to cut you off — interesting as this news is — but I gotta skedaddle. I'm working out now. Joined a gym. If there is a wedding dress in my future I'd sure like to look good in it, and I figure I need a huge head start on that. Emphasis on the huge. Get it?"

"Marta, you look great already."

178

"But I could look better!" she sang.

"I guess I'm going to go make chicken salad," Emily said.

"Atta girl," Marta said. "Make extra and take some to Brady at the bridge. I'm sure he'd just love lunch delivered by a ravishing widow. It's like a Hollywood movie!"

"Yeah, that'll happen." Emily grinned at her friend's penchant for pairing her off and admired her tenacity. "I'm not looking for love, Marta," she said for the umpteenth time.

"You know what they say though. When you're not looking for it is usually when you find it."

"Okay, I will take that under advisement. For now I'm going to try to help this girl."

"You're doing a good thing. And you know that when I come down I have got to see this guy for myself."

"I expected nothing less. See you soon?" she asked.

"Yeah, we'll firm up a date soon." They hung up and Emily had the feeling that as intriguing as Brady/Kyle was, Marta would still put off her visit in an effort to spend more of her summer with Phil. She put the phone down and went to make a list of items she would need from the grocery store to make her magic chicken salad. Magic because it would have to make Amber want to divulge her secret to her, when Emily suspected she didn't intend to tell anyone. She'd have to pray the whole time she made it, pray and add extra pecans. Maybe toast them too.

On the way back from the local Food Lion grocery store, her car trunk laden with more than just the ingredients for chicken salad, Emily slowly made her way over the bridge, thankful she'd caught it before it opened on the hour. She checked the car clock and saw she'd made it with only ten minutes to spare. She was getting better at timing her crossings, living by the bridge schedule like the other island residents. For the most part they handled it with good nature. She'd heard the stories at the meeting the other night — the times they'd been about to walk out the door for dinner and realized the bridge was about to open, so they'd poured another round of drinks, dealt a hand of cards, waited out the bridge in the comforts of home instead of waiting in the heat in a long line of cars.

As she reached the bridge tender's house, she couldn't help but slow her pace and glance over, hoping for a glimpse of him. With the bridge about to open, she figured he was doing whatever he had to do to get ready, if he was even working. She glanced over, then back at the windshield, then back over, then back at the windshield. All she caught was a glimpse of someone in the house, someone who seemed to have dark hair, but who knew if it was him. As she heard the wheels of her car make the *thump-thump* noise that meant the car was off the bridge and back on the road, she shook her head and laughed aloud in the empty car. She'd been reduced to her teenage years, just another fan girl hoping for a glimpse of her favorite star, though she tried hard not to think of him that way. He wasn't Brady. He was Kyle. She had to keep that in mind whenever she was around him, if she was around him.

She arrived home and began unloading the groceries, pushing him out of her mind. She put away the pantry items in the small cabinet used for storing food, wishing she'd paid more attention to the lack of pantry space that evening when she'd looked at the house. She'd been so taken with Ada's story and the serendipity of finding the place that she hadn't paid attention to details. And yet a lack of pantry space wouldn't have stopped her from buying the place. It would just be something she'd fix later. She had her eye on an unused corner where built-in storage would fit and planned to ask Claire later if she knew any good carpenters. With the groceries put away, she eyed the rotisserie chicken she'd bought — a shortcut to broiling the meat. "It's just you and me, buddy," she said. She eyed the clock as she began assembling the chicken salad. With any luck, she'd be finished in perfect time for lunch. She'd bought croissants and a precut fruit mixture and splurged on some potato chips — even though that was hardly good prenatal nutrition — but Amber was a teen and most teenagers could be plied with potato chips, in her experience. She added mayo and celery to the shredded chicken and hoped her plan worked.

As she stirred the grapes and pecans into the chicken mixture, she tried to remember the last time she'd had the recipe. She faintly remembered her mom making it and stocking it in the refrigerator after Ryan died, in those hazy days of grieving, the odd half-life between the funeral and when she decided to go back to work. She'd slept-walked through those days, staring at the television with no recollection later of what she'd seen. Taken phone calls and opened mail with no idea of who she'd heard from. Obediently spooned food into her mouth

182

with no sense of what she'd eaten. "Just take three bites," her mother would beg as if she were a child again.

After her mother left, Marta would sit down with a big plate of whatever was in the fridge. "If you're not going to eat it . . . ," she'd always say as she helped herself. And later, "I think I'm finding the weight you're losing, sistah." It was during that time that Marta had developed her love for that chicken salad, pronouncing it the best she'd ever had. She'd looked at Emily pointedly. "I think your mother's chicken salad is the meaning of life."

Emily smiled and shook her head at Marta's silliness. "I'm serious! Have you tasted this stuff?"

Emily hadn't tasted anything for weeks and Marta knew it. But she'd coaxed a genuine smile out of her and she knew Marta counted that as a hard-won victory. She'd been a true friend and hung in there longer than most people would have. In some ways, Emily thought as she gave the concoction a final stir, she still was hanging in there.

FOURTEEN

Emily found Amber at her usual spot behind the desk, Facebook open on the computer screen. The girl didn't even bother to hide it, her expression curious as she recognized Emily. "Hi?" she asked more than greeted. Emily thought she saw a glimmer of worry cross the girl's face. "Can I help you?" Amber sat up straighter, fumbled with the computer keyboard, and Facebook disappeared from the screen. Emily wondered if she was recognizing her from her recent stay or from the night before. Of course Amber had been so absorbed in her mystery man that she probably didn't notice anyone else last night.

Emily could feel her heart pounding as she cast about for the right thing to say. "Um, I was wondering if you'd had lunch yet?" The clock over Amber's head said 12:00 exactly. Emily doubted she'd eaten, hoped she hadn't. Amber's look in response told her she thought she was crazy. She found herself rushing to explain.

"I stayed here a few weeks ago and then I saw you last night at the ice-cream store. In Ocean Isle? It just made me think of you and, um, I got the idea to bring you lunch." She felt dumber by the second for letting Marta talk her into this scheme. They blinked at each other for a minute, neither of them knowing what to say. *Sometimes,* she thought in the silence, *it's better just to pray for someone and not feel the need to do something.* That is what she would tell Marta as soon as she got the chance.

And then Amber said something miraculous. "I actually haven't eaten."

Emily let out the breath she'd been holding and smiled. "Great! I made my mom's chicken salad. My friend says it's the meaning of life." She gave a little laugh. "I hope you like chicken salad. Wait right here!" She held up a finger and darted out, leaving Amber to determine, she was certain, just why she'd agreed to have lunch with a crazy woman who just might be a stalker to boot.

But she'd invited her in, and that was the first step. Out in the parking lot she looked up at the sky and gave a thumb's up, feeling goofy and out of her comfort zone, yet strangely euphoric at the prospect of being able to reach out to this girl. She felt more alive than she had in a very long time. The last time she'd felt her heart race like this was riding a borrowed bike back to this very motel on a warm, dark spring night, having just given a verbal offer to an old woman who had a house to sell. She pulled the lunch items from the car, thinking of the only other time she'd felt her heart race with that zinging erratic feeling of real living: whenever Kyle was around. But that was a silly schoolgirl crush, so it didn't count.

She balanced the items in her arms, making it back into the office with everything in one trip. As she entered the room, she saw Amber fiddling with her cell phone, then quickly put it back into her purse, a forlorn look on her face. Emily plunked the food on the desk. "I brought you croissants and chicken salad and fruit." She grinned, pulling the bright yellow bag of potato chips out last. "And potato chips!" she said conspiratorially. She saw the requisite fast-food cup on the desk near the computer keyboard. "I just thought you'd like something home cooked."

Amber reached for the food with a grateful look on her face. "That actually sounds perfect. I'm not sure what made you do this, but I'll take it." The two were back to awkward silence. In Emily's imagination they'd sat down and had lunch together, a conversation naturally opening up as they ate. She'd never considered that Amber would take the lunch and dismiss her entirely, an obvious sign of wishful thinking trumping actual planning. "Thanks?" Amber said, the question in her voice indicating she had no idea why Emily was still standing there like an idiot.

"Sure!" she responded with a brightness she didn't feel. "I guess I'll see you later?"

"Yeah . . . sure." Amber was already using a plastic knife to saw into a croissant. She barely looked up. The poor kid was hungrier than Emily realized. She started to walk away, to leave her to eat alone, her heart in her heels instead of her throat. She'd done what she was supposed to, so why did it feel so bad? She waved good-bye and slipped out the office door, all the elation she'd felt moments earlier evaporated.

She was walking down the sidewalk, her eyes downcast, when she ran smack into someone else — the guy from last night. Amber had called him and invited him to eat lunch — the lunch *she* was supposed to be eating with Amber, *her* magic chicken salad that was supposed to cause Amber to spill her closely guarded secret. Suppressing an urge to accost the guy right then and there, she merely mumbled an "excuse me" and stepped around him, heading for her car. She licked her wounds on the short drive home and spent the rest of the day sulking under the sun out at the beach, barely reading her newest novel as her thoughts kept returning to what a strange place Sunset Beach was turning out to be.

She was watching her tiny television that night when someone knocked on the door, so lightly she had to turn down the set to be certain that she'd heard right. Her heart thrilled for a moment, wondering if Kyle was back. Instead she opened the door to find Amber standing on the other side, her red hair pushed off her face with a white headband, her bright green eyes flashing under the porch light. "Amber, hi!" she greeted. She wasn't disappointed it wasn't Kyle in the slightest, she told herself. This was much better.

Amber held up the cut-glass bowl she'd put the chicken salad in for lunch that day. The bowl was a relic Ada had left behind like many of the other things Emily was still finding around the house.

Emily reached for the bowl, embarrassed that she'd been so flustered in the motel office that she hadn't even mentioned getting it back. Antique cut-glass bowls aren't usually considered disposable. Unless, of course, they weren't yours to begin with, Emily thought but didn't say. In the bowl was the embroidered napkin she'd tucked the muffins into, still bearing a chocolate smear. Emily eyed it and debated whether to call attention to the fact that she'd left the mysterious muffins, which Amber had obviously already deduced. Instead she said, "Thanks so much for bringing this by! Would you like to come in?" She opened the door wider, searching the street outside to see if perhaps he was waiting for her, but she saw no car.

"I walked," Amber explained, slinking past Emily with her shoulders slumped, not meeting her eyes. But she was in the room.

Emily closed the door behind her. "Have a seat," she offered, gesturing to Ada's couch, holding Ada's bowl. She looked down at it, still in her hand. "I'll just go put this away." She hurried into the kitchen, fearing for some reason that if she lost sight of Amber, she would disappear. Her pull toward this girl was unexplainable, and yet with her appearance on her doorstep, it also felt reciprocated. Emily felt a shade less ridiculous than she had earlier. She peeked her head around the corner to see Amber perched on the edge of the couch as though she was, indeed, about to bolt. "Can I get you a drink?" she asked.

Amber thought about it a moment. "Just some water? I'm kind of thirsty from walking."

Emily nodded and ducked back into the kitchen to fetch two bottles. One thing she would never get used to was beach tap water. She put one in Amber's outstretched hand. "How did you know I lived here?" she asked.

Amber shrugged as though she hadn't given it much thought. "Heard you bought Ada's house. Everyone around here knew her."

Every time she forgot how small Sunset Beach was, someone reminded her. She had a feeling that the residents — few as they were — were all interconnected, and that she would spend much time navigating all the loops and whirls that were their connections. She almost said as much to Amber, but chose to simply nod instead.

"I just wanted to say thank you for the lunch. I'm not really sure why you did that but it was nice." Amber gave her a small smile. "And delicious." When she smiled her green eyes crinkled at the edges. It occurred again to Emily that she had no idea how beautiful she was. Most likely his recognition of that was the opening that got Amber's older man what he wanted. It wasn't that her beauty wasn't there, she wished she could say to the girl, it was that it hadn't been recognized. She bit back the words and made small talk instead. Maybe someday she could pour into the girl in a deeper way. But they were far from that yet.

Amber looked around the room. "The place hasn't changed much since Ada left. I kinda thought you'd update it." Emily picked up the disappointed tone in her voice. She'd expected a transformation and might've just been curious enough to walk over, the bowl an excuse to peek inside.

"I hope to someday. I have some plans. But for now I'm just getting acclimated. Learning my way around. Getting into a routine. Meeting people." She smiled to indicate that Amber was one of those people. Amber barely returned her smile and looked down at the bottle of water, picking at a curled edge of the label. Emily pulled back, recognizing she'd gone too far. She could see the fences going up. And yet she wanted the girl to know she had someone in her corner. It felt urgent and she knew instinctively that this wasn't the time for looking cool. With Amber's green gaze directed at the water bottle instead of aimed at her, she bolstered her courage, took a deep breath, and plunged ahead with what she'd hoped to say at lunch. This was her second chance and she couldn't miss it. If the girl ran away screaming and avoided her for the rest of time, so be it.

"Amber," she began. "I wanted you to know that I know." She waited for a beat to see if Amber would respond but she didn't look up, although Emily noticed her hand stilled, the loose corner of the label left flapping. "I'm not going to tell you how I found out — that's not important — but I wanted you to know that your secret is safe with me, and also that I'm here if you ever need anything."

Amber jerked her head up. "What secret?" she asked, an edge to her voice. "I don't have any secrets." Though she was trying to sound tough, underneath Emily could hear her voice wavering, betraying her.

"I think we both know that's not true, and I think maybe that's why you came here tonight. Because maybe you need to talk to someone and you don't know who to go to."

Amber stood up, putting the water bottle on the coffee table a little too hard. "I don't know what you're talking about, lady," she said. "I brought your stupid bowl back to you because you did something nice for me today. And now I see that you only did it because you're trying to get me to say I have some secret when I totally do not."

Emily could feel her heart racing and wondered if her face gave her away. Struggling to maintain composure, she took a deep breath as she stood.

She looked back at her guest, who had taken several steps toward the front door, her eyes on Emily as though Emily might pounce on her, hold her captive like some crazy woman and not let her go until she spilled her secrets. "Look, I'm sorry. I have a longtime habit of this kamikaze-style helping thing. I didn't mean to creep you out," she said. She chuckled. "My husband used to give me such a hard time about it."

The mention of a husband, Emily could see, got Amber's attention. "You're divorced?" she asked, taking another step closer to the door, her movements stealth-like and calculated.

Emily pressed her lips into a thin line. "Widowed." She held out her arms. "This house was his last gift to me."

Score. She watched as her words hit home. The girl took in her age, her appearance, her presence in this room, understanding perhaps at least a bit more than she did before. She thought she saw something akin to sympathy cross Amber's face. Maybe this woman — this strange, meddling woman who bought Ada's house — could understand what it meant to be lost and alone, her face said. Seizing the moment Emily crossed over to her purse and extracted a pen and some paper. She scribbled her name and phone number on the paper, walked over, and put it in Amber's hand. "You don't ever have to do anything with this, but I wouldn't feel right if I didn't at least offer." Their eyes met — green and blue, the colors of the Atlantic Ocean. "Just call me if you ever need anything. Okay?"

Amber nodded, mute, the fight and bravado gone out of her. Gripping the paper, she slipped out Emily's front door without a good-bye, nearly jogging across the yard and away from the situation. But Emily knew better than anyone she wasn't going to outrun her problems. She said a prayer that the girl would call her and took a deep breath, filling her lungs with the sweet salt air before she exhaled. She missed her husband. She missed her best friend. She even sometimes missed her parents. And strangely, she missed Amber as she disappeared from view.

FIFTEEN

The next day she went with Claire and Noah and Sara to the beach, suckered into it by two sticky faces showing up at her door just after the sun came up, the air around them smelling of syrup. Their knocks on her front door jarred her from a fitful sleep on the couch.

"Mommy said you can come with us to the beach if you want to," Sara said brightly as Emily opened the door bleary-eyed, still trying to focus. For a moment she had thought it was Amber returning.

"You want to, don't you, Emily?" Noah piped up as Emily began to realize where she was, what was happening.

"Mommy said to tell you she's already made coffee," Sara added.

After mumbling to them to wait a moment, she pulled a sweatshirt on over the threadbare T-shirt and shorts she slept in most nights. "Your mommy's a smart lady," she said and followed the children next door.

The Connolly kitchen looked like a bomb had gone off in it, but the full coffeepot shone like a beacon in the middle of the warfare. Wordlessly Claire handed her a mug and pointed at the Splenda and half-and-half. She went straight to it, thinking of the night before, picturing Amber's near-sprint away from her house. She could almost hear Ryan's critique. *Taking the place by storm, are we?*

You got me into this mess, she argued in her head.

Well, you're doing an excellent job, she heard him retort, that little chuckle lurking behind his words. He always did get in the last word if he could. And with Noah and Sara clamoring for her attention she'd have to let him.

She moved over to their couch and took a seat, tucking her legs under her as she took a long sip of the hot coffee, inhaling the steam as if it would get the caffeine into her bloodstream sooner. She hadn't been up this early in a long time. Soon enough she was joined by Claire, who offered her a plate of pancakes dotted with strawberries and slathered with both maple and chocolate syrup, topped off with a squirt of whipped cream. Emily shook her head and pointed at her coffee. "Breakfast of champions," she said.

Claire shrugged and dug into the plate instead. Emily wondered how the woman looked like she did when she ate like she did. But as Claire jumped up to clean up Sara's spill, then jumped up again to pull Noah off the countertop before he toppled off it, she knew her new friend was constantly in motion. In the end she only got in a few bites of the pancakes before she lost interest and put the rest of the food down the disposal.

She turned to Emily, who was about to pour a second cup of coffee for herself, and grabbed her by the shoulders. "Please, please, please come to the beach with us today. I can't be responsible for my actions if I'm left alone with these two monkeys for another day."

Emily laughed as Claire pretended to shake her, her eyes wild. "I'm serious!" Claire continued. "I'm not sure I can have any more conversations about Legos and princesses or answer any more questions about how hermit crabs find new shells to live in without committing hari-kari. Rick comes in tonight and I just need a little help making it to the finish line."

Emily realized this was one thing she could do that would actually be helpful, that she couldn't mess up. "Ha," she wanted to say to Ryan, getting in the last word after all. She imagined him winking at her with that grin of his, aware that the ripple effects of his last gift would continue to keep spreading, reaching and affecting people in ways none of them realized yet. She couldn't help but think this was what he intended all along.

"Let me get my stuff together," she said. "But first I'm going to need another cup of your coffee."

They spent a lovely day at the beach and Emily didn't miss her novels at all. She quite enjoyed the break from her lonely routine, the company and clamor of a day with Claire and her children. Claire talked to her whenever the kids weren't, which wasn't often. Today she was the one answering questions about tides and tide pools, shells and sand dunes, a new source to probe for information for the curious monkeys, as Claire called them. Once she caught Claire making a face at her behind the kids' backs as she fumbled for the answers to basic science questions that had been long forgotten after her own elementary school years. Perhaps if she'd been a science teacher she would've made a better companion. She didn't suppose the kids wanted to discuss literary themes or character development.

When Sara took Noah down to the water to wade at the edge, she collapsed on a towel with a dramatic exhale worthy of Marta. Claire eyed her with a grin. "Try doing it 24/7," she said.

"I don't know how you do."

"I look forward to Friday afternoon all week long. Rick pulls his car into the driveway like a knight on a steed."

"I bet you give him the kids and run for the hills."

Claire tilted her head, pondering that. "I'm tempted, but if I did that I'd miss the little bit of family time we get. And I'd miss time with him. We don't get much of that."

"You should let me babysit one night. That way you two could get some alone time."

Claire reached out and clutched her forearm, her strawberry-colored nails digging into Emily's flesh. "Don't say that if you don't mean it." The desperation in her eyes made Emily laugh out loud.

"Sure I mean it. I'm right next door. People trust me with their kids back home — 'course, they're older kids — but how hard can it be? We'll survive for a few hours."

Claire let go of her arm and flopped back down on her own towel, raising her hands in the air above her. "Glory hallelujah, a miracle has occurred! A bona fide date night." She did a little shimmying dance, then rolled over and eyed Emily. "You'll have to help me pick out something to wear!" she squealed.

Emily smiled back at her. "Of course." She might've bombed in her efforts to help Amber, but she could be an angel of mercy to Claire. The tradeoff wasn't the same but made her feel a little better. She blocked out the image of Amber's near-sprint away from her house the night before, the empty glass bowl left on her counter.

Suddenly, beside her Claire sat up and Emily could feel tension emanating from her. She heard Claire start mumbling to herself, the mood going from festive to fearful in a moment. "That's too far," she heard Claire say. "Don't take him that deep."

She looked at Sara and Noah, who had rapidly moved from ankle-deep water to knee-deep and seemed to be moving deeper. She could feel Claire coiling tighter beside her on high alert in case her quick reflexes were needed. She wondered how it felt to never relax, never let go. In moments like this, she was actually glad she and Ryan had never had a child. She couldn't imagine being fully and solely responsible for another human being with no help, no white knight on a steed pulling into the driveway ever.

Both women were silent as they watched the children splash and laugh in the knee-deep water. Sara, taller, didn't realize how dangerous it was for her smaller brother and wasn't trying to be daring. Emily knew Claire wouldn't interfere unless they got deeper. She could feel Claire willing them to move in the right direction, to be safe. When Sara took Noah's hand and did just that, both women exhaled in unison. Claire laughed and elbowed Emily. "They are going to give me a heart attack. Just you wait and see." Their mingled laughter was the sound of relief, the joy found in safety in all its forms.

There were two moments from that day Emily suspected she would always remember, moments that in their own simple way added up to change everything. One plus one equals two. One came when Emily was alone for a bit, her eyes canvassing the beach as they often did. Claire walked along the water's edge with her children, patiently looking at another shell Sara presented, kicking water playfully back at Noah every time he kicked it at her. Emily watched the trio for a while. Then her gaze moved across the beach, taking in the scope of a summer's day at Sunset at the height of the season. People were everywhere, towels and chairs and umbrellas and coolers occupying every available patch of sand. She became just an observer and not a participant, seeing the scene unfold, a landscape painting entitled "Perfect Summer's Day." And as she watched the scenes around her, she felt a glimmer of what she'd felt on the massage table that day — that letting go, that openness. It wasn't a skein of yarn unspooling, more like a taut thread going the slightest bit slack. She felt more open, more connected to people than she had in a long time. She was among the living.

A heavily tattooed man played tenderly with a toddler. He looked like a giant lumbering grizzly as he tried to follow the pint-sized boy. And yet his awed look when he got down on the sand and peered at his child's little face brought tears to Emily's eyes. Near them a man and teenage boy played a game of lacrosse, sending the little ball sailing into the air and expertly catching it over and over, the ball making a whizzing sound as it passed over her head. She tried to decide if they were father and son, uncle and nephew, or not related at all. Perhaps the man was someone who had once reached out to the boy the way she'd tried to do with Amber. Maybe the boy was grateful he had now. But then she heard the man say something that ended with the word *son,* and Emily knew she'd guessed wrong.

Her eyes moved over to find two elderly women sitting side by side wearing matching floppy, wide-brimmed hats reading the exact same book. The image made her think of her and Marta someday, when they were old women. They would be that way, she thought. She would buy them matching hats and Marta would demand they read the same book so they could discuss it. They would compete over who could read faster, underlining passages to read aloud to each other. Perhaps by then Marta would be less enamored with Phil. Emily debated surreptitiously snapping a photo of the women with her phone and sending it to Marta with the words, "Us, someday."

Just beyond the women were three tween girls all sitting in a tidal pool as if it were their own personal Jacuzzi and they were enjoying a day at the spa. The girls were engaged in what looked to be an animated conversation, punctuated with lots of laughter and, Emily was sure, inside jokes built on history. Perhaps their families were friends and vacationed together every summer. Perhaps they were cousins who only saw each other once a year and crammed all the memories they could inside one week at the beach. Perhaps they'd only just met that day and formed the kind of instant bond that seems to happen in childhood. Either way, Emily wished them long and happy lives free from lost husbands like her, unexpected pregnancies like Amber, or the overwhelmed-ness she'd observed in Claire. And yet chances were of the three of them they'd face at least one of those things, and more. No one got to stay a carefree girl, laughing on a beach, her whole life waiting like a promise.

Finally her eyes landed on a couple walking along the beach, their fingers entwined as they moved slowly. Usually she immediately looked away from happy couples, but something about these two captured her attention in an unavoidable way. It was clear they had nowhere to be, no agenda to keep. They'd entered full-fledged beach time and had let go of whatever they'd crossed the bridge carrying when they arrived at Sunset. The girl leaned into him as she walked and he kissed the top of her head and, for a moment, Emily closed her eyes and held that image in her mind. Except in her mind it wasn't those strangers. It was her and Ryan years ago, making plans and allowing themselves to envision a future that would never come. She opened her eyes and the couple was past her, continuing on their journey down the beach. She didn't watch them go, and yet the image of them clung to her for the rest of the day, cropping up as they packed up to leave the beach, as she made her solitary dinner and settled down to eat in front of the TV, as she saw the headlights of a car sweep across the front of her house as it turned into the driveway next door.

She put her bowl of cereal down and went to her front window, barely pulling back the curtain so she could see Claire's husband arrive. From her hidden vantage point she watched as he parked the car and got out, standing for a moment in the glow of the interior dome light from his car. He was tall and even in the gathering dark she could tell he was handsome, a good match for Claire. She watched as Claire moved down the porch stairs and into his arms as he strode toward her. He wrapped her in his arms, Claire disappearing into his dark form as he pressed his lips into her hair. Emily backed away from the space, stung for the second time by a glimpse of such happiness. She knew what Claire was feeling in that moment, remembered it with every molecule of her being. Safe. Complete. Protected. Loved. She had had that once. Had soaked it in as much as she could for the time that she had.

Both images — the couple on the beach and Claire and her husband greeting each other — hunkered down in her psyche, becoming something that teased and taunted her for days, unavoidable no matter how much she tried to distract herself with more novels and household projects. It took her several days to finally admit why the two separate images had converged in her head and stuck there. It wasn't because she missed what she saw so much. It was, she realized, because she wanted what she saw. She wanted it again.

Sixteen

When the phone rang in the middle of the night, Emily reached for it, disoriented, forgetting entirely that she was in Sunset Beach, North Carolina. Instead she expected the voice on the other end of the phone to be a nurse from the hospital telling her Ryan was asking for her and to please come back, or worse, that he was gone. She blinked in the darkness and realized that that news — the worst news — had already happened. Instead she heard an unfamiliar voice say, "Okay, so you were right."

"Who? Who is this?" Emily asked, trying to place the deadpan delivery, the emotionless tone.

"It's Amber." This time the voice sounded smaller, less tough. Less certain.

"I was right?" Emily repeated, still not fully awake, still not tracking with Amber's middle-of-the-night timing.

"Yes," Amber said. "About what you said. I'm not sure how you guessed but I'm kind of glad you did now, because no one knows and . . ."

Emily listened to silence for a few seconds. "Amber?" she ventured.

"Yeah?" When she finally spoke, Emily could tell that Amber was fighting back tears . . . and losing.

"Honey, are you okay? Do you need me to come get you? Is your dad there?"

"My dad's never here. He always stays over with his girlfriend."

"Oh," Emily said. "Okay."

"And something's wrong. There's . . . blood. And I'm worried. I didn't know who else to call. No one else . . . knows."

She thought of her pull toward this girl, her desire to help her for no reason other than that the girl seemed like she could use someone in her corner. But God had known that this moment would come, that this girl would need someone to call. He had set it up, Emily could see, so that when the time came she'd have someone who cared. She closed her eyes and thanked Him, wondering what to do next.

Emily had never had a miscarriage but she'd known a teacher at school who had one. At lunch that day the other teachers

209

discussed the poor woman's tragedy like they were discussing something they had watched on TV, dishing about what happened. It had happened in the middle of third block and her husband, sheepish and ashen, had come to take her to the hospital. That, Emily thought, was what she needed to do. When it was over she would tell Amber that it was for the best and that when it was the right time, she'd have a baby, just like that teacher eventually did, bringing her bundle of blue to the school for all to admire.

"I'm on my way," Emily said, already moving toward the dresser to extract a sweatshirt to pull on over her old T-shirt, sliding her feet into flip-flops. She hung up the phone with Amber, who agreed to meet her in front of the motel office, and peered in her bathroom mirror. She looked awful, her hair messy and no makeup. For the sake of not scaring poor Amber with her appearance, she settled for running a brush through her hair and slicking it back into a ponytail. She swiped some light pink gloss onto her lips and ran the mascara brush across her lashes. Thankful that she'd gotten enough color on her face during her many days in the sun, she figured she looked passable, grabbed her car keys, and headed out the door.

She zipped down Beach Road, turned right, then left into the motel parking lot, skidding to a stop in front of the main office to find Amber sitting on the curb, her feet stretched out in front of her, looking miserable. She got up and slowly made her way to the car, stopping to put an old threadbare towel on the seat before she sat down. "Just in case," she said to Emily. The action brought tears to Emily's eyes and she blinked them back as she put the car into reverse and then drive again, racing forward until they reached the bridge, where they found the gates down and the bridge open.

"No way," Emily sighed aloud. She put the car in park and looked over at Amber, who was staring at her, open-mouthed.

"I have to get to a hospital," Amber said. "Like, now."

"I know," Emily said, opening the car door, the dome light shining on Amber's pale face as she did.

She reached out to grab Emily's shoulder before she could get out. "I know it sounds weird, but I, like, want to save this baby," she said.

Emily gave her what she hoped passed as an encouraging smile and slipped out of the car. She guessed that the pregnancy couldn't be saved. In her limited experience, blood in an early pregnancy meant a miscarriage was happening. But she didn't want Amber to lose hope and she certainly didn't want to be the one who broke that news to the girl. For that reason alone, she needed them to close that bridge so they could get to the hospital. She'd seen a rather large hospital up Highway 17 near Shallotte. With any luck she'd have Amber there in less than twenty minutes. She headed toward the closed gates, the lights flashing out a warning to not come any farther. Emily walked right past them, determined.

She walked to the water's edge and, with all the gumption she could muster, began to yell. "Hey!" she shouted. "Kyle? Bridge tender! Someone!" But they appeared to be doing something to the bridge and the clanking tools and machinations blocked out the sound of her voice. She yelled a few more times to no avail, even going far enough to flap her arms and jump up and down. But it didn't help. Defeated, she walked back to the car, and Amber.

She was trying to think of a way to break the news to Amber that they weren't getting over the bridge tonight unless they just happened to open it when she got back to the car. Amber handed her her cell phone with a number already plugged in. "Hit Send when you're ready," she said.

She looked at Amber with knitted brows.

"It'll call the tender house," the girl explained.

"They have a phone?"

Amber looked at her like Emily was perhaps a little slow. "Of course."

"And you just know the number? By heart?"

The look was still on her face as she said, "Everyone does."

Emily hit Send and listened to the phone ring a few times while she thought, *Well, obviously not everyone.*

The voice that answered was familiar. Of course. This wasn't the time to act like a flustered schoolgirl talking to her crush. She needed to be purposeful and direct.

"Hi, is this Kyle?" she asked.

"Yes, it is," he responded. "Who is this?"

"This is Emily Shaw, the woman who bought Ada's house?"

She heard him smile through the phone and — she couldn't help it — pictured him smiling as she did. "Emily, yeah, of course. What can I do for you?"

Oh, would Marta have had a field day with that question had she been there. But Marta wasn't there and Amber was. She looked at the girl who wasn't smiling at all. "I, um, need to get across the bridge. Now. It's an emergency."

His voice went from jovial to serious in a second. "What kind of emergency?"

"I've got a girl here — a teen — who is having some, um, issues and needs to get to a hospital. Can you please close the bridge just long enough for us to cross?"

"Is it life or death?" he asked.

She glanced at Amber, who didn't appear to be in pain, but who, she knew, was convinced that her baby would die if she didn't get to a doctor. And yet Emily knew that chances were that was already the case. Truth was, without an ultrasound or tests to tell them more, she didn't know for sure that Amber was actually pregnant at all. There had to be such a thing as false positives with those pregnancy tests.

"No," Emily answered, a little hitch in her voice as she spoke. "I don't think it is."

"I'm on orders from the state not to close the bridge unless it's a life or death emergency. We're reopening the bridge at 5:00 a.m. You can cross then. I'm sorry." He sounded genuinely sorry and Emily felt bad for putting him on the spot.

"It's okay," she said. She looked over at

Amber and made a face, then executed a perfect three point turn right there at the water's edge. She said good-bye to Kyle and handed the phone back to Amber before heading toward her house. She checked the clock. It was 3:00 a.m., which meant they didn't have long to wait for the bridge to be functional again. She turned to Amber. "The state is working on the bridge. He can't open it unless it's life or death."

Amber stared out the window as they drove. For a few minutes she said nothing. "I hate that bridge," she said as they pulled into Emily's driveway. "I wish they'd tear it down." In Claire's house she saw a light on and half wondered what they were doing up. She thought about the two sides of the argument, and the two women near her who were on either side — the romantic one who favored keeping the small-town access to the island in place and the practical one who favored safety and progress. Two generations held two opposing views.

As she watched Amber open the car door and carefully pick her way toward the front door of her house, she knew which side made the most sense, and she grieved not being able to help Amber the way she wanted to. Her throat tightened at the thought of yet another disappointment defining her life. She hoped that if she had miscarried, Amber wouldn't blame the bridge, wouldn't rationalize that this delay had caused her baby's death. Kyle had asked if it was life or death and as they each flopped down on opposite ends of the couch, she wondered if she had answered wrong.

After they both dozed for a couple hours, they got back in her car and headed toward the bridge. They were waiting when it swung shut to finally allow passage. She looked at the bridge tender's house, expecting to see Kyle's face and give him a wave, but she saw another man with gray hair instead. She told herself that she wasn't disappointed and that it didn't matter whether she saw him or not. What mattered right now was getting Amber to a doctor.

Thankfully there wasn't a crowd in the ER of the local hospital when they got there and they took Amber back right away. Emily was impressed at the girl's resourcefulness. She had her insurance card ready and filled out the forms with an efficiency that surpassed her age. She really was on her own, Emily realized. In that respect, Emily felt that they were kindred spirits. Each of them, when it came down to it, had no one to rely on except herself. She reached over and put her hand over Amber's. "It'll be okay," she whispered.

Amber, who seemed on the verge of tears, nodded. A moment later a nurse called her name. "I'll be right here," she promised as Amber walked away.

Emily flipped through old magazines — a *Woman's Day* from two years prior and a *Runner's World* from six months earlier. It was practically a new release, she thought with a smile. She was debating taking up running — maybe training for a marathon — when a nurse came and fetched her. "Ma'am," the nurse said. "Your daughter would like you to come back and be with her now."

Embarrassed, Emily started to tell her that Amber wasn't her daughter, but decided not to correct her. What difference did it make if that nurse thought wrong? At the rate she was going, Amber might be the closest she ever got to having a daughter. Never mind that — but for a teen pregnancy of her own — the girl couldn't be hers. She followed the nurse, thinking how touching it was that Amber had asked for her.

She found Amber in a small exam room wearing a backward gown, sitting up on a gurney with a blanket over her. "They're going to do an ultrasound," Amber said. "To see if there's a heartbeat." Emily crossed the room and took a seat on a small wheeled stool beside the gurney. She reached for Amber's hand and it didn't feel weird at all. Amber took it, looking grateful. "I just didn't want to be alone when I found out," she said.

In a few moments a tech came in pushing an ultrasound machine on wheels. "So," she said. "You've been having some bleeding?" the tech asked, all business, plugging the machine in and adjusting knobs as Amber began recounting the last few hours to the tech who nodded sympathetically but didn't seem to need to know the details.

Once she was happy with the machine, she pushed open Amber's gown in the middle, revealing a little pooch of stomach. She caught Emily's eye. "You mom?" she asked.

"No," Amber answered for Emily. "My mom's dead. She's a friend."

The tech just nodded. It was clear she cared nothing about this girl's life story or current situation. She was just another patient in a long line of patients, probably her last after a long night. "This is going to be cold," she said.

Amber inhaled as the gel was squirted on

her stomach. She looked at Emily. "She wasn't kidding." Emily smiled and was glad that after the drama of the night she could still make a joke.

They both watched as the screen came to life, a blur of gray and white images flashing. For a few moments there was no sound, just the efficient tech moving the wand across Amber's belly and entering numbers into the machine. "What do you see?" Amber finally breathed.

The tech pointed to a little flicker on the screen. "See that?" she asked.

Emily and Amber nodded in unison. The tech hit a few buttons and a noise filled the room. *Whoomp-whoomp-whoomp.* Emily thought she knew what it was and found she was holding her breath and fighting back tears as she watched the tech deliver the news to this girl who had just called her "friend."

"That's your baby's heartbeat."

Amber's breath caught in her throat and Emily noticed tears welling in her eyes. "Can you tell if it's a boy or a girl? Can you tell how far along I am? Can you tell when it will be born?" Her words came tumbling out and even the no-nonsense tech had to laugh.

"It's too soon to tell what it is — you'll be

able to find out around sixteen weeks along if you'd like. You're about ten weeks right now." She entered some more numbers and looked back at Amber. "Says here you're due around November 30."

Amber inhaled again. "Thanksgiving," she breathed. "It'll be right after Thanksgiving and before Christmas." She looked over at Emily. "That's my favorite time of year."

Emily did her best to smile and not go into how hard this would be on Amber, being a single teen parent with no parental support. She didn't want to tell her that this guy — whoever he was — would most likely stop visiting the motel once he found out about the blessed event to come. Though the harsh realities were on the tip of her tongue she chose to keep quiet and, after a very difficult night, let Amber have this moment of joy. She smoothed Amber's beautiful hair back, thinking of how pretty that baby — he or she — would be. She would focus on that and that alone for now. She turned back to look at the image on the screen, that tiny determined heartbeat. That baby was still a miracle. Life — as Emily knew all too well — always was.

After the tech bustled out, the two of them were left to wait for the doctor on call, who was somewhere in the hospital delivering a set of twins and "might be awhile," as the tech warned. Emily wanted coffee and was about to suggest she go find them something to eat and drink when Amber spoke. "I lied earlier," she said. She was sitting up again, her gown closed, her arm protectively resting across her stomach.

"About what?" Emily asked.

"About my mom. She's not dead. She left. A long, long time ago. I was a little girl." She was quiet for a moment, thinking, Emily imagined, about her mother. "My dad did the best he could. Bought the motel so he could be around. Before that he was a fishing boat captain. Took tourists out deep-sea fishing and stuff. He was never around, which is why my mom left, I think. He said she was supposed to come back and get me but . . . she never did."

She didn't meet Emily's eyes. "Do you think that someone who had a bad mother can be a good mother?" she asked quietly.

"Sure," Emily said a little too quickly, her voice a little too perky. "This is your life, not hers." She thought of her own mother's life in a fishbowl, consumed with appearances and ruled by what people thought, always pushing that mind-set on Emily. In coming to Sunset, she'd found a place where she didn't have to live that way. She wondered if maybe Ryan had thought of that each time he made those life insurance payments. "You can choose to do things differently than your parents."

Amber seemed to ponder that for a moment. She nodded, using her index finger to trace the edges of the ultrasound photo she held in her lap. "I want the best for this baby," she said.

"Of course you do."

She stopped moving her finger. "It feels so real, seeing it like that. The heart was beating."

Emily nodded, swallowed. "Are you going to tell the father?"

Amber shrugged. "I've tried a few times but I don't get to see him much, and when I do we never seem to get around to it."

Emily thought of him all over her at that ice-cream store. *I'll just bet,* she thought but held her tongue. "You should tell him," she said. "The next time you see him."

Amber nodded, ducked her head. "He's older," she said. "Out of college already. I'm afraid he's going to think I'm a stupid little kid for letting this happen."

Emily wanted to launch into a sermonette on how Amber wasn't the only one who "let this happen." But she held her tongue for a second time, choosing her words carefully. "You shouldn't have to face this by yourself though. If he cares about you then he should stand by you."

Amber looked up at her, a panicked look on her face. "But I don't know if he cares about me. We never exactly talked about feelings. We were just . . . hanging out. And stuff."

Emily sighed, her heart breaking for the girl. She was all alone in the world and she was getting ready to be even more all alone, Emily suspected. Except that now she was responsible for someone else. "Look, when the time is right you can bring it up, let him know and see how he reacts. And I'll be praying that it will go well." She forced a smile. "How's that?"

"You would . . . pray for me? About this?"

"Of course." She gave Amber her best "duh" look, being silly and trying desperately to keep things light.

Amber smiled back in spite of herself. "I just don't know if God wants to hear from me after the mess I've made. I'm not that much into . . . church and stuff."

"Well maybe now's the time." She reached across and put her hand on Amber's knee. "He does want to hear from you, that I can assure you."

Amber sighed. "Okay," she said. Emily was about to suggest they pray right then and there, but the doctor walked in and Emily was shooed from the room because she wasn't family. She found herself wanting Amber to say, "No, I want her to stay." But Amber didn't and Emily exited the room, using the time in the hallway to pray alone instead, asking Jesus to mend that girl's broken heart, and to somehow prepare her for what was to come.

SEVENTEEN

The doctor discharged Amber with orders to rest for a few days, but didn't appear overly worried about her or the baby. Though Emily wondered if the danger was truly past, she trusted the doctor and worked to put any lingering worries out of her mind. When she offered to take Amber home with her and let her stay over in her guest room, she didn't expect Amber to agree, but she did. "It might be best if I stay with you for a while, especially once I tell my dad that I'm pregnant. He's obviously not going to be very happy about that. And even though he's never around, he tries to keep tabs on me. So if I tell him I'm staying with you he'll think I'm safe without having the burden of actually having to take care of me himself." Her laughter was a forced attempt to make light of the situation and Emily felt a pang of regret for Amber as she drove them both home from the hospital, her hands at ten and two, her eyes on the road. Amber glanced at Emily. "If that's okay with you," the girl added.

Emily felt her eyes on her, the sense of desperation communicated in her piercing green gaze. Amber, tough as she acted, was afraid. Emily attempted to act nonchalant at the prospect of housing a pregnant teen, but the truth was she was afraid too. Afraid of the responsibility, the potential for making a bad situation worse, the emotional toll of being involved to this degree. She wanted to drop the girl back at the motel, pat her on the hand, and wish her luck before zooming away. And yet deep down she felt that her connection to this girl had led to this moment, here in the car. Amber had no one. She was afraid. Emily could be there for her, ease her fears.

"It's okay with me." She glanced sidelong at Amber, caught the relief that flickered across her face, and realized that this may be the best way to truly help this girl. "And maybe once your dad adjusts to the news and you get better, you'll want to go home." Beside her she felt Amber tense. "But no rush," she hurried to add.

"Thanks," she said, then turned her head to look out the window. Emily wondered what she saw as the scenery whizzed past.

Did she see a place she loved or longed to escape from? Did she ever want to live somewhere else? Had she ever dreamed of doing something more with her life? At her age, Emily had had big plans and bigger dreams. She was going to be a teacher in Africa, marry a doctor who would work alongside her in the mission field. He would treat the people and she would teach them, a partnership forged by a shared passion for ministry and each other. She never intended to live five miles from her parents, marry a guy who wanted nothing to do with Africa, teach at the same private Christian school she had attended. And yet she'd also never dreamed that such a "boring life" could be so full and rich. Amber's life was ahead of her, and yet it was already hindered because of her bad decisions. Emily wondered if she could help her change that. She would do her best.

Once home, the two of them collapsed, Emily falling into her own bed and pulling the covers over her head, sleep enveloping her much quicker than she expected it to. She'd envisioned tossing and turning, anxiety building as she processed what she'd just taken on. But once she got Amber settled in the room Marta had used — the one just a few steps from her own — wished her a good sleep, and closed the door to her own bedroom, a numbing fatigue set in, the bed in front of her shining like a beacon. She could worry about Amber later, deal with the ramifications of housing her through a long, private phone call with Marta, who would surely tell her she'd gone too far. "Oh well," she said in the quiet house. "I'll have to think about all of that later." She surrendered to sleep, grateful for the sweet oblivion of unconsciousness.

When she awoke, she heard Amber on the phone in the next room, her voice a steady murmur from behind the closed bedroom doors. Emily wondered if she was talking to her father, confessing it all or just telling him she wouldn't be returning to work and that the aunt who had stepped in to help out at the motel today would be needed on a more permanent basis. Emily rose from her bed, reluctant to leave the room but feeling hungry. She looked at the clock and was shocked to see that it was already two o'clock in the afternoon.

She opened the door to her bedroom and found she could hear the conversation going on behind Amber's bedroom door a bit clearer. Though she couldn't make out every word, she heard bits and pieces. She hoped that things went well with her dad, that somehow he would understand her need to be in a home, with someone looking after her. Or maybe this whole situation would be the wake-up call he needed to start paying his daughter the attention she needed. Was it right to blame the father for Amber's situation? For sure leaving a girl alone in a motel all the time was negligent. Of course Amber could've made different choices, but was she even capable at her age? Alone and uncertain, this guy's attention was more than she could resist, a child unable to turn away from the candy even though it would surely lead to a stomachache.

Amber's laughter was the first clue that she was not talking to her father. No matter what she'd told him or how well he took it, she doubted that there would be cause for laughter, and certainly not the flirtatious giggle she heard. Frowning, Emily crept closer to the door, but as soon as she stepped on the threshold the floor creaked loudly. Amber's voice quickly silenced. Her heart racing, Emily scurried into the kitchen, attempting to look as if she'd been there the whole time. She entered the kitchen to find the remnants of a sliced apple, a stray slice left to brown on a plate, the peel curled in the sink. A big glob of peanut butter was also smeared on the plate. Amber had been up for a while.

Suppressing a martyr-like sigh, Emily busied herself with the cleanup, running the plate under hot water and running the disposal after she pushed the peelings into the drain. Amber, she reminded herself, had been under a lot of strain. Cleaning up was probably the last thing on her mind on a good day. And while sleep had come easily to Emily, it had obviously eluded her young friend. The girl was probably exhausted and, no matter who she was talking to, was dealing with the reality of what she'd seen on that ultrasound screen. Emily would need to tread lightly. And yet in the back of her mind, she could hear Marta warning her. She wondered if Ryan would've expected this. She smiled to herself as she turned off the spigot. He probably wouldn't be surprised at all. She might not have made it to the mission field, but he knew her proclivity for finding a mission field everywhere she went.

The door squeaked open behind her and she turned to see Amber emerge from the guest bedroom, blinking and looking around as if she was surprised to find herself there. "You okay?" Emily asked brightly.

Amber nodded and gestured at the plate

Emily held in her hands. "Thanks for cleaning that up. I was going to but I got a phone call."

"It's no problem," Emily said, feeling guilty for being miffed with Amber, if even for a moment. If this was going to work, she was going to have to extend much grace. "Did you get any sleep at all?" She put the rinsed plate in the dishwasher and pulled out an apple for herself. Taking a big slurping bite, she followed Amber into the den and took the seat opposite her on the couch.

"Some," Amber said, resting her hands primly on her knees, looking like the guest that she was. "I was doing some thinking." She eyed Emily. "I know I can't stay here forever and I gotta figure out what to do, you know, long term."

Emily took another bite of apple, making a loud chomping noise that made Amber smile. "Well, don't feel any pressure from me," she said after she'd chewed and swallowed.

"I don't," Amber rushed to say.

"What did he say?" Emily asked, working hard to make her face emotionless. She'd love to have some words with the man. Or better yet, sic Marta on him. She suppressed a smile at the thought.

"I didn't tell him," Amber said. "Yet."

"Was that him on the phone?" Emily asked.

Amber nodded again and started picking at her fingernails, chipping off the blue polish in little fragments. Seconds passed as Emily waited for her to say more. She had enough experience with adolescents to know that sometimes silence was the greatest tool. Eventually, growing uncomfortable, they would attempt to fill it. This time it worked.

"He's coming here soon. When he does, I told him we need to talk. He asked about what, and I said I'd have to tell him face-to-face. I think he suspects but . . ." She raised her eyes to meet Emily's. "I'm just scared to tell him," she whispered. "I don't want to lose him."

The raw vulnerability in Amber's eyes silenced Emily. She had said those very words many times after Ryan was diagnosed — to her mom, to Marta, to God. She'd gone through denial and anger and fear, all things she expected Amber was going through — or would go through — herself. Now wasn't the time to lecture Amber on the importance of telling this guy, or coaching her on dealing with her father. She would give Amber time and space and when she needed it, a listening ear. That, as far as she could see,

232

was the best thing she could do, the one thing no one else seemed to be offering. She gave Amber a smile and rose from her seat to throw away the apple core. "I'm thinking about tomato soup and grilled cheese sandwiches," she tossed out as she headed to the kitchen. "Think you could go for that?"

When Amber gave her an enthusiastic yes, she took it as a sign that she was doing something right.

After their late lunch/early dinner, Amber said she was going out to sit on the dock and think. Emily noticed she took her phone and wondered if she would use it to call her father or him. She needed to ask Amber what his name was, maybe get her talking a bit about him instead of being so secretive. She watched her walk across the yard, wondered when her slim figure would start showing signs of pregnancy. At a certain point whether to tell wouldn't be an option.

The knock at the door startled her. She crossed the room to answer, hoping she wouldn't find the adorable faces of her pint-sized neighbors on the other side. She had a real soft spot for Noah and Sara, but she was too exhausted to handle their exuberance today. The look of relief on her face when she saw Kyle standing there could've been misconstrued as interest in him. Later she would wonder if he'd taken it that way.

"I came by to see if the girl is okay. The one you were trying to get over the bridge last night?"

"How did you . . . ?" she started to ask, thinking that this was indeed a small place if he'd already heard. Then the events of the night before came rushing back to her sleep-addled brain. "Oh, never mind. We talked. I kind of forgot with everything that went on. Sorry." She held up her hands and shook her head. "Obviously I need some caffeine."

He took it the way she feared. "There's a great coffee shop just over the bridge. Near the Food Lion? I could take you . . ."

Feeling foolish for putting him on the spot with her stupid caffeine comment, she waved her hand in the air. "Oh, uh, that's okay, I can just make some coffee here."

Did he look disappointed? Was she hoping he was? She missed being married, missed having all of this . . . uncertainty off the table. She never wanted to be here again. And yet here she was. And here he was. She forced herself to look past him, just over his shoulder. He was just too good-looking and sometimes the reality of who he was sunk in all over again, filling her with that giddy fan-girl euphoria. She needed to get a grip.

"So is she okay? I wanted to apologize for turning you all away. But I could lose my job for messing with scheduled maintenance. If it had been an emergency vehicle I could've done something but . . ." He looked at her and she forced herself to look right back.

"She's fine. We got over the bridge as soon as it opened back up and it was no big deal."

"I should've offered to get you a boat," he said regretfully.

"Really. It was fine to wait. She wouldn't have liked all that effort anyway."

And yet something still nagged at her about it, the sentiments of those proposing a more reliable bridge echoing. She understood what they were saying. While the old bridge was sentimental and romantic, it wasn't always safe. Thankfully her emergency hadn't been that urgent, but what if it had been? What if seconds had counted? She hated to think of what would happen if that were the case. She was thankful that all was well with Amber, but what if the delay had cost her the baby? While she wanted to be on Kyle and Claire's side, the practical part of her said that replacing the bridge was the smarter way to go. Of course, she thought as she leaned against the doorjamb, she wasn't going to tell him that.

"Did you want to come in? I could make that coffee," she asked, attempting to look nonchalant, as if she invited the star of one of her favorite movies of all time inside every day. When he said yes, her heart did a little leap and she internally scolded herself for being ridiculous.

He followed her into the kitchen and surveyed the rest of the house as she busied herself with dumping grounds into a filter and putting water in the coffee maker. "Need any help?" he asked.

She shook her head. "No thanks."

"You haven't done much with the place," he observed, then chuckled. "It looks like Ada's going to walk back in here any minute."

"Well, she left me a lot of her things. I haven't really had the heart to get rid of any of it." She looked around. It really did look like an elderly person's house. Maybe it was time to purge.

He shrugged. "If you want to start, I'd be willing to help you haul stuff away. A buddy of mine's got a truck we could use."

"Thank you, that's a very nice offer. Maybe someday I'll take you up on it."

He let out a dramatic sigh and leaned forward. "Is there a reason why you keep turning me down?" He gave her that grin of his.

Her heart racing, she cast about for the right thing to say in response. There was a reason, but she didn't want to get into it with him. Actually, there were a lot of reasons. "I didn't know I was turning you down," she finally offered weakly.

He laughed. "I offer to take you to get coffee, you say no. I offer to help you out around here, you say no. I come by here and it takes you, like, five minutes to invite me in. I thought you were going to shut the door in my face!"

"I'm sorry," she said and gave him a rueful smile. "I didn't see it that way." The coffeemaker burbled and she pulled mugs from the cabinet and cream from the refrigerator. She gestured to the sugar sitting beside the coffeemaker and handed Kyle a spoon.

He took it and with his back to her continued talking. "You sure you're not just playing hard to get? Or maybe you're mad about the bridge thing." He carried his coffee to the table and she focused on hers, trying not to think of how surreal it was to have him sitting at her kitchen table sipping coffee.

"I'm not mad! I promise." She smiled as she doused her coffee with cream and then added a packet of sweetener.

"So you're playing hard to get then."

She carried her coffee over to the table and sat across from him. Was he seriously hitting on her? "No! I'm not . . . I just . . . I don't really know what I'm doing," she confessed. "I'm not exactly . . . experienced in this type of thing."

He held up his finger and made quotation marks in the air. "This type of thing," he said. "So it's like that?" His grin told her he was teasing her, and enjoying it. She couldn't help but think that Ryan would like this guy, ex-movie star or not. They would've been friends. The thought warmed her like the summer sun beginning its descent in the sky. She'd missed a gorgeous beach day, slept it away. The nice part of living at Sunset was that there were always other days ahead.

His face lost all traces of teasing as he braced his elbows on his knees and tried to catch her eye. "I'd like to take you out. So if not for coffee or to the junkyard" — he smiled — "then for dinner?"

She took a sip of coffee and stared down into her mug. In *Just This Once,* her favorite scene was when Brady asked the awkward girl out over the phone. The girl thought it was a joke, a prank he'd been put up to. Emily had always savored the moment on film when she realized he was totally serious, that he actually liked her. As a teenage girl watching that movie, she had become that girl, her heart had soared as if she were the one being asked out by this gorgeous guy who should've never noticed her. It was her dream come true on film. And now her dream was coming true in real life. She realized she'd stopped breathing and exhaled loudly, knowing all attempts at playing it cool were lost.

"Sure," she said. "I could do that. I mean, if you want." She put the mug back down.

One corner of his mouth turned up. "Now we're getting somewhere." He took another drink from his mug.

The back door opened and their heads turned in unison. He looked from Amber to Emily, then back again, addressing Emily. "So you brought her . . . here?"

Emily nodded once, then looked at Amber as she gestured in Kyle's direction. "This is Kyle Baker. He's one of the bridge tenders and was on duty when the bridge was closed. He came by to check on you."

Amber waved at Kyle. "I know Kyle," she said dully, unimpressed. No one here seemed to be all that enthused about Kyle and Emily couldn't figure out why. Granted, he'd starred in a hit movie years ago and not everyone felt about it the way she did, but still. He had been a movie star, if however brief his stardom lasted. That was worthy of more than the banal response he seemed to garner from the other residents of the island.

"I'm fine," Amber continued. "So you can tell my dad to stop checking up on me."

Kyle blinked and looked over at Emily before addressing Amber. "I didn't come by because of your dad. Really!"

Amber let out a little sarcastic sputter. "Sure," she said. Turning to Emily she said, "I'll be in my room," and slipped away. Emily cringed a little at how cozy she already sounded and questioned her offer to let her stay. But the last thing Amber needed was to feel that she didn't have a safe place.

He waited until Amber closed the door to speak. "Her room?"

Emily shrugged as if the phrase meant nothing, but it had taken her aback slightly, how easily the girl had laid claim to Emily's home. "She's staying here. Temporarily."

"You sure she knows that it's temporary?"

"I'm not sure about anything. I kind of offered and now . . . she's here." She spoke in a hushed tone, not wanting Amber to hear. "It's kind of a mess but I want to help her."

He drained his mug and carried it to the

sink, washing it out and placing it in the dishwasher. She couldn't decide what was odder — that Brady Rutledge just had coffee at her kitchen table or that he did his own dishes. Without being asked.

"Thank you," she said, an incredulous tone creeping into her voice.

"No problem." He shrugged. "Just be careful. Her father can be a pretty intimidating guy. And he's not really into outsiders."

"Yeah, he sounds like an . . . odd guy."

Kyle shook his head. "You don't know the half of it. Look, thanks for the coffee. I'll let you take care of things with Amber. I'm sure things'll work out." Looking at his face, she could tell he wasn't sure at all. "Maybe on our date you can tell me how you got involved with her . . . and why she's here. How's tomorrow night?" He took a few steps in the direction of the front door.

She should say she was busy, that she needed more warning, play hard to get. And yet after the last twenty-four hours she just didn't have the energy for games or manipulation. She took a few steps toward him, her bare feet suddenly cold on the wood floor. "Sure," she said, rubbing one foot up and down her calf to ward off the chill. She would grab her favorite pair of Ryan's socks as soon as he was gone. She followed him the rest of the way to the door.

He opened the door, held it there for a moment, studying her. "Don't worry so much. It'll all work out." He winked and was gone, leaving her to stand, blinking and trying to take his advice long after he left.

EIGHTEEN

That night she logged onto her computer and went straight to Google. Now that she had accepted the date with Kyle she wanted to learn whatever she could about his story. Why did people seem hesitant around him? And what was with the tragedy Marta had found when she Googled him? Claire treated him with outright disdain, and he seemed to accept it. And why had he abandoned Hollywood for this beach hamlet? They had oceans in LA. If memory served, he'd even had a pretty hot and heavy romance with his costar. Emily remembered because she'd felt jealous at the time. She had to laugh. If she'd been able to tell her former self what her future self would be doing one day, her former self would've never believed it.

There was surprisingly little on Kyle — or Brady, as he was known then. A search of his real name turned up some old records from his high school years and a small article in the local paper about his being discovered at a casting call in Atlanta he had attended on a lark. At the time of the article he was filming the movie. He called the whole experience "a whirlwind" and said he missed his girlfriend back home. Emily knit her brows together over that. Girlfriend back home? She wondered who that could be. Soon she would pin Claire down, insist she tell her the whole story. Of course, to do that she'd have to admit that she was going out with him and she wasn't exactly ready to discuss that with anyone.

Dissatisfied with her findings, she erased the search bar of Google and sat staring at the empty space, knowing there was one more thing she had to do, something that had nothing to do with Kyle and everything to do with what she felt about the bridge debate. It had been nagging at her ever since she'd found the bridge closed as a frightened teenage girl whimpered beside her in the dark of night. She couldn't pretend that hadn't happened and — while it had all turned out okay — there was no guarantee that someday it wouldn't. The threat of harm coming to someone was too real to avoid. At the meeting the state representatives had urged citizens to leave comments, expressing why they were for or against the bridge. "We will read every comment and take it under advisement," the guy who seemed to be in charge had said.

"And then do just what you were going to do anyway," Claire had muttered beside her.

But whether it made a difference or not, Emily wanted to register her thoughts, to try to relay the danger she had felt in being closed off on the island with no way to cross. Sometimes it was really important for someone to be able to get to the other side and for nothing to hinder that from happening. She stared at the picture of the proposed new bridge that came up on the state site, the sturdy structure rising into the sky. That bridge, she could see, would not keep people from crossing. She scrolled down to the comment section, took a deep breath, and began to type, silently apologizing to Kyle — and Claire — as she did.

She finished her comment, revising and amending it so many times she finally gave up and just hit Send, feeling a little sick as it went flying into the Internet Neverland, irretrievable and, even worse, bearing her actual name that the state had required for submission. Emily supposed this was to deter hacks and prohibit people from using the site to incite arguments on the topic. People hid behind anonymous commenting opportunities, grew bolder and more outrageous if they didn't have to own up to what they'd said. She guessed the state was trying to avoid that, especially on this hot-button issue.

Emily had felt the undercurrent of people's emotions running through the meeting room that night and recognized the bridge debate was potentially charged. There were those who were powerfully attached to that bridge, and she suspected they all had reasons of their own, memories and feelings conjured by the past. She knew what that was like better than most. And yet in this case, she couldn't go along with the desire to hold on to what was, not after she felt the danger that night in the car.

She looked up and saw Amber sitting on the couch, staring at her. She had no idea when the girl had entered the room. "Hi," she said. "You okay?" She seemed to be asking Amber that a lot.

Amber nodded. "I just got up. I fell asleep for a while. Then when I came out here you seemed pretty absorbed in whatever you were doing." She gestured at Emily's laptop. Emily was glad it was turned at an angle that prohibited Amber from seeing what she'd been doing. She didn't want to explain or leave Amber to draw her own conclusions why she was on the state's site devoted to the bridge debate. She closed the laptop.

"What would you like to do tonight?" she asked. "You hungry?"

Amber thought about it for a minute. "Not especially. I mean maybe, like, a snack?"

"What if I made popcorn?" Emily stood up, stowed the computer on the shelf where she typically kept it. "And not that micro-wave kind either. The old-fashioned kind, on the stove. My —" She stopped short of saying, "My husband taught me how." She didn't want to bring Ryan up to Amber, not when she'd just seen Kyle there. It was all too much to get into for now.

Amber shrugged. "Sure, I guess." She got up and followed Emily into the kitchen, watching attentively, as if she would be quizzed later on the process, as she took out butter and oil and popcorn and got out the big pot Ada had left behind that was just tall and heavy enough for the task. Emily found herself talking about each step as she did, trying hard not to think about the night Ryan had taught her when it was clear he wasn't going to beat the cancer. Though he hadn't spelled it out for her, she knew he knew he had to pass it along to her, seeing as how she loved his popcorn so much. She had to learn to make it on her own. She'd cried her way through the first batches she made after he died, but the sight of popcorn kernels no longer brought automatic tears to her eyes.

Moments later she was finished with a huge batch. She dumped the popcorn into a large stainless steel bowl and carried it into the den, plopping it between the two of them. "We'll never eat all that," Amber remarked as she saw the bowl. She had already turned on the television and was flipping through the channels at lightning speed. "There's nothing on," she informed Emily in a monotone.

She landed on a sitcom and left it there after turning to see if Emily objected. "Nothing else better," Emily said as shoulder to shoulder they took in the activity and the canned laughter on the screen, robotically popping pieces of popcorn into their mouths. Not paying attention to the storyline at all, Emily wondered what to say to this unexpected roommate of hers. She wanted to dole out some wise advice but could think of nothing at all.

During a commercial Amber spoke up.

"He was a guest at the hotel," she said as if in answer to a question Emily hadn't asked. But in truth, she'd asked it internally many times, never brave enough to come out and say it. Amber must've sensed her curiosity. Amber swallowed hard. "He was cute. Older, but not so much older that it was gross, ya know?"

Emily barely nodded. She was afraid any sudden movements might scare Amber off, put her back into closed-off, secretive mode.

"He would flirt with me whenever he checked in or out. Tease me about how our motel wasn't exactly five star or whatever, but that he couldn't afford more." A look of pride crossed her face and she sat up a little straighter. "He's starting his own business: T-shirts that say really funny things on them that he sells at the different beach stores." She quieted for a moment, thinking. "He just graduated from college and had made T-shirts for his fraternity. He got the seed money for this business from doing that." She smiled. "He's really smart.

"He calls me 'Cheerleader' because he said that he knew I was a cheerleader, even though no way was I a cheerleader. For one I'm uncoordinated and for another I work too much to do that." She made a face. "Anyway, when he says it, he always makes me feel pretty, you know?" She searched Emily's face, willing her, Emily knew, to understand. And she did understand. Emily imagined there wasn't a woman alive who didn't understand that part.

"So one day he called down from his room and said there weren't any towels and could I bring some up?" She looked down at her lap, studying her hands, folded there, her fingers shiny from the buttered popcorn. "I knew there were towels up there because I had put them there myself. And I knew if I went up there everything would change. Between us. For me." She sat motionless for a moment, then turned to look at Emily. "I just didn't know how much."

She looked away quickly, staring at the television. Another sitcom had started but she didn't bother to turn up the sound. "It's been going on for a while. We never talk about the future except when he tells me I should go to college, that I'll have the time of my life. We never say 'I love you' or even talk about when he's coming back. Every time he leaves I never know if that's the last time I'll see him. It took him months just to give me his cell number. And now . . . I just don't know."

Amber's voice trailed off and they both sat silently. Emily cast about for the right words, the perfect piece of wisdom to share. "Are you going to keep the baby?" she finally asked.

"I'm not sure if I can keep it or if it would be best to give it up for adoption. I want to talk to him about it, I guess." She shrugged. "Not that he's ready to be a father. I mean, he's trying to get that business launched and it's not like he's got extra money." She gave a little ironic laugh. "Or any money." She brought her fingers to her mouth and licked the butter and salt from the tips, one by one. "I was all set to just, like, give it up for adoption or whatever but then when I saw the little heartbeat, I was just like, 'That's our kid.' And it made me think, what if we could make a go of it? I know I'm young and everything but I just want it to work out so much." Her beautiful green eyes widened. "I love him so much."

"Then you should tell him. Be honest. The next time he comes in town, just go for it."

Amber nodded. "I know. I need to. I will." She lowered her eyes, embarrassed. "Thanks for letting me talk. I don't really, um, have someone to, you know, talk to."

Emily patted her and stood up. "That's what I'm here for." She walked toward the kitchen, giving them some emotional and physical distance after such raw honesty.

"Want some sweet tea?" she called out over her shoulder, doing her level best to seem unruffled. She hoped she could act as well as Marta, could pretend that all was well when it completely was not.

NINETEEN

Amber stood in the doorway watching Emily, who was turning from side to side in front of the bathroom mirror. She had decided on white jeans paired with a black sleeveless crocheted top and black wedges. She'd gone with simple silver jewelry and barely any makeup. With her tan face and sun-streaked hair, she looked, she hoped, shiny and healthy. She'd looked weighed down and blah for far too long. Tonight she liked what she saw in the mirror, feeling her best even if Amber wasn't looking all that convinced. "You're sure about that top?" she asked. Emily had worked with kids long enough to know a veiled insult when she heard one.

"What's wrong with this top?" Emily tried not to sound defensive but maybe the girl knew something she didn't.

Amber shrugged and turned from the doorway. "It just looks kinda old-ladyish to me." She laughed. "But too late to change. He's here." Amber laughed harder at the look on Emily's face. "I'll get it," she said and dashed for the door, leaving Emily to stare into the mirror one last time. For better or worse, Amber was right. It was too late to change a thing.

She walked into her room and took a few deep breaths, looking around at the place that had become familiar and comforting to her in recent weeks. It was, she had to admit, starting to feel like home. She looked at her bed, thinking how nice it would be at that moment to crawl into it and hide under the covers, pretend she'd never said yes to this insane idea. What business did she have going out with any guy, much less a guy whose poster she used to have taped to her wall? She laughed when she remembered the movie tagline scrawled across that poster: "Tonight they take their one big chance." The irony was almost too much.

"Why do I feel like somehow you're behind all this?" she whispered, her eyes scanning around the room, wishing somehow he would answer. She'd give anything to hear his voice again, see his smile, feel his arms around her. Even now, even with the prospect of going out with someone she once had a crush on. That someone didn't —

couldn't — live up to the reality of who Ryan had been to her, who she still wished he could be in her life. She waited a moment longer, giving him a chance to come rushing back into her life like she wanted, before putting on her bravest smile and going out to rescue Amber and Kyle from small-talk purgatory.

Kyle walked Emily out to his car, his body stiff, his smile tight. She wondered if he was regretting taking her out or just feeling nervous like she was. Marta had called and given her a pep talk that afternoon, speaking to her like a coach might address his team during halftime at the Super Bowl, her speech punctuated with exclamation points and peppered with superlatives. If the night kept going like it was so far, Marta had oversold the event. She gave Kyle a little smile as they neared his car, then heard her name being called and turned her head to see Noah standing in the front yard of his house, holding the water hose and dripping wet. "Hey, Emily!" he called.

"Hi, Noah," she replied, thankful that she was standing far out of the hose's reach. She started walking toward the car, silently praying that the boy would become engrossed in whatever he was doing with that hose again.

"Where ya goin'?" Noah continued. The hose dribbled a little stream of water from the end as Noah arced it through the air. Emily guessed he was pretending to be a fireman. She thought of her comment on the state's site, about the access to emergency vehicles that a new bridge would allow. Her stomach fell at the thought of Kyle finding out how she really felt about the bridge. Somehow she didn't think he'd understand her position.

"Out to dinner," Emily said, trying not to think about what could go wrong for once.

"Who's he?" Noah asked.

"This is Kyle. He lives here. Your mommy knows him." She couldn't be sure but she thought she saw Kyle wince as she said it.

"Oh. You're going to eat dinner with him?"

"Yep!" She gave a little wave and tried to hurry the rest of the way to the car so she could duck inside it and close the door on this little exchange. Noah was cute but Lord knew what he would say next.

"Noah!" she heard Claire call before she could see her. "Do you have that hose?" Claire rushed into the front yard, looking frazzled as usual. "I told you you were not allowed to play with the hose," she continued, snatching the hose from the boy's hand as he started to holler.

"He didn't have it on very much," Kyle said, defending Noah and shocking Emily when he spoke. Up to that moment he hadn't said a word since they left the house.

Claire startled and glanced over to find Emily and Kyle standing there. She did a double take. "Oh! I didn't know you two were out here."

Emily pointed at Noah dumbly. "We were talking to Noah."

Claire, holding the dribbling hose, nodded. "Well, I guess I'll let the two of you get to wherever you're going." She looked from Emily to Kyle to the car and back again, clearly confused. Emily had almost gone over and told her about the date, but with Amber there she hadn't had a moment to slip away and relay the whole story. And truth be told she hadn't been dying to confess that she was going out with Kyle or that she had taken in Amber. It would take more than a few minutes to catch Claire up on everything that had happened in the past few days. She made a mental note to pay Claire a visit first thing tomorrow.

"Have a nice night, Claire," Kyle said. "And go easy on the kid," he added. "He wasn't doing anything wrong."

Claire narrowed her eyes at him, her tone

turning from civil to surly in seconds. "Mind your own business, Kyle," she said. Then she turned her back on the two of them and busied herself with getting Noah inside the house.

Emily watched her go until Kyle made a move toward the car. "Shall we?" he asked, pulling the passenger side door open for her and gesturing toward the seat with a flourish and a silly grin. He really was handsome, she thought, and her heart did that fluttering thing that she thought had died with Ryan.

She nodded and slid into the car, watching as he walked around and joined her. He closed the door and looked at her. "You ready?" he asked.

She smiled back at him. "Yes," she said, not wanting to bring up why Claire didn't like him. Tonight she didn't want to think about Claire or Noah or Amber or — truth be told — even Ryan. She studied Kyle's profile as he concentrated on backing out of the drive. It was a very nice profile indeed.

He drove her to Southport, a quaint little town on the water about an hour away, for dinner. They ate outdoors, the setting sun warming her bare shoulders as they indulged in hushpuppies and corn on the cob, steamed shrimp and crabcakes. He told her stories about working on the bridge, entertaining her with funny things that had happened — the teenagers who tried to jump the bridge as it was closing, in their truck à la *Dukes of Hazzard,* or the boat that tried to race through the closing bridge and got snagged on one of the cables, ripping part of its motor away in the process. Around them boats bobbed on the water and happy children dashed up and down the docks where the restaurant was located while seagulls hovered around in hopes of scraps, their shrieks punctuating the meal every so often.

After dinner they walked along the road until they found a bench and flopped there, stuffed and content to just sit for a while. Around them vacationers swarmed, enjoying the atmosphere of the town just like they were. "I've never been here," Emily admitted.

"To Southport? Really?"

She shook her head. "It's nice. I'm glad you brought me."

"Yeah, sometimes it's good to get out of Sunset for a while," he said. He crossed his legs at the ankle and folded his hands across his stomach, tilted his head up to the sky, and closed his eyes.

"Need a nap?" she joked.

He shook his head without opening his eyes. "Nah, just relaxing. Enjoying this night."

"It's really beautiful out," she agreed. "We couldn't have ordered better weather."

A seagull swooped by them, calling out as it passed. In the distance a boat cruised along the horizon. "So tell me your story," he said.

His eyes were still closed so he couldn't see the shocked look she gave him. She closed her mouth. "My . . . my story?"

He nodded and cracked his eyes open to peer at her. "Your story. I've heard rumors as to what it is but I'd like to hear it from you, directly."

She laughed. "And what about your story?" she countered.

He nodded. "That's fair, but you already know more about mine than I know about yours. I mean, I told you all about working at the bridge. As for the rest . . ." He shrugged. "I tried acting. It didn't suit me. I came back here." He held his arms out to take in the ocean, the seagulls, the boats. "Home." He sat up a little straighter and balanced his elbows on his knees, leaning toward her. "I don't normally take out girls I know nothing about. I think it's only fair I know more about you."

She raised her eyebrows. "See if I pass the test? Is that it?" She was pretending to be more confident than she felt. Marta would be impressed.

He smiled without showing any teeth and nodded. "Something like that."

"What do you want to know?" she asked, her voice lower and shakier than she wanted it to be.

"How about I tell you what I heard and you tell me if it's true or not?" He propped his arm up on the back of the bench, almost as if it was around her, but not quite close enough.

She shrugged. She could smell the scent she was coming to recognize as him — a unique blend of sea air and skin and the cologne he wore, mixed with a metal smell that must've come from working on the bridge. She found herself leaning slightly forward as the breeze picked up and carried his scent that much closer. "Sure," she managed to say. "We can do that."

"You're a teacher from Rockingham. You came here to buy a house because you inherited some money. You bought Ada's house after finding it for sale by owner while on a bike ride one evening. Now you live next door to Claire — my sympathies, by the way — and you have a friend who comes to visit from time to time, but mostly you seem to live alone. Of course, now you have the girl from the motel staying with you. So that's not exactly true anymore, I guess." He paused to take a breath and glanced over at her. "How'm I doin' so far?"

She elbowed him hard and he leaned over and pretended to fall off the bench. "You sound like some stalker!" she said, unable to keep from laughing as he slumped across the bench, still pretending to be wounded. She watched for a moment until he composed himself. "I'd say those acting lessons paid off," she added.

"I never had an acting lesson," he retorted, a cocky smile on his face.

"Well, I didn't want to say anything but . . . ," she came back, matching his cocky smile with one of her own.

He studied her for a moment, all the teasing suddenly gone out of the moment as he fixed her with those gorgeous eyes of his. But it wasn't just that they were gorgeous; it was what was behind that gaze — something deeper, something that told her he knew her, and not just the random observations he'd thrown out. And yet she wasn't ready to broach any of that. So she looked away and did her best to keep up the banter. "So did you actually follow me or just happen into that information?"

Thankfully he went along with her and didn't try to keep things serious. "I hear things. People talk. There're not many new residents around here these days. The people who do buy houses mostly use them for rentals. It's not often you have someone stay around. Especially a young single woman." He paused to watch as a man with spiky hair walked a little black-and-white dog past the bench.

When the man was gone, he spoke again. "The one thing no one seems to know is how long you're staying in town." When he looked at her, his eyes said more than the question he was asking. If she didn't know better, she'd say his eyes were hoping for a certain answer. She blinked and watched the man with the dog start to fade from view. Maybe she was reading more into this than he intended. Maybe he was just making conversation.

Then his hand covered hers, causing her breath to catch in her throat as he spoke again. "Or why you're single but you wear that ring." He twisted her wedding band around on her finger and then his hand was gone before she had time to register how his skin felt against hers. "You don't have to answer that if you're not ready to talk about it. I just want to know I'm not out with a married woman." He looked away and for a moment they both sat, silent and still.

She searched for the right words to say. She wasn't ready to talk about Ryan with him, and yet she did owe him some sort of explanation. She'd been a dummy to forget about her ring. It had been such a part of her — and for so long — she didn't think of it much anymore. There had been the initial question after Ryan died about whether or not she should keep it on. (Everyone had had an opinion they were only too glad to offer.) Once she decided she felt best keeping it on, she'd stopped thinking about it. Other than those really lonely nights when she got out their wedding album, lit candles, and had a good cry, did she really let herself think about what having it on still meant?

But how to tell him all that? The last thing she wanted to do on their first date was weigh down the conversation with her sad story. When she tried to speak, the words caught in her throat and she coughed and swallowed as he watched, a look of mild amusement on his face. "Didn't mean to choke you up," he quipped.

She gave him a strained smile, thinking as

she did of Ryan and wondering if being with Kyle meant she was getting over him. Did it have to be either or? She twisted the ring on her finger and looked down at it, trying to push from her mind the day he'd given it to her out on the quad at school. Bystanders had stopped to stare as Ryan dropped to his knee and began to propose. When he pulled the ring from his pocket, people had actually clapped. And when she said yes and they kissed, well, they had cheered. She would always treasure that moment, that feeling of being the most blessed and special girl in the world. And now, sitting with someone she once thought was the most good-looking guy on earth and having him look at her the way he was, well, it was a close second.

"I'm not married." She smiled. "I'd never have agreed to go out with you if I was. But would it be okay if we talked about it later? I'd like to have a nice time tonight and leave the past where it is, for now at least, if that's okay."

He leaned over and cupped her face with his hand, rubbing his thumb across her cheek. "I think that's an excellent idea." He drew her to him and kissed her on the cheek. "But can I just say that I'm really glad to hear you say you're not married?"

He pulled away, stood up, and reached his hand out to her. She placed her hand in his and let him pull her up too. As they started to walk to his car, she realized she had no idea where they were going next and she didn't care. All that mattered now was that as they walked he hadn't let go of her hand.

After Southport they stopped in Shallotte to check out the movies playing there, standing in front of the marquee scanning the listings as people rushed past. She couldn't keep her mind off the fact that she was standing in front of a cinema with none other than Brady Rutledge. The irony made her grin and, while she was getting more and more used to the idea of him being Kyle and not Brady, she still had these little fan-girl moments, her inner teen thrilled with the development.

"Something look good?" he asked, mistaking her grin.

"Not really, to be honest," she said. "I'm just having a good time. It's such a beautiful night. I wouldn't mind just sitting out on my dock and talking if that sounds good to you."

His face broke into a grin to match hers. "I knew I liked you." He couldn't know the fireworks those words set off in her heart.

She coached herself to cool it as they walked to the car. Just because her inner teen was lurking didn't mean she needed to completely show up.

And so the night ended with them out on her dock, listening to the rippling water and the sounds of an occasional fish breaking the surface, agreeing that this beat any movie, hands down. They watched the lights of the bridge in the distance as it opened and closed. He explained the process that was going on behind the scenes. "I'd like to go there sometime and see it up close," she said, then wondered if that was too forward. He hadn't said he wanted to see her again, and yet he hadn't rushed off. Wasn't that a good sign? She was so out of practice at this dating thing.

"I'd like that," he said, his eyes on the bridge, his face serious. She wondered if he was thinking about the fate of the bridge and felt a pang of guilt course through her as she remembered what she'd written. It wasn't that what she'd said wasn't true, it was that her words betrayed the cause he was so passionate about and could contribute to the destruction of something he loved. She wrestled with fessing up as much as she'd wrestled with telling him about Ryan. But there was never a right moment to do it. No sense making a first date so serious. Instead she concentrated on his every move, hoping — even though she couldn't believe it — that he would kiss her again. Her stomach was filled with butterflies — monarch, painted lady, and swallowtails — all doing laps.

She could almost feel both Amber's and Claire's watchful eyes on her, eyes peering from the windows of their respective houses. She would have to introduce the two of them so they could coordinate their spying. All they needed was her mother and Marta to complete the picture. But there was nothing to see except two people making small talk on a dock on a summer's night under the stars. The setting was beautiful and perfect and she tried to focus on how already she'd gotten more than she ever expected when he'd first shown up at her house looking for Ada.

He yawned and she felt a little crestfallen. She knew what that yawn meant and resolved not to make it hard for him to leave. She would be cavalier and fun, not serious and dry. He would like being with her because of it and maybe he'd ask her out again. And if not, she'd had this night, which was more than she'd ever dreamed of when she'd tacked that poster on her wall so long ago. She thought of the words on the poster: Tonight they take their one big chance. Going out with him at all had felt like taking a chance to her, a big, good first step to a life apart from Ryan. Perhaps there would come a time when she could explain that to him. She hoped he could understand when she did find the words.

"You tired?" she asked.

He nodded. "I've got an early shift tomorrow. Promised myself no matter what I'd make this an early night." He looked over at her. "But it's hard to leave. I've enjoyed just relaxing with you." He stretched his legs out ahead of him and leaned back to look at the stars.

"I'm glad. I had a nice time too."

"Nice enough to do it again sometime?"

She glanced up at the stars above them, the quarter moon hanging just over the bridge. "Yeah, I'd really like that," she breathed, unable to keep a victorious smile from filling her face.

"Good," he said and pushed himself to a standing position. He looked down at her and for a moment she thought he was going to extend his hand again. "I can show myself out," he said. "Don't get up. I like thinking of you out here, enjoying this view. Now when I look in this direction while I'm working I'm going to picture you sitting here." He stretched and shook his head. "It'll be the highlight of my day."

"Unless of course someone else tries to jump the bridge with their truck," she said, looking up at him.

He leaned down so that his face was inches above hers, so close she could feel his breath on her face, smell his skin. "Can I kiss you good-bye?" he asked.

She meant to say yes, of course, please, ask him what he'd been waiting for. Instead her heart raced and she fumbled for the right words, her brain short-circuiting at the time when she most needed to think clearly, her heart stuttering when she needed it to pound. This wasn't the fantasy of kissing Brady Rutledge. This was the reality of kissing Kyle Baker. This wasn't *Just This Once;* it was real life. So instead of merely nodding — which would've been just fine and what people in the movies did as the music soared — she began babbling, her mouth working independently from the rest of her as she tried to offer an answer to his question.

"I just can't believe I'm here, with you. I mean, you're Brady Rutledge. Of course I know you're not Brady Rutledge, I mean, duh, of course I know that now. But I mean, to me you were Brady Rutledge for so long and I guess in some ways I'll always think of you that way and so the idea of kissing you — I mean, my goodness, I just can't even process that."

She stopped babbling and noticed that he'd moved his face away and that obviously she'd ruined the moment. "I'm sorry. I shouldn't have said all that. I mean, it's just that we hardly know each other. I mean, last night I was Googling you, for crying out loud, just to know more about you. And you asked me earlier about this ring and, well, that is a story and it's a sad one. And isn't it weird to think of kissing someone when you don't even know their sad stories? I mean, I found a story on you that said you came back here because of some sort of tragedy. So that means you have a sad story of your own."

He took a step backward, his face registering his shock over her outburst. And as she said it, she realized this was why she hadn't wanted to kiss him. "I mean, what if one of us doesn't want to deal with the other's sad story?"

He stood motionless for a moment, blinking at her as if he didn't speak English and had no idea what she'd just said. "Point taken," he finally mumbled. "I guess I'll see you around." He started to walk away and she could see in the set of his shoulders that she had hurt him.

She jumped up, humiliated at what she'd done and wondering why in the world she'd sabotaged what could've been a beautiful, relationship-defining moment for them. What was wrong with her? Barefooted, she ran across the grass, already wet with dew, forgetting all about the sand spurs that lurked in her yard. "Ow!" she hollered as a spur caught her flesh, embedding itself in the sole of her foot. She tried to hop forward, but the injury made it impossible to keep going. She began to feel around in the dark for the offending element to pluck it out of her skin when she felt him coming near.

"You okay?" he asked.

She felt his hand on her shoulder, steadying her as she yanked out the burr. "Dang it, that hurt!" she said as she tossed the burr back into the grass. As she did, she knew why she'd ruined the moment. Just like she wasn't ready to tell him about Ryan, she wasn't ready to kiss him like that. As much as the girl inside her found it appealing, the woman she'd grown into was still grieving her husband. And while Kyle was a nice distraction, he wasn't Ryan. She looked at him, flustered, her foot throbbing as he put both hands on her shoulders and pulled her to him, wrapping his arms around her, somehow knowing that what she needed most in that moment was a hug.

"I'm sorry I'm such an idiot," she said, her voice muffled by the fabric of his shirt, which smelled like him.

"You're not. You're just not sure what you want. And no one said you had to be." He pushed her back slightly, his hands on her shoulders so he could look her in the eye. "I had a nice time," he said. He pointed to her foot. "I'd pour some peroxide on that if I were you." Even in the darkness she could see the smart-aleck grin cross his face. "Sure you don't need help getting inside, oh wounded one?"

She shook her head. "Nah, I'll hobble in alone, thank you. I'd actually prefer you walk away so I can try to reclaim some scrap of my dignity."

He took a few steps away. "See you around?" he asked.

"Yes," she said, noticing that his phrasing pretty much meant there would be no more dates. And who could blame him? She'd acted crazy, babbling on instead of kissing him, dodging his questions about why she wore a wedding ring. Most men avoided crazy like tearjerker chick flicks.

As promised she waited until he was gone to half hop, half limp inside, wishing that her wounded pride would heal faster than her foot. She'd just gone on a date with a movie star and managed to blow it in the last fifteen minutes of the night. Maybe this was Ryan's doing too, proof that he wasn't any more ready to let go of her than she was of him. Before she went inside she looked in the direction of the horizon. But it was too dark to distinguish the sky from the water.

TWENTY

"I rambled, Marta. Babbled. Like an idiot. Pretty much came out and said, 'I'm a complete loony and you should run.' And he did, Marta. He practically broke into a run to his car."

"I'm sure you're blowing this out of proportion," Marta said. She was at Phil's house taking this phone call. He was washing her car for her out in the driveway and wasn't that sweet? Marta had gushed. Emily had never heard Marta gush over a guy before. She didn't quite know where to put it. And frankly she just didn't want to hear about Marta's happiness at that particular moment. Not when she'd single-handedly ruined any chance at her own. Unless of course Ryan wasn't really dead and this had all been a big mistake. Sometimes she wished he would walk in the front door of the house, smile at her, and thank her for getting them the perfect house. She'd give him a tour that ended in the bedroom. Then they'd go to the beach. Walk back to that house that was sliding into the ocean and marvel over how their dreams came true.

But of course that was as likely to happen as Kyle ever speaking to her again.

"Marta, you weren't there. You didn't see his face. He was scared. Polite because he's a Southern boy and he can't help but be, but I'm telling you he was out of there. He said, 'See you around.' What do you take that to mean? That doesn't sound promising."

"Okay, I admit that's not really what you want to hear at the end of a date, but I'm sure he'll come around. You can't judge the whole date off the three little words he said at the end."

She thought of the three little words most women want to hear and wondered if she would ever hear them again. If she would ever want to. Was her love reserved just for Ryan forever? Emily listened as Phil came into his house and spoke to Marta who laughed uproariously at whatever he said. Phil, as Emily recalled, wasn't that funny. "What did he say?" she asked, not really caring but just wanting to get off the subject of her disastrous first-and-only date with Kyle.

"Oh, inside joke," Marta said. "It would take me too long to explain and then it wouldn't even be funny."

Emily tried not to let it hurt her that Marta was forming inside jokes with Phil, that their relationship had grown to something that excluded her, that they had formed a couple world where only the two of them existed. It was normal, natural, and Marta deserved it. She had waited so long. She wanted to be genuinely happy for her friend, not petty and selfish.

"So," Marta said. "I have an idea. Since that girl is living in *my* room" — Emily had spent the first part of the conversation filling Marta in on all that had happened with Amber and, to her credit, she hadn't once said how crazy Emily was — "and I'm not bitter at *all* about that." She paused to let Emily laugh. "But if I am recalling correctly, there are still two unclaimed bedrooms, no?"

"Ye-es? What are you thinking?"

"I'm thinking Phil and I should come down there. Spend some time with you. Assess this situation with the girl — Phil is a lawyer, after all — and get your mind off things."

Emily sighed in relief. While in a perfect world Marta would come alone and not bring her own personal attorney, beggars couldn't be choosers. Marta would make her laugh, help her stop obsessing over her ruined night. Maybe it was for the best that things had ended with Kyle before they really started. He hadn't seen what she'd written on the state site, taking a public stand against something he cared about. That probably would've been the end for them and maybe it would've been harder than this. Sometimes things just weren't meant to be no matter how much you hoped they were.

"I would love that," she said. "When can you come?"

"Tomorrow?" Marta said. "We could stay through the weekend."

"I wish. But I actually have plans to babysit for the people next door tomorrow."

"Babysit? How in the world did that happen?"

"My next-door neighbor never gets to see her husband because he only comes down on weekends. But he's here for the week and she caught me in a good mood because I was excited about going out with Kyle —"

"You mean Brady," Marta interrupted.

"No, I mean Kyle."

Marta laughed. "I was kidding. I just like saying that my best friend is going out with

Brady Rutledge."

"Your best friend is most certainly *not* going out with Brady Rutledge — or his alter ego."

"Anyway, getting back to the story of how your neighbor took advantage of a weak moment and capitalized on your happiness," Marta said.

"She didn't. I mean, she had no idea I was going out with him. She doesn't really care for him for some reason. In fact, I'm seeing her tonight. I should ask her about that."

"Maybe he's secretly a violent criminal. Maybe he's a terrible person."

But Kyle wasn't a terrible person and Emily knew it. Deep down in her soul she knew he was kind and caring, the type of person who had the foresight to leave himself an escape hatch out of Hollywood because he couldn't be a celebrity. He'd rather be an anonymous bridge tender, making a way for other people to get where they were going.

She pushed those thoughts out of her mind lest she start obsessing over what she'd done again. "Maybe so," was all she said. She and Marta made arrangements for them to come the day after tomorrow and stay for several days. She hung up the phone choosing to feel happy over the visit, forcing her mind to think about the things she could control and not what had already happened that she couldn't go back and make any different. Water under the bridge, she told herself. And smiled at the irony.

"Now, they will beg you for ice cream, but do not give it to them," Claire was saying as she and Rick left for their evening out. Claire looked stunning, a vast difference from the bathing suit top paired with old track shorts she usually wore, her face bare of any makeup. Even then she looked beautiful, but in an ordinary way. This Claire — the dressed-up, made-up version — was movie-star gorgeous. Emily was having a hard time not feeling jealous. It was Sara's good fortune that she looked just like her mother. Emily glanced over at Sara, pouting on the couch at being left behind.

Rick, who already had one foot out the door, pulled on Claire's hand. "They will be fine," he said softly. Behind Claire's shoulder, he grimaced comically for Emily. "Tell her you will be fine and to stop worrying," he pleaded.

Emily could tell Rick wanted his beautiful wife to himself. And soon. Maybe she'd have a chance to ask Claire about Kyle when they got home.

Claire looked from Emily to the kids. "I'm just a little worried because Noah was acting puny this afternoon," she said. "You have my cell, right?" Her eyes darted back to Noah who was watching cartoons, oblivious.

"I've got it," Emily said. "Go have fun. Please."

From over Claire's shoulder, Rick gave her the thumbs-up sign. "See, honey? She's got it all under control. They'll be fine." He emphasized the word *fine* and this time, when he pulled on her hand, Claire let herself be pulled away. Emily waved at both of them and shut the door before Claire could rethink things and come rushing back in. She felt better when she heard the car actually leave the driveway.

She turned to the children, who were alternately engrossed in the TV and pouting over their parents' departure. "Who wants chicken nuggets?" she said, forcing her voice to sound cheerful and certain. Children, she knew, could smell fear just like bears.

"I don't want chicken nuggets," Noah said.

"Me either," Sara echoed.

Emily looked over at the package of frozen nuggets Claire had pulled from the freezer. "They love these," she had said, sounding so certain.

"Well, if you don't want nuggets, what do you want?"

"Grilled cheese!" Noah called out.

"Yeah!" Sara agreed.

Emily walked over to the refrigerator and searched around for some cheese. She found a package of American slices, wrapped in individual plastic. She found a loaf of bread on the counter, thinking of that first night Amber was with her, how she'd made her grilled cheese and tomato soup. It was comfort food. For two kids upset about being left with a sitter, comfort food was probably just what the doctor ordered. Claire had said something about lactose intolerance but she was probably just fretting needlessly. Emily had been surprised she hadn't bolted from the house as soon as she showed up, taken the chance to be alone with Rick for a few hours and literally run with it. Instead Claire had been clearly conflicted about leaving Sara and Noah. Motherhood was more complicated than Emily knew.

Her thoughts wandered to Amber again as she got out a frying pan and heated butter. She had offered for Amber to come next door with her, but Amber had begged off, saying she was tired and wanted to rest. Amber didn't seem to be struggling with nausea much but did sleep a lot. Since Emily had never spent a lot of time around a pregnant person, she assumed this was normal, though sometimes she wondered how much of Amber's lethargy was pregnancy related and how much was mild depression.

Emily would be depressed if she was Amber — unmarried, basically homeless, and not much hope for the future. She needed to help the girl figure out how to change at least one of those three things as soon as possible. Maybe refocusing on Amber would help her forget Kyle, who hadn't called and was clearly out of the picture. She thought of what Amber had said about him when she came in from her date: "He's cute, for an old guy." Emily had told her it didn't matter and slunk off to her bedroom to pour peroxide on her foot like Kyle had recommended and sulk. To her credit Amber hadn't pressed for details.

She finished grilling the sandwiches, plated them, and called the kids. They took their sweet time coming to the table, but once there they wolfed down the sandwiches. "Mommy never lets us have these!" Sara said, a big approving smile on her face. Emily felt proud of her babysitting ability.

She had scored big with the kids and the evening was going smoothly. Claire and Rick deserved a nice evening out and she was making that possible for them. It almost made her feel better about how badly things had gone with Kyle.

After dinner she gave into the begging and scooped ice cream for them, being careful to only give them one little scoop. They whined and begged for more, but she stood her ground, distracting them from the ice cream with an offer to play a round of Uno. She had to help Noah a bit, explaining to Sara — who objected — that they were a team. She thought the game would pass the time, but after several rounds the clock only said six forty-five. They had another hour before she could put them to bed. "You guys want to watch a movie?" she asked. They agreed, rushing over to turn the TV back on.

They all snuggled together on the couch, Emily enjoying the feeling of closeness. That was the thing about being single again. She often went days — even weeks — without physical contact, missing the time when she had a husband, when she could always count on a kiss or hug or hand to hold at any given notice. She missed a lot of things about being married, but that was perhaps the biggest. She thought of Kyle holding her hand the other night and how familiar yet strange it had been to her. She had been terrified of it, yet craved it all the same. Touch was important, and anyone who said it wasn't didn't understand the human heart. A person could starve for physical affection the same way they could starve for food. She was sure of it.

The feeling of comfort overtook her and she could feel her eyes growing heavy the longer they sat there. She wasn't interested in the cartoon movie the kids had chosen and she hadn't slept well since her date with Kyle, tossing and turning as she sorted out her complicated array of emotions. She figured Kyle hadn't lost a wink of sleep since their date — probably hadn't given the night a second thought — and that only made her feel worse. She felt herself slipping into the sweet oblivion of sleep, the noises from the TV and the wiggling children fading away as she did, dreams replacing reality.

In her dream Ryan was still alive. She could hear his voice, feel his arms around her, watch his eyes crinkle as he laughed. He teased her, sometimes disagreed with her, offered her advice. In her dreams it was as if they were still married. She often woke up confused as to which world was real —

the one in her dreams or the one she found herself in when she awoke. This time her dream took place in Claire's house, only Sara and Noah were her children, her and Ryan's. The three of them were waiting for him to come home, the kids asking her again and again when he would be back. The more they asked, the more desperate she became, pacing in front of the window that overlooked the street, watching for a car that never arrived. After what seemed like hours in the dream, little Sara pulled on her arm. "Is Daddy ever coming back?" she asked. She opened her mouth to say yes, but instead she just started to cry. And as she cried, Sara joined in, her howls escalating until Emily put her hands over her ears.

She woke up with wet cheeks, her eyes blurry from tears when she opened them. She blinked them away, looking around the room, confused about where she was for a moment. That was when she realized that the crying from her dream was still reverberating through the house. She looked around as it started to dawn on her what had happened. She had fallen asleep and the kids were not on the couch beside her anymore. She jumped up and headed in the direction of the crying.

She found Sara in the kitchen sobbing, a

trail of sticky ice-cream droplets leading from the table to the sink where she had tried to wash away the evidence. A bowl lay cracked in the sink, and a melting carton of ice cream sat on the counter, the scooper still sitting inside. She took in the mess and the crying child, realizing in a split second that the other child was nowhere to be found. "Sara," she said, crouching down beside the little girl, "where is Noah?"

Sara turned her sticky face to Emily. "His tummy hurts. I tried to help him."

"Oh, Sara honey, you should've woken me up," she mumbled as she turned and went in search of Noah, calling his name. The house looked like a hurricane had hit and she wondered how she could've slept through all of it. There were more ice-cream drops leaving a trail through the house and she followed it like bread crumbs. The closer she got to Noah's room, the more she could detect a faint moan. She rushed inside feeling more and more like a failure the more she uncovered. How long had she been asleep?

She found Noah sprawled across his bed, moaning and hugging his pillow. He looked up at her. "I don't feel so good," he said.

"Oh, Noah, how much ice cream did you have?"

"Just a little bit more. Sara made it for me while you were sleeping."

Emily realized that the ice cream was probably enough to send their lactose intolerance into overdrive. She pulled Noah to her and hugged him close. "I'm sorry I fell asleep," she whispered.

He groaned and crossed his arms over his stomach. "I'm sorry I ate the ice cream."

She ruffled his hair. "Get your PJs on, honey. I've got a mess to clean up in the kitchen." She slipped from the room and went back to the kitchen where little Sara was tearfully trying to clean up by herself. "Sara, I'll do it," she said. "You go get your PJs on." She took the sponge Sara was using out of her hand and put her hands on the little girl's thin shoulders. "I'm sorry I wasn't watching you guys like I should've. This is my fault." She wanted to plead with Sara not to tell her parents, but held back. She scanned the kitchen and checked the clock, gauging whether she could clean up the place before Claire and Rick got back. Maybe it would all work out and the kids would be sleeping like little angels in a clean house by the time they arrived home.

Sara shook her head. "I shouldn't have gotten Noah the extra ice cream. He begged and begged and I thought it would make him happy. Now he's sick."

"Look, we're going to get this cleaned up. And Noah will feel better soon. Right now I just need you to get ready for bed so I can clean this up before your mommy and daddy get back." Sara looked doubtful, surveying the mess with a pinched expression on her face. Emily tucked a stray strand of hair behind the girl's ear and smoothed down her hair, thinking of how Sara had had a similar expression on her face in the dream. Now, and then, she had only wanted to put the child's mind at ease.

Thankfully Sara trotted off to her room while Emily quickly and efficiently tackled the mess in the kitchen. She rinsed the dishes and stowed them in the dishwasher, then began wiping down the counters. She was about to mop the floor when Sara came running back into the kitchen. "Emily! Emily! It's Noah, he's really crying bad!"

She grabbed the mop from Emily's hand and motioned for Emily to follow her. Panicked, she ran back to Noah's room. She found Noah in a fetal position on his bed saying, "My tummy hurts," over and over. She sat down beside him on the bed and attempted to pull him into her lap to comfort him. But it turned out that moving him was not the smartest decision. As soon as he sat up, he vomited all over Emily, himself, and his bed. From the doorway, Sara gasped as Emily sat frozen, stunned by what had just happened, the warm contents of Noah's stomach pooling on her shirt and in her lap. She and Noah blinked at each other and for a few seconds there was complete silence.

The silence was broken by the sounds of voices in the kitchen. She heard Claire calling for her, heard Rick's heavy footsteps clomping through the kitchen. "Mommy," Sara said and walked toward the sounds of her parents' voices before Emily could respond. She held her shirt away from her body to keep the liquid from seeping through but she could feel it soaking through her pants. She was grateful she hadn't worn shorts that night. Noah sat up and was struggling to get down from the bed when Claire walked in. "What is going on?" she asked, her voice not angry but confused.

"Mommy," Noah said, reaching for Claire, who started to pick him up until Emily stopped her. "I wouldn't do that if I were you," she said, flipping on Noah's bedside lamp so Claire could see what had happened. Claire grimaced as she simultaneously registered what she was smelling and seeing. Instead of hugging her little boy to her, she helped him out of the bed and led him to the bathroom, motioning for Emily to follow them. Uncertain what to do first, she followed like one of the children and came to stand in the bathroom with Claire and Noah. In the other room she could hear Sara's bright voice relating to Rick all that had happened.

"From the looks of things," Claire said to Noah as she removed his shirt, "you guys got into the ice cream."

Noah nodded seriously, coming clean in more ways than one. "And we told Emily we wanted to have grilled cheese. It gave me a tummy ache just like you said it would."

Claire looked at Emily, biting back a smile. "Mommy tells you things for a reason, Noah. That's why God gave you a mommy. And Emily didn't know the rules but you did."

"I fell asleep," Emily confessed as well. "The kids were watching a movie and I don't know what happened. I'm sorry."

Claire pointed at Emily. "You need a clean shirt," she said. "And maybe some yoga pants?" She gave Emily a look that told her she didn't blame her. Emily nodded in response. Claire disappeared from the bathroom and returned quickly with an old

T-shirt and some worn yoga pants. "Use my bathroom to get changed and cleaned up while I finish with him and get his bed changed."

"I'll help," Emily offered.

Claire held her hand up. "You just get dressed. I'll handle it from here." Though Emily knew she was being nice, she couldn't help but wonder if deep down Claire was disappointed to find the chaos she'd come home to. Emily would've been if the tables were turned. Poor Claire had so looked forward to going out alone with Rick. How positively unromantic it was to walk back into vomit and mess after a romantic evening alone. In the privacy of the bathroom Emily dressed quickly, balling up her dirty clothes and carrying them out to the kitchen in search of a plastic bag to stow them in. She found Claire stuffing the soiled sheets into the washing machine in the laundry area just off the kitchen, her expression pinched. Emily couldn't help but notice her face looked a lot like Sara's. She started to say so, but sensed this wasn't the time.

"I'm really sorry about tonight. I thought I had everything under control. This was the last thing I wanted you to walk into. I was hoping I could get it cleaned up before you got home." She checked the clock. "You guys are home much earlier than I thought you'd be."

Claire looked over at her, her expression grave. "We kinda got . . . in a fight. So I said we should just come home and he said fine."

Poor Claire, this night was just bad all the way around. There was no way she was bringing up Kyle to add to it. "I'm so sorry."

Claire shrugged. "Rick wants me and the kids to come home. He thinks that our original plan isn't working. He says this way of living is just too hard. But I love being here so much and I told him that he should find a way to spend more time here. He said I wasn't respecting how hard he has to work to provide for us because I was pressuring him." Claire started to cry. "So the night was already ruined. You didn't ruin it." She gave Emily a weak smile. "I mean, I could've lived without dealing with throw up, but I know how relentless they can be. Trust me."

"I shouldn't have fallen asleep," Emily said. Rick walked into the kitchen and leaned against the counter, staring at the two of them as they both fell silent. Emily looked from Rick to Claire and back again. It was clear he wanted to speak with his wife. "I'll just, um, go. Now. Just tell the kids I'll see them later."

293

Claire gave her a little wave as she squared her shoulders and turned to face Rick. Emily let herself out, crossing the yard toward her house. She noticed the lights were off and assumed that Amber must've already gone to bed for the night. Slipping into the house, she fumbled with the light in the kitchen, switching the darkness to light.

She didn't know whether it was the sound or the movement that caught her attention first. But either way, she was instantly aware that there were people in the dark den. She saw the flash of skin, the flurry of activity, and heard someone curse as she realized what was happening. "Amber?" she called out, crossing toward the den as whoever was with Amber fled, scurrying into the room Amber had been using and slamming the door. Amber, left on the couch under an afghan, blinked at her, her breath coming in frightened gasps. Emily looked down at her, understanding what was going on, yet still wishing it wasn't true. She looked from Amber to the closed bedroom door and back again.

"You're home early," the girl said, her eyes wide.

Emily clenched her fists and took a deep breath. She was too young to have a teenager, but she felt that in that moment she knew what a parent of one must feel like, the warring emotions of wanting to string the child up and wanting to protect her from herself wreaking havoc inside her.

"One of the kids got sick," she managed to say, surprised at how level she'd managed to make her voice sound.

"Oh," Amber said. She pulled the afghan closer to her chin and looked away.

"Is that him?" Emily asked, gesturing to the closed door.

Amber nodded without looking up.

"Did you tell him?"

Amber shook her head no.

"So you — what? — invite him over here for a little romantic rendezvous while I'm out of the house? What did you think would happen after that? Why would you do that, Amber?" She couldn't keep the betrayal out of her voice. She knew she should be more diplomatic, less emotional, but she couldn't. She had offered this girl shelter and friendship, reached out to her when no one else did.

"I wanted to see him," Amber said weakly. "You didn't say I couldn't." She played with the fringe of the afghan, still not looking up.

"I would assume you would know that wouldn't be cool with me," Emily said.

"But I was going to tell him."

"When?" Emily's voice was getting louder.

A few seconds ticked by as Emily watched Amber wrap the fringe of the blanket around her finger and let it go a few times, resisting the desire to yank it out of her hand. "Later," Amber finally said.

"You are being a fool," Emily spat out, unable to hide her frustration. This had been a monumentally bad evening and this new development was salt on the wound. She was past politeness and decorum.

"Well, I'm sorry I'm not so under control like you," Amber countered. "I'm sorry I have feelings for him."

"But he doesn't have feelings for you, Amber! He's using you!" She was being too harsh, spitting out all the things she'd held back from saying since she became aware of Amber's situation. Her anger was getting the best of her and she suspected she would regret her outburst later. But in the moment she couldn't hold back.

Emily watched as a look of hurt flitted across Amber's face that was quickly replaced by a look of steely resolve. Her eyes flashed as she stood up and gripped the afghan to her. "Maybe I should just leave then."

Emily stepped back, leaving room for Amber to walk away. "That's your choice, Amber." A lump rose in her throat. This wasn't her child; she wasn't even really her responsibility. Yet somehow she was. This girl had captured her heart, made her feel an unexplained connection almost from the minute she saw her. She couldn't help but feel saddened at the thought of her walking out the door. And yet she also couldn't ignore the fact that Amber had been wrong to invite him over in her absence. She willed Amber to admit it, to say she was sorry, to beg Emily to let her stay. But instead Amber just walked away with her head held high, disappearing behind the door to the room Emily had quickly come to think of as hers. She waited until the door closed behind Amber to cry.

TWENTY-ONE

Marta and Phil would arrive that afternoon to a sunny, clean house and fresh-baked cookies artfully laid out on a platter, a pitcher of fresh-squeezed lemonade beside it. In an effort to keep busy and ward off thoughts of the night before, Emily had thrown herself into scrubbing the house and getting ready for her guests, a welcome distraction. She thought of Ryan's messiness as she cleaned, remembering how angry she used to get as she tidied and scrubbed — and how oblivious he seemed to it all. She pushed harder on the sponge in her hand, the elbow grease relieving the stress, sadness, and confusion she'd been battling.

Though she still wished Marta was coming alone, she was determined to make the best of things. No matter how she got her there, it was still good that her best friend was coming on this day of all days. She needed to process all that had happened,

talk about the sequence of events ad infini-
tum as they had always done. Marta's wry
sense of humor and no-nonsense approach
to things always helped set things straight
for her, and she looked forward to the visit.
Marta would help her figure out what to do
about Amber, how to talk to Claire even
though she felt totally awkward after the
babysitting fiasco, and get her mind off
Kyle. So far in Sunset everything she
touched turned as sour as the vomit that
coated her clothes the night before.

That's a nice image, she imagined Ryan
saying.

You hush, she silently retorted. *You're the
one who got me into this in the first place. If it
wasn't for you, I'd be well on my way to becoming a master landscaper back home and
maybe have run off with the yard guy.*

You wouldn't do that to me, would you?

She stopped moving around, her industri-
ousness forgotten for a moment, her hand
on the pitcher of lemonade she'd made.
How she wished she really could talk to
Ryan, that these internal conversations she
had with him were not imagined. Sometimes the sadness ambushed her from behind the bushes, reducing her to tears she
never saw coming. She allowed herself to
cry for a moment, remembering her hus-

band and missing him so much. She would trade this house for him, this beach haven for the humble abode they had shared, this new life for her old one in a minute. This new life didn't suit her, and she was starting to doubt it ever would. Was there anything more hopeless than thinking your life — and your chance for happiness — was over at twenty-seven years old?

"You left me," she responded, aloud this time. But Ryan didn't have the chance to say anything else because her guests arrived. So she went outside to greet them.

The rock on Marta's left hand caught the light almost as soon as she stepped out of the car, winking at Emily as if she was in on a joke. She watched Marta grab bags from inside the car, unaware that she had spotted the ring. Her heart fluttered and she was grateful she had a moment to collect herself before she had to face Marta. *Be happy,* she instructed herself. *This is good news and she's your best friend.*

After Marta and Phil had stowed their bags in their respective bedrooms, they convened in the kitchen, gathered around the cookies and lemonade. Marta looked around the house. "Where's the girl?"

"Oh, she left last night." Emily tried to

sound like it was no big deal, but a quiver crept into her voice.

Marta stared at her, open-mouthed. "She left? Why?"

"I got back early from babysitting and interrupted her and a *visitor.*" She raised her eyebrows. "When I tried to talk sense into her about how unwise that was, she balked. Said she should just leave if that's the way I felt." Emily sighed, shrugged. "I didn't try very hard to stop her."

"And now you feel bad about it?"

"I don't know what I feel. She's just . . . dumb about this guy. He's taking advantage of her and she's letting him. I've tiptoed around it long enough and last night I snapped. I finally said what I've been holding back." She could read the disappointment in Marta's face. "I know, I know, it wasn't my finest hour. But it was not a good night and I wasn't exactly firing on all cylinders." She rolled her eyes skyward and exhaled. "I blew it. And now I don't know how to make it up to her."

Marta reached out and patted her shoulder, the ring catching the overhead light as she did. "Em, this girl isn't your responsibility. You couldn't let her stay here and take advantage of you. You did what you could and you can't go around second-guessing that."

"I thought about going by the motel today, see if she went back there. But I chickened out." Anxious to change the subject, she pointed at Marta's hand. "So let's talk about something else. Like, for instance, when were you going to tell me about that?"

Marta and Phil looked at each other and grinned like fools. "Now!" Marta said. She held out her hand so Emily could properly admire her ring.

"Oh, Marta. It's gorgeous," Emily breathed, thinking of the ring she still wore, the one that had confused Kyle. *Don't think about him now,* she coached herself. She turned to a beaming Phil. "You did good."

He nodded, running his hand along Marta's back. "I did." She knew he wasn't talking about the ring and she let herself feel happy for her friend. Marta had gotten what she'd always dreamed of. And, Emily couldn't help but realize, it had only come through Emily's personal tragedy. Without Ryan's death and insurance policy Phil would have been just another coworker at his firm, just another nameless suit filing by to pay respects. She glanced around the kitchen Ryan had never seen, the kitchen he bought her. She looked at the happy couple he had brought together and saw, for perhaps the first time, the good that had come out of the bad. Romans 8:28 ran through her mind. "All things," she whispered.

"What?" Marta asked. "Did you say something, Em?"

"Nah," she said. "It was nothing." But that wasn't true. It was something. In the wake of losing Ryan, it was the good she needed to find.

That night she walked out on her deck after a nice meal with Phil and Marta. She had managed not to feel like a third wheel, thinking of all the times she and Ryan had been the couple at the table and Marta had been the single girl across from them. They had laughed and swapped stories. Less than twenty-four hours after the babysitting debacle she had already found some humor in it, her outlook considerably brighter than it had been when she'd been thrown up on. Marta and Phil had laughed hard at that story, but the mood became somber when he casually asked Marta if she was ready for all of that. Marta wasn't just getting married, Emily noted. She was starting a family, a family that wouldn't include her, no matter how nice Marta tried to be.

Wanting some time alone to think, she shooed Marta and Phil outside to the dock where she had kept those two chairs she and Marta had first dragged down there. After dinner was cleaned up, she walked out onto her deck and saw them, their hands joined across the space between the chairs. She had intended to go down and join them but thought better of it. "I wish you well," she whispered. And she did. She glanced over at the Connolly house, to the open windows of their kitchen. She'd meant to get over there and check on the kids but between cleaning for and entertaining her guests, she hadn't had a moment. The four of them were gathered around the table, their heads bowed in prayer. Noah was fidgeting but Sara was dutiful. She turned away from the scene — from both scenes, really — and retreated inside to the safety of the house Ryan bought her, his last gift that sometimes didn't feel like a gift at all.

A knock at the door an hour later made her heart race. Could it be Amber returning? Or even Kyle? She raced to the front door and pulled it open so forcefully she scared Claire, who was standing on the other side. "Eager much?" Claire asked. She looked around. "Expecting someone else because I know you're not that thrilled about me coming over." She gave Emily a grin. "Kyle maybe?"

"No, not Kyle. You don't have to be worried about me and him anymore. I haven't heard a word from him since our disastrous date."

Claire frowned. "I'm sure I should feel bad about that, but I just don't. He's not my favorite person, as I'm sure you've picked up on."

Emily nodded. "I did indeed. Wanna tell me about it?"

Claire shook her head. "If you're not seeing him anymore there's no point in going into it. It's old history. Best forgotten." She shrugged. "I really don't like to talk about it."

Emily nodded. She understood not wanting to talk about painful memories better than anyone. "No problem," she said. She gestured for Claire to come inside. "I'd love for you to meet my best friend and her fiancé. They're right outside on the dock but I'm sure they'll be in soon." She glanced outside at the sky turning pink and orange, threading the clouds with an array of colors. The island had come upon its name for good reason.

"Sounds great. Anyway, I just mainly wanted you to know no hard feelings about what happened last night. It was a bad evening all the way around." She gave a rueful grin. "You weren't to blame in any way. I told you the kids can be little monsters." She laughed. "You were just their latest victim."

Emily shook her head. "You told me about the lactose issue. I knew better than to make them grilled cheese, but to be honest I just never thought about the cheese being milk. I'm not used to thinking about anyone's eating habits except my own."

"Well, you're not a mother so you don't have to." Emily winced and Claire noticed, quickly adding, "I mean, you will be someday. And then you'll get used to keeping track of every morsel of food that crosses another person's lips. It's so fun. And rewarding. You'll see." She made a face that made Emily laugh.

"How are things with you and Rick? Did y'all make any decisions?"

"No, not yet. There's never a moment to talk. The kids are so demanding and by the time they finally collapse we're too exhausted to talk." She shook her head. "I know all you single girls make a big deal out of being married, having a family, but it's not always a fairy tale." Emily noticed Claire's eyes travel to her ring. "But I guess you've already figured that out."

Emily pressed her lips together and gave a barely perceptible nod.

"Divorced?" Claire asked. "You never talk about it so I figured it must've been a messy one." She gestured to the house. "Figured you bought this with the settlement money or something." She shrugged. "That was my theory, at least." She pointed at the ring. "But sometimes it's hard to let go."

Claire began to shift and shimmer before her as her eyes filled with tears. "It is," she managed to say.

"Sorry I guessed," Claire said. "I mean, I didn't want to be right but I'm pretty good at figuring stuff like that out. Rick says I'm just nosy but I call it intuitive." She raised her eyebrows and gave a sly look that made Emily laugh, a welcome feeling.

"Yeah, it's still kind of hard to talk about." She looked down at her finger and didn't bother to correct Claire. "I keep forgetting I even have this on. I guess I need to take it off soon, but I'm just . . ."

Claire reached out to squeeze her hand. "You're not ready," she said with an ease that relaxed Emily. "When you are, you'll know. In the meantime, don't stress about it."

"Thanks," Emily said. She heard the footsteps of Marta and Phil coming back in. "I want you to meet my friends who are here visiting." She made introductions all around once Marta and Phil got inside.

"So you're the one with the lactose-intolerant kids," Phil said as Emily cringed.

"I told them all about the fiasco last night. How I loaded your kids down with both grilled cheese *and* ice cream."

"Well, let's not forget that they helped themselves to even more ice cream."

"Yes," Emily added, "while their stellar sitter managed to fall asleep." She felt the nagging memory of the dream she'd had during her nap at the Connollys', the way that she had been waiting for Ryan even though she knew he would never come. She looked at Claire and felt bad for letting her believe the wrong thing. She had to start being honest with people about Ryan, to tell them how she came to own this house. If for no other reason, it was a tribute to him to tell the truth about his one last self-less act.

But not today. She listened in as Claire and Phil and Marta exchanged small talk. Where were they all from? What did they do for a living? How long had they known Emily? When she realized that the next question might be how they met Emily, she interrupted before Phil could explain and contradict what she'd just let Claire believe.

"Phil and Marta just got engaged!" she said, knowing that would redirect the conversation.

Marta held up her shiny new diamond and Claire gave the obligatory approval noises. "When's the big day?"

The two of them looked at each other. "We were just talking about that, out on the dock. We've got a few potential dates. Let's just say ASAP." They both laughed.

Claire nodded knowingly. "You want to have kids and need to get this show on the road, right?" She gave Emily a look that said she knew that was painful for her to hear. It made Emily like her new friend all the more. She was trying to be tactful and sensitive. Marta and Phil, bless their hearts, couldn't see past their own bliss. Emily gave her a look back that told her not to worry about it. She was a big girl and this was her new life. People were allowed to be happy, to move forward, around her.

"We do, very much," Marta gushed.

"And we just know we want to be together so why prolong that?" Phil added, wrapping his arm around Marta's shoulders. Emily noticed that Marta looked thinner, already anticipating wearing that white beaded gown and looking her best, if she knew her friend. She hated that Marta hadn't talked to her about her wedding plans, but guessed that Marta was afraid to bring it up. She wished she wasn't someone people felt they had to tiptoe around.

"Well, I better go before Rick sends out a search party. And by search party I mean my six-year-old daughter who can find me better than any bloodhound." She laughed at her own joke. "But listen, Emily, I want you to come tomorrow night to the meeting about the old bridge. Word has it there's going to be some surprise announcement. It helps to show community interest." She gestured to Marta and Phil. "Heck, you guys come too. Bodies in seats is what it's all about."

Marta and Phil looked confused so Emily explained. "The community is pretty divided over the state's proposal to take out the old bridge and add a new one. They're having information meetings about replacing the old bridge."

"And you're in favor?" Phil asked, focusing on Emily. "Of replacing the old bridge? Or are you against it?"

She gave a little laugh and looked over at Claire. "I'm new here. I don't really have a dog in this fight. I'm just showing my community spirit by going, I guess." She felt the little hitch inside that she always felt when she didn't tell the whole truth.

"So you'll come?" Claire asked.

She looked at Marta and Phil. "I'll come. I'm not sure if these two will be all that interested, but you can count on me."

"No, we'll come," Phil said. "Why not? Maybe we'll buy a house down here too and get involved ourselves!"

Marta leaned against Phil, content and dreamy. Something simmered below the surface in Emily as she did. It wasn't fair that Marta might get the husband, the kids, and the house at the beach. Not when she had only gotten one or the other. She looked away from the picture of contentment and focused on seeing Claire out. "See you tomorrow night," Claire called brightly as she trekked back over to her own house to see her handsome husband and perfect children. Emily waved and smiled and did what she did best: acted as if everything was fine.

TWENTY-TWO

The restaurant dining area turned meeting room was full again. This time Claire didn't have the kids in tow since Rick was able to stay with them. She seemed lighter as she buzzed over to welcome Emily and Marta and Phil, who had spent the better part of the day talking about both wedding plans and real estate in Sunset. Emily wished they hadn't decided to come with her and was starting to hate the sound of Phil's voice. She had learned that Phil considered himself an expert on many topics. And Marta thought he was brilliant. Emily couldn't decide if she was truly put off by him or just jealous.

Emily stuck by Claire's side, observing the meeting as an outsider while Phil joined in conversations as if he'd lived there for years, Marta grinning and nodding by his side. There was an electricity in the air at this meeting that she hadn't felt at the last one, a buzz generated by everyone's speculations about what the surprise announcement was. Pockets of Sunset residents gathered to speculate, their guesses ranging from boring to outrageous. As they waited for the meeting to begin, Emily scanned the room for Kyle. She couldn't help but wonder if he knew what the surprise was. And if he did, what he thought of it.

Though they had only spent a handful of moments together, she missed talking to Kyle, hearing what he thought about things and sharing stories. She had been surprised to find that her teen crush went deeper. She actually liked the guy, found him interesting. Though they hadn't talked about what his plans were beyond the bridge, she found she wanted to know. She wanted to know a lot of things about him that she hadn't had the chance to know. Not since she'd ruined their date and he'd turned tail and run. She didn't blame him but she had held out hope that he'd call and ask for them to try again. In one of their rare non-wedding conversations during her visit, Marta had said she should call him but she had steadfastly refused. "You weren't there. I'm not into humiliating myself further. He's not interested. Let's just leave it at that."

Marta had shrugged and gone back to

313

talking about the color of her bridesmaid's dresses and the many ideas she was gaining from the Internet. But Emily's mind had stayed on Kyle as she half paid attention to what Marta was saying. If she had the chance again, would she take it? And why *was* she still wearing her wedding ring? Was she that intent on sabotaging herself? In some ways, she saw, it was the same thing as pacing in front of a window waiting for Ryan to return. That night as she got ready for the meeting she had slipped the ring from her finger and stared at the white ring of flesh where it had been. She had kept the ring off the whole time she was getting ready, then slipped it back on at the last minute, just before they left. Now, sitting in the room full of people, wondering if Kyle would be there and what she would say to him if he was, she twisted it around and around.

From the corner of her eye she saw bright lights enter the room and a group of people moving through the doorway. A murmur started as those seated speculated on what was happening. It didn't take long to see that the lights were clearly attached to cameras and the cameras were clearly trained on the entourage that was entering the room. "Do you think it's someone famous?"

Marta asked Phil.

"Nah, probably just the local news," he confidently assured her.

Emily suppressed a smile when it became obvious that he was wrong. This wasn't local news coverage. Her smile evaporated as she realized that it *was* someone famous attracting the cameras' attention. But that someone famous was not someone she wanted to see. Not when she saw the very thin, very toned, very tan arm slip around the shoulders of the guy she had been thinking of moments earlier. She watched in pain as Xandra Noble, former costar and girlfriend of Brady Rutledge, gave him a kiss on the cheek and grinned at the crowd. Kyle blushed as he held out his hand and gestured for her to take the podium at the front of the room. Beside her Marta inhaled, starstruck. "That's Brady Rutledge and Xandra Noble," she hissed, squeezing Emily's hand. Then she remembered herself. "Sorry," she added and blanched.

Xandra stood behind the podium and gave the crowd the megawatt smile the world had come to love. Kyle might've bailed on Hollywood, but Xandra had stayed and made her mark long after the movie that began both their careers had become a cable channel mainstay. She'd been nominated for awards, gotten a star on the walk of fame, become a humanitarian with multiple charities she funded. Xandra, much as one might want to hate her, seemed to be lovely inside and out. Emily had never guessed that she and Kyle stayed in touch — not after he left her behind to take refuge in this small coastal haven. And yet as a look passed between them, it was clear that they had. There was obvious affection there, and Emily knew right then that her chances had slipped from zero to negative ten.

"Unbelievable," she heard Claire say. As Xandra began to speak, Claire excused herself from the meeting and awkwardly navigated through the tight maze of chairs and out the door. But no one watched her go. Everyone was too focused on what Xandra had to say. As she listened, Emily couldn't help but wonder what had upset Claire enough to leave.

"I was asked to come here by a dear friend who cares very much about this island," Xandra said. Flashes went off as people began taking shots with cell phones and their own cameras, commemorating a celebrity sighting in Sunset Beach. Kyle, Emily knew, didn't count as such to the citizens. As a hometown boy who'd long since blended back in, he didn't hold the allure that this beautiful woman did. He certainly hadn't achieved the same kind of fame she had, and Emily wondered if sometimes he wondered if he'd made the right call by coming back and giving up on the movie business.

"I'm sure most of us can attest to the fact that, when someone we care about cares about something, we can be drawn into the cause — whatever it is — by their passion. When my friend Kyle called me this past week to ask if I could come and speak out on behalf of keeping the swing bridge, I told him sure." She paused and flashed that smile that had made her famous, baring her perfect white teeth and razor-sharp cheekbones as she did. "Kyle loves that bridge and has spent the last several years quietly working as a bridge tender, choosing this quiet, anonymous life over one of fame and fortune. His work is truly a labor of love. To think of that love being all for nothing — that the bridge could be removed by the state and replaced by a large, impersonal bridge with no sense of history — is unacceptable. And so I have come here tonight to voice my support — both personal and financial — to saving the bridge." Xandra turned to the state officials lined up along one side of the crowd and gave a succinct nod, as if that summed it all up and the decision was made. Emily had to hand it to her, she sure knew how to command a room.

Xandra summoned Kyle, who ducked his head with good-ole-boy bashfulness and shuffled up to take his place behind the podium. Emily was probably imagining things but she could swear he had absorbed some of Xandra's celebrity light. He was positively glowing as he stood under the lights, looking like a natural with the cameras trained on him. If the bridge did close, Emily thought, he could definitely head back to Hollywood. Maybe he had plans to do just that. Her heart sunk at the thought.

"I hope that as this story hits the different news outlets, this issue will hit home with people beyond our little community. I hope that people who care about this state's history will let their representatives know that we need to preserve this bridge. It might be sentimental, and I might be all heart. But if we stop thinking with our hearts, we've lost who we are, as a state and as human beings."

At that moment Kyle found Emily in the crowd, his eyes resting on her so briefly that she would spend the rest of the evening convincing herself it was just a coincidence and hadn't meant a thing. No man was going to give her a second glance with the lovely and talented Xandra Noble standing by his side. Not to mention the fact that Xandra had flown cross-country to stand up for the bridge while Emily had left a comment against the bridge online like a coward, too fearful to admit to Kyle how she really felt about the bridge or anything else. In every way, Xandra was the clear winner. Emily needed to forget all about him and burn that particular bridge. The irony made her smile as the meeting broke up and people flocked to the front to shake the hand of Xandra Noble, asking her and Kyle to pose for pictures and sign their "Save the Bridge" flyers.

"Okay, so I'm just going to say this once but, wow. It's them. Together. Here," Marta said. Emily started to say something in response but Marta held up her hand. "Nope, don't wanna hear it. I'm done talking about it." She patted Emily's shoulder and cast a sympathetic look in the direction of Kyle and Xandra. "Sorry, hon. But that's a hard act to follow."

Emily rolled her eyes. "Don't I know it," she agreed. "Let's just get out of here." She stood. "I want to go find Claire anyway. She sure got out of here in a hurry."

Marta and Phil stood. "Yeah, all this ce-

lebrity brilliance is hurting my eyes anyway," she said, making a visor with her
hands and pretending to shield her eyes.
Emily laughed and they started to work
their way through the crowd.

"Why did Claire leave?" Marta asked.

Emily shook her head. "She doesn't care
for Kyle. Actually, they both make no bones
about their lack of love for one another, but
I have no idea why. I guess it made Claire
mad that he was using his celebrity status
to garner support for the bridge."

"Yeah, but if it helps the bridge I'd think
she wouldn't care."

Emily nodded. "You would think. But I'm
learning one thing about Sunset. Things
don't always make sense here."

Phil spoke for the first time since before
the meeting began — an uncharacteristi-
cally quiet few minutes for him. "Sweetie,
that's not just Sunset. That's the whole
world." They walked silently for the rest of
the way toward their car, Emily pondering
what Phil had said, begrudgingly admitting
he was right. Things rarely did make sense
in this world, and yet Emily was still compelled to look for the logic and the reason
at every turn, around every corner. Maybe,
she thought as they waited for their turn to
cross the bridge, to grow up was to stop at-

tempting to find sense and just start embracing the nonsense. Maybe maturity meant you stopped expecting life to fall into place. Maybe instead of her chicken salad being the key to life, it was that simple truth.

Emily stood in the tiny corner dressing room at Victoria's Ragpatch, studying herself in the full-length mirror as Marta waited outside. "Well?" her friend asked from behind the curtain that didn't quite hide the dressing area from the rest of the store, but did a good enough job. Emily felt self-conscious changing in the small space, fearing exposure. She checked out the dress Marta had talked her into trying. It was a bit more daring than the clothes she usually chose for herself, but that was to be expected when Marta was in charge.

"I want to buy you something in exchange for this amazing weekend we've had," her friend had said that morning after breakfast. No matter how much she had argued that Marta and Phil didn't need to pay her back, she kept insisting until Emily gave up and agreed to go shopping. Hardly the retail mecca that nearby Myrtle Beach was, the two had ended up at the upscale boutique near Ocean Isle, exclaiming over the unique beachwear hidden inside its unassuming exterior. "I am so coming here to shop for my honeymoon," Marta said more than once.

And now Emily studied herself in the mirror contemplating Marta's choice. It wasn't the way the dress looked. It was the way it looked on her. And it wasn't that the dress looked bad. It looked nice, she supposed, flattering to her figure. Emily had worn the same size since high school, her weight fluctuating up or down a few pounds depending on what she was going through (there really was such a thing as fat and happy in her case) but never enough to do any real damage.

Her mother used to warn her about what would happen when she had kids, speaking ominously about the havoc pregnancy wreaked on a woman's body. But with Ryan gone, that didn't seem likely so she supposed she had nothing to worry about there. And yet as she turned from side to side and debated the purchase, all she could think of was how Xandra Noble would look in that dress. No matter how much she stared at her own reflection, she knew she could never measure up to that standard. The thought made her sad, even though Kyle was out of her life before Xandra showed up. Xandra's appearance — the way she smiled at him and the way he looked at her — only confirmed it. They were beautiful people, a former couple, and they belonged together. A better person, Emily told herself, would wish them well and forget that one little jaunt to Southport had ever happened.

But Emily found it hard to forget.

"Are you ever coming out of there?" Marta sighed from behind the curtain. "How bad can it be?"

Emily obliged and pushed the curtain open to give Marta a glimpse of herself in the dress. "Vavavavoom!" Marta said, her voice so loud in the small store that heads turned. She added in a low voice, "Hubba hubba." Emily blushed and shook her head.

Marta threw up her hands and the onlookers turned back to their shopping. "You have got to let me get you that dress. It looks amazing on you, and since it's our last night here, we're taking you out to dinner. And you're totally wearing the dress. We'll go to the restaurant where the meeting was last night. I heard people saying it's a little more upscale and the food's good. I mean, I love Calabash of course, but I'm not thinking that dress and fried seafood go together, ya know? Oh! Maybe we'll get to sit out on that balcony that overlooks the intercoastal." She sighed dreamily. "Wouldn't that be nice?"

Since Marta and Phil got engaged, Emily had noticed, it didn't take much to make Marta happy, her voice hovering constantly at that wistful level. Emily was working hard to rectify this Marta with her old friend, the snarky, jaded, "romance is dead" version of the same girl. The new Marta snapped the curtain shut between them and ordered her to change out of the dress so she could pay for it. Emily obeyed, looking once more in the mirror before changing back into her faded denim shorts and polo shirt.

Marta was right. She did look pretty. Maybe not movie-star pretty but pretty. The dress showed off her tanned legs and accented her curves without being too clingy. And it was a pretty hot pink and vivid blue pattern that was bright and fun. She had some sandals at home that would match perfectly. She would go out tonight and make the best of the evening, forgetting about the newspaper headline Phil had showed her this morning, the *Brunswick Beacon* touting Xandra's arrival in their little town and speculating about Kyle's relationship with her. Before she'd turned away from the article, not wanting to see any more, she'd noticed the paper had used

324

a photo of the two of them from years ago, paired with a photo of them from the night before. In both photos he had his arm around her impossibly small waist, their smiles wide and bright, a matched set. Maybe, Emily thought now as she handed off the dress to Marta, he would return to Hollywood with her. Maybe he was already gone.

TWENTY-THREE

Emily emerged from the house wearing her new dress and feeling good — really good — about things for the first time in quite a while, as long as she didn't think about the babysitting fiasco, Amber's exit, or Xandra's entrance. She expected to find Marta and Phil waiting on the porch as they had said they would be, but instead saw them both in the yard next door, their heads bent toward Claire, their eyes darting over to Emily's house, faces concerned as all their mouths seemed to move at once. When Marta's eyes met Emily's and darted quickly away, she knew something was amiss. And all that good feeling she'd mustered whooshed out of her like one of Noah's beach balls with the valve opened. Always the actress, Marta plastered on a bright smile and waved her over. "We've been getting to know Claire," she called out.

When Emily reached them, Marta

wrapped her arm around her shoulders and squeezed in a most un-Marta-like display. "She's been filling us in on all things Sunset Beach. We just love it here," she said. Marta's happiness was over the top and unnatural, but Emily seemed to be the only one who noticed. Claire and Phil just stood by, their grins doing nothing to hide whatever it was they were up to.

She glanced at all of them, wishing someone would fill her in on the real story. What had they been talking about so earnestly? She had a feeling it was her, or something to do with her. And yet she also didn't want to know. "Well, I'm finally ready," she said. "Are you guys?" They weren't the only ones who could act like all was well. After all, Emily had had over a year's worth of practice.

"We are ready!" Marta sang back. "And don't you just look amazing." She turned to seek Claire and Phil's agreement. "Doesn't she just look amazing?"

They both nodded vigorously, a couple of mute bobblehead dolls on Claire's lawn. Emily idly wondered where the children and Rick were. Then she wondered again what they were talking about. Then she decided she didn't really like her two worlds colliding — her at home world with her Sunset

Beach world. The two were meant to run on parallel but separate tracks, like those lines in her geometry book in high school. Those lines never converged because they weren't supposed to. She made a mental note to call her mother and let her know a visit wasn't the best idea. Not with everything going wrong. Emily wasn't so sure she wanted to stay any longer herself.

"Well." She gave them her best fake smile. "Let's get going. I'm st— I'm hungry." At school she always told her students not to say they were starving, because none of them truly knew what starving was, and yet those very words nearly escaped from her lips. She was so off her game.

"Bye, you guys," Claire called after them as they trailed off to the car. "Have a nice night. We'll just be here shooting some fireworks." She put a finger to her lips. "Shhh. It's a secret."

Fireworks were illegal but easy enough to get away with, considering they were plentiful just over the South Carolina state line. And during the month of July, they could be heard all up and down the beach. Sometimes at night Emily would catch a few zooming above the water, their red, blue, green, and yellow bursts reflected there. It was pretty and no one minded a little law breaking if it was all in good fun.

She waved good-bye to Claire and closed the car door to the rear passenger seat, studying Marta's and Phil's heads as they pulled away. Soon a child of theirs — maybe even children if all went as planned, and Emily bet that all would go as planned if Phil had anything to do with it — would occupy this spot. She wondered what life would hold for the two of them. Wondered if their marriage would be happy, their future blessed. It wasn't that she wished them ill. It was just that sometimes she wished for someone who understood her pain, who could share in the loss she'd sustained in a way that was sympathetic and not just empathetic. People always thought they knew how she felt — and said as much. But she suspected that only those who had actually lost someone like she had — someone they loved more than life — could truly know the hole it created, could give voice to the way it felt when the wind blew through, as it still did.

When they drove over the bridge, she didn't turn to see if Kyle was there. She was forcing herself to stop that habit. She didn't need to see what didn't involve her any longer. She wished they would tear out this old bridge, and the bridge tender house

329

with it. Without a bridge, there would be no bridge tender, and without a bridge tender, he would be free to leave. Maybe that was what everyone needed, permission to go. She leaned her head against the car window and wondered just where she would go if she had permission. She studied the water and thought that she was where she was supposed to go, and yet the place had offered none of the solace she had thought she'd find. It was starting to occur to her that there was simply no way out of grief, no bridge that could get her there.

There was a line in front of the restaurant, a crowd of people milling around on the front porch waiting their turn for a table. Phil had, of course, thought ahead and made reservations so they were shown to their table almost immediately. Phil gave them a knowing smile as they followed the hostess to a lovely table upstairs, in the same room they'd used for the meetings, now set up once again for diners. "It's not the balcony, but I guess we can't have everything," Phil said, pulling Marta's chair out for her. When he reached out to do the same for Emily, she declined and grabbed her own chair. It made a horrible screeching noise when she tugged too hard on it, and other patrons glanced over with dramatic grimaces. She took a quick seat, chastised, and busied herself with arranging her cloth napkin in her lap, her mother's instructions from childhood echoing in her mind as they always did when she was out to eat.

> Sit up straight.
> Put your napkin in your lap.
> Be aware of where each piece of silver goes, and what order in which to use them.
> No elbows on the table.
> Think of things to keep the conversation going.
> And please, above all, remember who you are.

Embarrassment was a fate worse than death to her mother, who worked overtime to make sure her husband the pastor was always in good standing. Sometimes Emily looked at her mother and felt very sorry for her. Sometimes she wanted to shake her. This summer had been a good break from all of that and, beyond a phone call every few days to check on things, she dared say her parents had enjoyed the break from her, their grieving daughter. Emily knew she hadn't made the most socially acceptable widow. She wondered if her parents would've been surprised to hear she'd gone out on a date. Of course her mother would've wanted a complete religious history on Kyle, preferably with a written testimony of his decision to follow Christ. She and Kyle had scarcely gotten that far. But he had thought to bless the food before they ate that night.

Marta's hand gripped her arm, knocking her out of her reverie just in time. "Don't look now," she said through gritted teeth. "But the movie stars are out on the balcony having what looks to be a *private* dinner." She leaned over and elbowed Phil. "No wonder we didn't get to go out there. No one did."

Emily glanced over, trying hard not to be obvious and praying her eyes didn't meet Kyle's. She would rather die than have him see her see him, looking like some rejected wannabe still pining away. And yet if he looked into her eyes at that very moment, she knew that's exactly what he'd see. With a quick glance through the window she took in his dark hair and her blonde. Saw a flash of jewelry as Xandra reached for him, her hand resting on his shoulder. Emily had rested her head on that same shoulder, been just that close. She reached for the water the waiter had put on the table and took a big sip.

She looked around the restaurant, seeing the other people who were also trying hard not to look at the bona fide movie stars in their midst. Funny how Kyle had existed in this autonomous fog all this time, the citizens of this hamlet content to let him be, a humble bridge tender who scarcely warranted a second glance. But let a star fall from the sky and land among them and his star suddenly began to shine again. Suddenly the men wanted to be him and the women wanted to date him. If she hadn't lost him before, she most certainly had now.

Dinner was a quiet, stilted affair, with Phil pontificating and Marta readily agreeing, an eager, adoring expression on her face that made Emily uncomfortable, as if she was witnessing something meant for just the two of them. Or that she was witnessing a transformation no one should see another human go through. She hoped her friend wasn't contorting herself just to fit into whatever mold Phil had for her. But it was none of her business. Her friend deserved her chance at happiness and if this was all she ever got, who was she to tell her not to take it?

Emily was almost finished with her she-crab soup (the mildest, blandest thing she could find on the menu with her stomach doing flips because of Kyle) when Marta brought up their conversation with Claire. "Em," she said. "I didn't realize you'd never told Claire about Ryan." Emily looked up, avoiding looking at Phil, aware of Kyle's presence, forcing herself to focus solely on what Marta was saying. "She seemed confused about your . . . situation. Said she'd assumed you were recently divorced and it had been painful and that was why you were still wearing your wedding ring. Did you know that?"

Emily put her spoon into the bowl, watching the whole thing slip into the creamy white soup until it completely disappeared. "We started to talk about it one time and I just . . . changed the subject. I didn't want to go into it."

"Well, I set her straight."

Emily sat up a little taller. "What do you mean, you set her straight?"

"I told her. She's your next-door neighbor. She's been a friend to you. I'm not sure why you wouldn't have told her. It's kind of odd. I mean, it's been over a year. And what he did for you. That house. It's all part of your story."

Emily wanted to leave, to get away from

all of them. She didn't want to have this conversation in front of Phil, with Kyle just a few feet away from all of them. She could feel a warm blush move across her chest and up her neck. She couldn't look at Marta so she studied the bowl of soup, the outline of the spoon barely visible just under the surface, like a sunken ship. "It's my story to tell, though, Marta. When I'm ready."

Marta glanced in the direction of the balcony and back at Emily. "You didn't tell him either, did you?" She hitched her thumb in Kyle's direction and it was so obvious Emily wanted to reach across the table and grab her hand, but that would've been even more obvious. Sometimes a best friend could be so dead-on that it hurt. Marta's mirror was much harsher than her own. Hers had softer lighting, better angles. Marta's had that fluorescent glare only found in department stores and waves that made her look like the funhouse version of herself. And yet Marta's mirror was one she needed to force herself to look into.

She had withheld her story from these new people for reasons she couldn't explain. She'd made it through weeks, spent hours with Amber, Claire, and Kyle, yet never told any of them the truth about what brought her to Sunset. In her silence, they had filled in the blanks on their own. They'd been wrong about her, yet she'd felt no need to correct them. Was that even a real relationship if she wasn't being real? And what had stopped her from talking about Ryan's last gift to her? Grief? Shame? Fear? None of those reasons made any sense.

When she looked up at Marta, she didn't see judgment in her friend's eyes, just understanding and compassion. The last few days — and all the changes — had made her less certain of Marta's friendship, but in that moment, she knew that in spite of it all, she still had her back. Marta spoke up. "Maybe the reason things didn't work out between you is because you're holding back. Not because he is."

She glanced over at the table outside and saw that Kyle and Xandra were getting up to leave. She watched him move and smile and felt a sense of loss as she did. She looked back at Marta with a sad expression behind her pasted-on smile. "No, I think the reason things didn't work out is because I can't compete with that." She nodded toward the balcony just as the door opened. Heads turned as Kyle and Xandra breezed through the dining room, a buzz of whispers flowing through the room as people watched the two most beautiful people in

Sunset make their exit. She forced herself to look down at her bowl of soup, busying herself with extracting the spoon just as Marta punched her in the arm. "Ow!" she yelled and looked at her friend like she'd lost her mind.

"He was looking over here. At you," Marta hissed. "He was trying to catch your eye."

She looked in Kyle's direction but he and Xandra were already past them. She watched him walk away, and as she did, something fell into place. Sometimes, she reasoned, life was just like that — a series of near-misses and almosts, all signaling that, for whatever reason, something just wasn't meant to be. She had to let this go and stop obsessing. She had to quit living in a dream world and start rooting herself in reality. Maybe this little foray into romance had been just something God used to show her happiness with another person was possible someday. Her love life didn't have to be over. And God knew that just any guy wouldn't have gotten that far, so he sent Kyle. She had to hand it to Him. He knew what motivation to use.

She looked at both Marta and Phil. "I think I might go home with you guys to-morrow if that would be okay," she said. "I could follow you back."

Marta's mouth fell open and Phil knit his brows together. "I thought you were staying the summer."

She shook her head. "I never knew how long I wanted to stay. I figured I'd know when it was time to go."

Marta chuckled. "And now that he's off with her that's your cue to exit stage left?"

Emily shook her head. "No, not really. I mean, sure, it's not easy to see your crush find his way back to the girl who got away all those years ago. But I just realized God used Kyle in my life for a purpose and I think that purpose was accomplished." She rested her hand on Marta's forearm. "I think I was supposed to just be open to love again, to realize I could have feelings for someone besides Ryan again. And who better than Brady Rutledge to help you figure that out?"

Marta laughed out loud. "You got that right." She gave Phil a sidelong glance. "Sorry, honey." He held his hands up to show no harm done. "But what about Amber? And Claire?"

"Claire said she might go home with Rick. He really wants his family together and I don't blame him. This place is nice but it gets lonely just like anywhere can. And as for Amber, I wish her well. I tried to help.

But you can't help someone who doesn't want your help." She shrugged. "I did all I could."

"Well, if that's the way you feel about it, then I guess you're right. Maybe you could go home awhile. Then come back here toward the end of summer. It's close enough that you can divide your time."

"Exactly." Emily felt better as she said it. She loved Sunset. She wanted to have time here and she was glad she'd bought the house, grateful to Ryan for his last gift to her. It had been his place; then he had shared it with her as only he could, and in a way that lasted. And yet it made sense to go home. She could see her parents, go to her church, tend to her yard, and maybe take that landscaping class. She could get ready for school to start, get a jump on her lesson plans and communication with the students' parents. Maybe she'd get a puppy.

The bill came and Phil looked at the two ladies. "You ready to go?" he asked.

"Yes," Emily said. And she meant it.

She didn't mean to see Kyle and Xandra inside the bridge tender's house when they drove back over the bridge after dinner. But when her eyes traveled that way she caught sight of that blonde hair, a perfect, expensive rendition of a color that mostly occurred only on young children. She saw that yellow hair and his black hair, two heads inclined in the same direction. It was just a flash, but it was enough to cement the rather impulsive decision she'd just made. She would return home tomorrow.

She wouldn't pack up the whole house, just take the essentials she would need for some time back home. Phil and Marta could help her pack and load. She'd come back for a few weeks at the end of summer. By then she was willing to bet that Kyle would be gone back to Hollywood with Xandra, coaxed back into the limelight by her megawatt smile. Emily hoped that her leaving might inspire Claire to go home with Rick. Maybe she and Claire could time it to come back for a last hurrah at the end of summer. She'd like more time with her new friend and Noah and Sara. She'd grown quite fond of the children and hoped she could serve as a kind of summer aunt to them. And when she got back she'd make a point to drop by the motel and check in on Amber. She was sure the girl wanted her space, but she also knew she needed to show her she still cared. Amber didn't have enough adults in her life who did care and her failure to really help the girl still nagged at her. Merging tough love and unconditional love was harder than it looked. It had given her a new perspective on parents of teens.

She was thinking of Amber and her absentee father as they turned on her street and saw the smoke, the people in the street looking up and gesturing, the cars parking haphazardly as more people jumped out. Something was on fire. Emily was willing to bet it was someone's house. Her heart began to pound. What if it was hers? She thought of Ada's heirlooms, the few happy memories she'd managed to make there thus far, the journal Kyle had come in search of the first time she'd met him. What if there were other things inside that mattered to the history of the island? As one of the oldest houses there, it was surely possible.

"Is it my house?" she asked Marta and Phil, who in the front seat could see just slightly ahead of her. "Can you tell?"

Marta looked back at her, a panicked look on her face. "We're not far enough yet. Don't worry. It won't be your house."

"Oh, what if it's Claire's? She loves that place."

Marta reached for her hand and she took it, grateful for the human contact and the show of support. Marta squeezed. "It'll be fine," she said.

But Emily didn't know it would be fine. Not anymore. Once she had been a girl who had believed that everything did turn out fine. She believed that God took care of those He loved and a happy, blessed life was a sign of His care. She knew God didn't play favorites, but she also knew that, as the daughter of a preacher, she and her parents had enjoyed a good life because they lived a good life. Church attendance, volunteering, and living the Golden Rule paved the way to safe living. But then Ryan had gotten sick and she'd felt the walls of her spiritual fortress begin to cave in. Blackness swirled in the air where once there had been light. All the memory verses and rote prayers and knowing the books of the Bible in order had done nothing to keep it away. And while her faith in God had stayed mostly intact through the loss of Ryan, her certainty of a good life was as dead and buried as her husband was. Nothing would ever be fine again.

She strained forward to see ahead, sticking her face in the space between Phil and Marta as all three sets of eyes focused on the point of origin of all that smoke. She steeled herself, expecting to see her house in flames. She'd learned to hold all things lightly since she lost Ryan, but this house, she realized, had become precious to her. In a way it was all she had left of him, a haven he'd provided when his arms were no longer available. And while she'd made the decision to return home for a while, she didn't want to lose it entirely. Tears filled her eyes as she faced what she'd decided was the inevitable outcome. Of course it would be her house on fire.

Except it wasn't. And it wasn't Claire's house either. It was the house on the other side of Claire's that was usually rented each week to a new set of vacationers. But Emily didn't think she'd seen people there this week. She heard Marta expel the breath she'd been holding and Emily let out a sigh of grateful relief, even as she felt terrible for whoever's house it was.

"I knew it wouldn't be your house," Phil said, pulling the car to a stop and parking on the side of the road. "I could tell by the direction of the smoke."

She ignored him and got out of the car, spotting Claire standing alone near the house on fire. She hurried over to her. "What happened?" she asked, looking around for Rick and the children. "Are the kids okay?"

Claire nodded, her eyes filling with tears.

"It's our fault," she said. "Rick's got the kids inside calming them down. They were in the backyard shooting off fireworks and one just caught the breeze and flew up to that roof deck. We thought it just fizzled out up there but then . . ." She gestured at the flames and smoke. "We saw that."

Emily realized something. "Wait. Why aren't there any fire trucks here?"

Claire pressed her lips into a grim line. "The tide's too high. The truck can't make it across the bridge until it goes down."

"But that could be hours!"

Claire nodded, her face unchanging. "The house is going to burn down unless a flash storm comes along to put it out or God sends along a wind to magically blow it out." She pointed at a pickup truck with the fire station insignia on the side, parked off to the side with a few other police cars. A collection of men in uniform stood staring up at the disaster with strangely impassive faces. The group of people had resigned themselves to the loss of the house. And most of them, she suspected, were just glad it wasn't their house affected.

Emily had seen that same response so many times from people when Ryan was sick. They felt bad but there was nothing they could do. And while they wanted to

344

bring food and write cards and offer pithy words of comfort, mostly they just didn't want to catch whatever dose of misfortune Emily had contracted. They still held on fiercely to their belief that things would be fine. Their faces were always kind, but distant. Get too close and you might breathe in the bad air around her.

She didn't blame them, exactly. On a certain level she understood it. And now she understood it all over again as she remembered the moment when she realized it wasn't her house on fire. She was relieved for herself and Claire. And while she felt sorry for whoever owned this house, she was mostly just grateful.

When someone approached her, she assumed Marta was coming to get the lowdown from Claire. But when she turned to fill her in on what she knew, it wasn't Marta she found standing next to her. Kyle's large form filled the space beside her, his salt-and-sun scent lost in the acrid, smoky air. Just behind him trailed Xandra, looking sheepish and frightened. Emily squinted up at him and over at Claire, who had noticed him too.

"What's going on?" he asked them both. He looked stricken by the sight of the burning house, but also nervous to talk to either of them.

Emily was about to answer when Claire interrupted. "Kyle, just take the princess back wherever you came from. This doesn't concern you." Claire's venom toward Kyle never failed to surprise Emily. She wanted to pin her down and make her explain its origin.

"I live here, Claire, so it does concern me." He swept his hand out, indicating the onlookers all around them. "If you haven't noticed, not everyone here lives on this street but you don't seem to have a problem with anyone else's right to be here. I was here to see if I could help. I thought maybe I could clean up after the fire's put out."

"Fine," Claire said. She gestured at the police and firemen. "Go talk to them. I'm sure they'd love to fill in the local hero."

"I never said that, *Claire.*" When he spoke her name, it sounded like a loaded weapon.

"You never had to, Kyle. Or should I say Brady? Which is it this week?"

Kyle smirked at her. "You beat all, you know that?" Emily and Xandra, the onlookers, blinked at each other and looked at the house on fire, the ground, the ridiculously lovely setting sun above them. "How long has it been, huh?" Kyle continued. "And you still can't let it go." He shook his head. Xandra moved closer to him, placing her hand on his bicep, a movement that was at once protective and proprietary. Emily took a step back.

"Please. Just. Leave," Claire said. "I can't handle this right now."

Kyle looked from Claire to Emily. He opened his mouth and, for a moment, she thought he was going to say something to her. Her heart fluttered erratically in response. She was pathetic and had clearly not advanced much beyond the teeny-bopper who once loved him from afar. Mustering all the gumption she had, she spoke to him in defense of her friend instead of following her heart and waiting to hear whatever it was he had to say to her. "You should probably go. Claire's upset enough right now."

His shoulders slumped and he gave her a sad smile as he leaned toward her. "I wish things hadn't turned out like they did," he said and, with Xandra hanging on his arm, turned to make his way over to the police and firemen, leaving Emily and Claire alone again. She glanced over at Phil and Marta, who had watched the whole scene from a few feet away. She gave Marta a wide-eyed, "No idea what is going on" look and turned back to Claire, who was still seething.

"I hope Kyle knows he can kiss his beloved bridge good-bye now. The state's gonna tear it down for sure after this. Guess that means he won't be able to hide in that tender house anymore." Claire wasn't really talking to anyone but herself, that was clear. Her voice was angry and tense. She turned to face Emily, as if she only just realized she was there. "Ten bucks says he's back in Hollywood before the week ends." She hitched her thumb in Xandra's direction. "She'll make sure of it." Claire shook her head with disgust. "I literally cannot believe he brought her here." She gave a bitter laugh.

Emily wanted so badly to ask what was going on, but she knew better than to say anything more at that moment. Instead they stood silently and watched the fire, a sense of reverence in the air as more and more of the house succumbed to the flames, the police and firemen keeping a perimeter so the onlookers were safe, their eyes always watching the house with a hopeless look on their faces. She noticed that Marta and Phil gave up and went inside her house. A policeman strolled over to Claire. "Claire, the fire trucks are on their way. The tide's gone out enough now to get them over the bridge. Once they're underway, we'll need to take your statement and talk to your husband." The man looked over his shoulder, in the direction of Claire's house. "He inside with the kids still?"

She nodded mutely. "They were pretty upset." Her eyes as she searched the policeman's face were pleading. "It was an accident."

"We know that. Kyle and I were just talking about it. Coulda happened to anyone. Especially this time of year. We're not supposed to shoot off fireworks but we all do it." He snickered. "But you didn't hear me say that."

Claire grinned in spite of herself. "Don't try to make me feel better," she said.

He clapped her on the back. "Don't be so hard on yourself." He nodded at Emily. "Ma'am," he said and walked away.

Claire leaned in after he was gone. "His name's Roy. He's a good guy. Single. Cute. Gainfully employed."

Emily looked at her with a shocked expression. "Claire!" she said.

Claire shrugged. "I'm a hopeless matchmaker," she said. She gestured over to where Kyle still stood beside Xandra, who was being grilled by two women who had lost interest in watching a house burn down and turned their interest on her. "You can do better than him."

Even with everything that had happened, Emily doubted that. "I don't want to be match-made, anyway," she mumbled.

Claire linked her arm through Emily's and pulled so that the gap between them was closed. There was a beat of silence. "When you're ready then," Claire finally said.

Emily nodded.

"I'm sorry," Claire added. "For your loss." She caught Emily's eye and gave her a look of understanding. "I couldn't imagine."

Emily wanted to say that no one should have to imagine. But the lump in her throat was too big to talk around. She nodded as a tear escaped from her eye. Claire slid her arm around her and together they watched the house burn, the flames leaping up to try and touch the sky.

TWENTY-FOUR

It was late that night when the last flame was extinguished and all the city officials and onlookers finally left. The burning house had become somewhat of an odd party site, people both repelled and attracted by tragedy, as people are. They wanted to be close to the action but they also wanted to make sure it didn't come anywhere near them. Sitting on the dock with Phil and Marta, they rehashed the events of the evening, the smell of smoke strong in the air, the sky above them hazy. But they could still see the stars and the lights of the bridge twinkling in the distance.

"You sure you want to go back tomorrow?" Marta asked. Her voice sounded skeptical.

Emily considered Marta's question. She hadn't thought again about leaving in all the excitement. There hadn't been time. Did the burning house change anything? She thought about Xandra's hand on Kyle's arm, pictured Claire's face when she went inside, whispering before she did that she had no choice but to leave town for a while now. She glanced over at her house, sitting still and safe a few yards away. She had discovered how much she loved her house when she thought she might lose it. And yet she didn't feel the need to stay. Not when Claire was leaving, and Kyle would surely be gone as well now. Staying would only amplify her loneliness. She glanced at the bridge, the lights a kind of touchstone she'd come to rely on in all her nights on this dock. Soon they would be gone too, and that thought made her sadder than any other.

"We might all sleep a bit later, but yes, I'd like to follow you guys back home if that's okay."

"Fine by me," Marta said. "Maybe we could stop for lunch on the way home?" They both wanted to return to the little hole-in-the-wall barbecue place they'd found by accident on their first trip down.

"Sounds perfect." She stood up, stretched, and looked at her friend and her friend's fiancé, who had been there for her in so many ways lately. "Thanks, guys. For dinner tonight and for . . . everything. I —"

The sound of a slamming car door and squealing tires silenced her. They all glanced at each other in confusion. Emily wondered if perhaps the owners of the house had arrived and were upset. Or maybe an emergency personnel had left something behind at the house and was returning for it. But the noise sounded closer than a few houses over. It sounded like it came from her own front yard. She found herself heading toward the sound as Marta called for her to wait up.

The three rounded the corner of the house in time to see a figure crouching on all fours in Emily's front yard. They heard the sound of sobbing. Whatever car had been there was long gone and the person — whoever it was — had clearly been left behind. Whether by choice or not remained a mystery. "Excuse me?" Emily called out to the figure, bolstered by Marta's and Phil's presence. "Can we help you?" She took a few steps closer and the sound of the crying got louder. In the darkness, Emily couldn't make out the face. Her heart hammering in her chest, she crouched down beside the person and put a tentative hand on the shoulder. "Is there someone I can call? Do you need a ride or . . . something?" she asked, her voice qua-

353

vering. Marta and Phil had come to stand directly behind her but were silent.

The figure turned her face toward the light coming from Emily's house, her eyes searching for, Emily knew, a sense of home or welcome or at least not outright rejection. She heard Marta gasp when she realized who it was. "I . . . I didn't know where else to go so I told him to drop me here," the familiar voice said. Amber raised her hands toward Emily with a hopeful look that nearly tore Emily's already fragile heart in two. She glanced over her shoulder at Marta with a fraction of hesitation. This girl here, now, when she was so close to making a nice clean break, was the last thing she needed. Marta nodded vigorously and Emily turned back to nod at Amber. Taking both her extended hands she helped her to her feet. And then she wrapped those hands around Amber's neck and gave her a hug that told her she was welcome.

After settling Amber down with a warm blanket and a glass of water, Marta took it upon herself to pepper her with questions while Emily stood by and listened. Amber probably wouldn't have answered the same questions coming from Emily, but Marta's teacher persona was working for her, goading the girl into submitting to authority. Amber looked like the child she was as she picked at the blanket and avoided their eyes while relaying her story. Phil had gone to bed and Emily was glad for that. When Amber had stood and walked beside her across the yard, Emily had noticed she had started to show, her body pushing her to finally tell the truth because she just couldn't deny it anymore. She'd watched how Amber's hand had gone to her belly, a protective gesture that touched Emily's heart and told her this girl wasn't a lost cause.

"He doesn't want a baby, that's what he said," Amber said now, tears sliding silently from the corners of her eyes and making tracks across her face. She had put on more makeup than usual, Emily noticed, dressed up a little nicer than she normally did, probably in preparation to tell him about the baby, to make him want her more. The fact that it didn't work probably only made her feel worse. Was it possible to feel more rejected?

"He said I was a stupid kid and he should've known better than to mess with me. Said I wasn't to tell anyone about him and not to even think of asking him for a dime of help."

"That's illegal. He doesn't get a choice,"

Marta said, taking a seat across from Amber. Emily noticed her movements were slow, the way one might move around a grizzly bear or lion. "We can help you with that part of it," she said.

Amber raised her eyes to meet Emily's for the first time. "You knew this is what he would do, didn't you?"

Emily thought about lying, but then decided against it. "I suspected."

"That's why you were trying to get me to go ahead and tell him, wasn't it?"

"I figured it was better to know right away what you were dealing with. It helps with decision making, to know all the facts." That is what Ryan's doctor had told them when he delivered the diagnosis. Was that even true or was it just something people said? Was it possible to make a good decision when there wasn't one to be found? "I just wanted you to know what you were facing." She sat down beside Amber and rested her hand on the girl's knee. "I didn't want to hurt you but I guess I suspected the hurt was coming."

Instead of pulling away as Emily expected her to, Amber leaned over and put her head on her shoulder. "I'm sorry I didn't listen. I should've." Amber yawned.

"What does your dad say?" Emily asked.

She could feel Amber's shrug. "He says I'm no better than my mother. That I'll end up like her. He says my life is ruined and don't count on him for help. You know. What I expected him to say." The girl's sigh was world-weary. "God forbid he should act like a father."

Marta and Emily exchanged glances. Marta's said, *This girl is all alone in the world.*

And Emily's said, *What do you think I've been trying to tell you?*

"Well, your room is still all made up for you, if you want it," Emily said, running her hand through Amber's auburn hair, her fingers catching in the tangles and snarls.

Amber looked up. "You kept my room?" she asked.

When Emily looked into those gorgeous green eyes, her heart nearly broke. How could she ever help this girl see how beautiful she was, how valuable? How could anyone possibly undo the damage her own father, and now this jerk, had done to her? She wasn't a piece of trash to be discarded, and yet Emily doubted she'd believe anything else for a long time to come.

"Of course I did," she said, her voice falsely bright, full of a hope she didn't have for a future she couldn't see. She led Amber to her room, hoping at the very least they could all get some much-needed sleep and that things would look brighter in the morning, like her mother always said.

Her mother. She would call her in the morning, ask her if she knew of any charitable organizations who could help Amber. If she had to take her home with her she would. For sure no one would miss her here. She yawned, her body shutting down in spite of her. Tomorrow. She would think about all of it tomorrow. For now she just wanted to lie down and quiet the many thoughts zipping through her brain at the speed of light. She tucked Amber in first, pulling the covers to her chin and saying a quick, quiet prayer for the girl as she did. Before she could walk away, Amber grabbed her hand. "Thank you," she said.

"It's nothing," Emily assured her.

"Huh!" Amber scoffed at Emily's downplay. "To me? It's everything." She rolled over to face the wall.

Emily didn't know what to say in response so she just offered a weak "thank you." She started to slink out the door so Amber could drift off to sleep, but she heard Amber sniffing and worried she was starting to cry all over again. "Are you okay, Amber?" she asked.

"Yeah, I'm just wondering what I smell?

Is that . . . smoke?" she asked.

Emily laughed with a kind of manic relief. There were no more tears to soothe for now. "You missed a lot of excitement around here tonight. I'll tell you all about it in the morning, okay?"

She started to walk out but Amber's sleepy voice stopped her once more. "I wish you were my mom," the girl said.

Emily pretended not to hear and slipped from the room, closing the door behind her.

She woke the next morning and, for a moment, thought that perhaps she had dreamed the events of the night before — seeing Kyle and Xandra at dinner, coming home to find a neighbor's burning house with the community gathered to watch, her decision to go home, and Amber's unexpected return. Of course, she thought as she stared at the ceiling, Amber's presence locked her into staying a bit longer. At least until she could figure out what to do with her. She would call her mother later, beg her to call in favors at whatever maternity homes she could think of. Their church had supported several different ones so surely her mother had some pull. She just had to talk Amber into going to one.

She opened her bedroom door to find a

quiet house and was relieved to have a few moments to herself before the chaos of the day hit full force. When she took a deep breath, she could still smell the smoke that lingered from the night before. She went to the front door and pulled it open so she could see the burned out house, part of her wanting to verify that the odd night *had* actually happened. She'd heard the owners of the burned house were driving up today to see the damage, that they'd been on the phone with onlookers who knew them throughout the night trying to process what was happening.

"They should've taken out that bridge a long time ago," she'd heard that the man who owned the house had said. According to the talk among the crowd, he'd added a few expletives to make sure everyone knew how he felt about the bridge and said he was going to file an official complaint with the state, and possibly even sue for damages. It wasn't that the man didn't have a point, people had said to each other. Suddenly the public sentiment about the bridge began to change. She hoped no one told the angry man exactly who was responsible for the fireworks that started it all. Claire certainly didn't need him showing up on her doorstep. She was already feeling enough guilt. Although it was an accident, Emily suspected there would be some sort of charges filed. It was probably best that Claire was already looking toward leaving town for a while.

She stepped out onto the front porch to get a look at Claire's house, see if anyone was up and moving around. Perhaps Claire would want to talk. But no one was milling around and she stepped back, not wanting to look like she was spying. When she stepped back, her foot came down on some foreign object — a sharp foreign object. She hopped around, trying to grab her foot without being too loud while trying to see what she'd just stepped on at the same time. When she looked down, she saw a beautiful pink conch shell resting on her deck. Beside it lay a creamy white envelope with the word "Emily" written across the front in sharp, black ink. The handwriting was unfamiliar and blocky. She stopped hopping and reached for it, her curiosity overcoming her pain.

She carried the offending shell and the envelope inside, wondering who could've left it for her. In spite of the rather masculine handwriting on the envelope, she told herself it was from Claire, probably saying what she couldn't say last night. That sounded like something Claire would do. Unable to sleep after Rick and the kids fell asleep, she'd probably decided there were some things she needed to say before she left. Things were changing, she was upset, and the emotions were flowing. Hence the letter Emily held. That made perfect sense.

She ripped into it, using her thumb to dig into the seal and tear an opening large enough to pull out what was inside. Impatient, she bent the paper because she pulled it out before she'd made a big enough opening. She didn't care about the condition of the paper, she just wanted to see what the words on it were. She closed her eyes as if in prayer before she opened them and focused on the words that someone had written to her.

Emily,
Last night I wanted to talk to you but with Claire around I didn't think it was a good time. I'm sure she's told you why she hates me. It's not like she doesn't have a good reason, but sometimes I wish she could let it go. Claire was probably the hardest part about coming back here. Her and people like her. People who don't understand.

I wanted to explain about Xandra being here and tell you that I'm sorry that things went wrong with us. When you didn't want to kiss me, I should've been happy with a hug. I should've stuck around and not let you push me away.

I left you the shell because it reminds me of you, and of me. I found it a long time ago and kept it to remind myself to let people in. If you look at it, you see it's tightly coiled, one protective layer after another. For a long time, I was like that. After everything happened and I came back here, I had so many layers around me, no one could get to me. I suspect you're the same way. I know what it feels like to not want to be hurt again, to lose something, or someone, you care about. I know it feels safer to stay wrapped up tight, and to be afraid to let anyone else in. But I also know how lonely that can feel. I don't know your story, but I'd like to hear it. I think we'd have a lot to talk about. Which leads me to why I'm leaving you this note.

Please meet me tonight at the bridge. I have to work, but I'd really like to see you, to tell my side of the story so you don't only hear Claire's. I know I don't deserve it, but I hope you'll look past that and agree to hear me out. After that, if you don't want anything to do with me, at least I'll know I tried. If you come by around 9:30, I'll have some time to talk. I hope you'll come. I'll be in the tender house and we can talk there.

See you then?

Kyle

Emily read the letter through twice before she realized she'd stopped breathing and exhaled, the air coming out of her in one loud *whoosh*. Kyle wanted to see her. Kyle wanted to talk to her. Kyle actually thought she might not respond to his humble, precious request. She clutched the letter to her chest with a big smile and kissed the shell, then held it aloft to inspect the coils he'd written about. Was she like that shell? She'd invited Marta and Phil into her life, and Claire and the children, even put herself out there with Amber. She'd beg to differ with him when she saw him this evening. He might not know her as well as he thought, but it was sweet that he was trying to. She wasn't afraid to open up to others. And she hadn't not kissed him because she was closed off. It was just because she'd been overwhelmed by the reality of kissing him. That was all. Somehow she'd find the words to explain all of that — preferably without sounding like a ninny — when she saw him.

But first she had to get over to Claire's and find out just what he was referring to. She'd make Claire tell her why she hated him even if she had to drag it out of her. Without bothering to make herself more presentable, she marched off the deck and over to Claire's. She walked around to the back door, knowing she'd find a messy kitchen and cartoons on the TV, sleepy children being trailed by sleepier parents. Maybe Claire and Rick would already be packing to go.

But when she peered into the glass on the back door she saw no evidence of breakfast, heard no canned animation noises coming from the TV. There were no signs of life at all, the kitchen and family area sitting still and undisturbed. She held her breath again as she scanned the rooms, wondering where they were. Wild scenarios raced through her mind — they'd ducked out in the middle of the night, the police had come for them, the angry homeowner had taken them hostage. Suddenly Sara appeared, her pensive face looking more pensive than usual as she opened the door for Emily.

The little girl held the door open only

slightly as she informed Emily that no one was awake at their house yet. "We had a very late night," she said in a voice that sounded very grown up. Emily imagined that Sara had grown up some last night. Growing up seemed to be a process of facing and sur- viving the hard things in life, each instance pushing you a little further forward down the path of maturity. Sara had witnessed that firework taking flight, then turning in the wrong direction and setting a nearby house on fire. No one could protect her from that reality anymore. Emily saw the burning house in her mind's eye and said a silent prayer of thanks that it wasn't her house, then felt guilty all over again for thinking that way. Just a shift in wind direc- tion and it could've been her house. She couldn't pretend she wasn't glad it hadn't been. She glanced over at her still-standing house, her gift from Ryan, her consolation prize. With life came bad and good, and sometimes one came out of the other. She thought of Amber and her baby, a good and bad situation all wrapped up in one messy package.

"We're having family time right now," Sara continued, drawing Emily's attention back to her as she used her body to block Emily's entrance. "Just us," she added.

Emily knew Sara cared for her, had enjoyed her presence during the long, lazy days of summer they'd spent together. And yet it was clear that her welcome only went so far. Sara was protecting her family, circling the wagons after a confusing and unsettling night. She didn't blame the child. And yet she felt left out. In so many ways she was just on the outside of things — Phil and Marta, Claire and Rick, even Amber wasn't her family, much as the girl needed her right now. If Ryan had lived she'd have a family of her own by now. She would belong somewhere, with someone. She could have family time.

"I'll just come back later," Emily said, an unspoken apology in her voice. "You can tell your mother I came by. Okay?"

She heard Claire's voice coming from the back of the house. "Sara? Who's at the door?"

Without missing a beat, Sara called out, "No one," and unceremoniously shut the door in Emily's face. Emily stood blinking at the closed door for a moment before turning with a shrug and walking away, still holding Kyle's letter and shell, her grip just a little tighter.

TWENTY-FIVE

Marta and Phil had gotten away late after they realized that the weather was going to be too perfect to miss a day out on the beach. Even Amber had hesitantly agreed to come along with them, wearing a bikini that showed off, rather than hid, her growing stomach. "Can't hide it anymore, huh?" the girl asked Marta and Emily as she rubbed the melon-sized mound under her skin. Though they tried to assure her she still looked great, the girl pushed away their compliments, insisting she was "a cow." During the day Emily stole glances at her and thought she looked more beautiful than ever. Emily hoped the baby — whatever it was — would look just like its mother, with her shade of red hair and startling green eyes. And she prayed that someday Amber would know how truly beautiful she was. If Amber had a normal life one day, it would only be because of the grace of God.

When she left, Marta promised she would track down Emily's mother, who'd been strangely unavailable by phone. Emily tried not to worry and resolved that though she couldn't leave quite yet, she needed to get home and at least look in on her parents. Marta had hugged Amber and made her meet her eyes rather than looking away like she usually did. "We're going to take care of you and your baby. Don't you worry," she'd assured her. Then Amber had looked away, down at her toes painted with metallic purple nail polish, and mumbled her thanks.

The two of them stood in the driveway and waved until Marta and Phil's car disappeared. "They're so nice," Amber said, instinctively knowing that Emily needed a moment to compose herself. "I told Marta I want to come to their wedding."

Emily looked over, surprised by this revelation. She found it strangely heartening to hear Amber talk of a future that included them. "I'm sure she would love to have you there," she responded.

Amber blushed and nodded. "I'll be even fatter then."

Emily laughed. "You're not fat now." She wrapped her arm around the girl's shoulder and ignored the stiffened reaction she got when she did. "Let's go get something to eat."

"Music to this fat girl's ears," Amber joked as she used an elbow to Emily's ribs as an excuse to get out of her grasp.

At that moment she felt a stream of water hit her back, followed by an unmistakable laugh. She spun around to find Noah on the front porch of his house, armed with a Super Soaker water gun that was trained on her. "Ha, ha, I got you, Emily!" he called and, try as she might to get angry with him, she just couldn't when she heard his laugh.

"Noah! You little scamp! I'm gonna get you for that!" she called back.

Undeterred by her threat, Noah turned the gun toward Amber. "Who goes there?" he called. "Identify yourself or meet your fate," he said in an ominous voice.

"I'm Amber," Amber said.

"I don't believe you!" Noah called back and began shooting the water gun in her direction, the stream catching her right in the head.

Noah cracked up laughing again when he saw her shocked expression. "Ha, ha, ha, I got you too!" He was so busy laughing he didn't see Claire coming up behind him, a finger pressed to her lips so Emily and Amber wouldn't give her away. She reached out and grabbed him, lifting him up high in the air, his mouth forming a perfect O as he dropped the gun with a loud clatter.

She spun him into a cradle hold and began to tickle him. "That'll teach you," she was saying over his laughter. Emily and Amber watched for a moment, both of them smiling. Claire finished tickling him and told him to go inside for dinner, then turned to Emily. "I heard you came by earlier. Sara finally confessed that she sent you away."

"She needed some family time. I understood."

Amber pointed to her wet head. "I'm going to get a towel," she said and went back inside, leaving Claire and Emily alone. Claire walked closer and Emily did the same, the two of them meeting in the middle.

"We're going to take off tomorrow," Claire said. "Rick thinks it would be best. Both kids are pretty upset about what happened. They feel like it was their fault. It's been hard."

"I'm sure. And I'm sorry."

Claire shrugged and pointed at where Amber had been. "So she's back?"

Emily nodded. "For now. I'm trying to figure out how to best help her."

"You will," Claire said. The certainty on

371

her face as she spoke was its own kind of compliment. "So why did you come by this morning when my daughter the bouncer prevented your access?"

Emily laughed. "Actually, I had a question for you. I got this . . . note. From Kyle. And in it he alluded to why you hate him so much. He assumes I already know the story." She smiled. "I guess Amber's not the only one who's not talking around here."

Claire looked away for a second, then back again. "I try not to talk about it. It hurts too much." She wrapped her arms around herself as if it were cold. But it was ninety-seven degrees outside. She sighed. "I guess you want to know?"

"It might help. Considering he thinks I already do."

"And you're seeing him? Even though he's with that . . . star." Claire said the word *star* as if it were the worst curse word ever spoken.

"I'm not with him. He just wants to talk tonight."

Claire shook her head. "I wouldn't go if I were you."

"I can't not go, Claire. The fact that you don't want me to isn't a good enough reason. If there's really something awful about him then please tell me."

Claire let out her breath in a huff. "He's just a jerk, okay?"

"Did he dump you for her? Is that what it is? And you're still hurt even after all these years?" Emily had guessed this was the case but she'd never had the courage to say it out loud.

Claire smirked at her. "You honestly think I'd be that petty? After all these years and even though I have Rick and the kids? That I'd still be nursing some old wound like that?"

When she put it that way, it did sound unlikely. "I'm not sure what to think. So tell me."

Claire plopped down in the grass and motioned for Emily to do the same. She did, but not without thinking about how much grass made her legs itch. She'd have to shower again so she wasn't scratching the whole time she was with Kyle.

"He was with my best friend when he got 'discovered.' We'd been together for as long as we could all remember, a big group of us hanging out every summer, all summer." She smiled wistfully as she remembered. "We'd go to the beach, the pier, get summer jobs at the same restaurant so we could all be together even at work."

"The restaurant where we met?" Emily asked.

Claire nodded grimly. She had a special connection to the town, as Emily had suspected. The fire they'd started meant the end of the bridge, and that end would hurt a lot of people. She reached out and squeezed her friend's shoulder. No wonder she was leaving. She didn't feel she deserved to stay.

"So," Claire continued. "He wanted to go out to Hollywood and see what happened. I mean, of course we knew he was good looking but he was just Kyle, you know? We never expected anything to come of it. Lily — that was her name — thought it was funny. We took bets on how soon he'd come back." She sighed. "And then he gets out there and starts these modeling jobs and he's going on all these auditions and then there's all this talk about this movie." She cut her eyes over at Emily. "And then we find out he's changed his name and he's just . . . different. And of course Lily was like, 'Come home. Now. Enough's enough.' And he's all, 'Just let me see how this movie thing goes. It could set us up for life.' And Lily believed him. Of course she believed him. Because Kyle was a good guy."

Claire continued, "But Brady Rutledge

374

was someone else altogether. Someone none of us liked or even knew anymore. He would come home for visits and be this totally different person, all impressed with himself. So the last time he came home he was on a break from filming and he told Lily that she was going to hear some rumors about him and his costar but not to believe them. Lily told him she wasn't feeling well and was going to the doctor but it was like he didn't even care anymore. He just raced back to Hollywood and left her behind."

"She was sick?" Emily asked, her voice shaky. She knew about sickness, about facing a terrible illness with someone you loved.

Claire nodded, her eyes filling with tears. "The day she got diagnosed was the day the news of his affair with Xandra hit the entertainment news. So she had to face his betrayal at the same time she had to deal with the fact that she might not live. And the worst part was, he was so busy filming and then doing all the promotion when the movie came out, he wasn't there for Lily. At all."

"But you were?"

Claire nodded again, swiping the tears away. "I was there for all of it. I was with her every minute. I even shaved my head when she lost her hair. We called ourselves the Bald Beauties." Claire looked over at Emily. "The worst part is, I really believed she would live. I spent so much time focusing on how she was going to get Kyle back after she was better. Meanwhile I was finding Lily's hidden fan magazines with his pictures, and back issues of *People* with gossip about him and Xandra. He just broke her heart and didn't even care." She leveled Emily with a look. "He came back one month after she died, talking about how sorry he was and it couldn't be helped and yada, yada, yada. But it was too late and I was like, 'I don't want to hear it.' "

She rested her chin on her knee. "And I never did want to hear it. Not then. Not now. There's nothing he could say that would explain why he treated my best friend like that. Why he let her die alone with a broken heart." She sighed. "And I wouldn't be a good friend to you if I didn't warn you that he's not who you think he is. Xandra being here is only proof of that. Don't you see?"

Emily nodded, sobered by all that she'd just learned. She thought of the shared pain the two of them had experienced — both losing someone they loved so much, both the survivors who carried the memories of suffering. She wondered what Kyle could say that would possibly explain any of what she'd just learned about him. What did he have to say in his own defense like his note suggested? And what *was* his relationship with Xandra? None of it sounded very good. If she was smart she'd find a place for Amber, get her squared away, and then steer clear of this place for a while. Maybe once the bridge was gone, Kyle would go back to Hollywood and then she wouldn't risk running into him. In the meantime she could just dodge him.

But would it be fair to not at least give him a chance like he'd asked for?

Rick knocked on the front window, alerting Claire that her few moments of reprieve were over. "Don't go see him," she said to Emily, her eyes imploring her. "I don't think I could take another one of my friends getting hurt by him." She stood up and then reached down to help Emily do the same. Claire smiled at her. "You know how much I love to match-make, but this isn't a good match. Just take my word for it."

Emily nodded her assent, because what else could she do? Claire had made a good point, one she couldn't ignore. And yet as she waved good-bye to her friend and headed inside she couldn't ignore Kyle's plea either. He had asked for a chance to be heard. Didn't everyone deserve that?

That afternoon while Amber napped, Emily snuck away to the end of the beach, to the place she had avoided all summer, the place where the house was falling into the sea. She wanted to see how much was left, and if the place still felt as special to her as it had that day on their honeymoon. Ryan had been alive and well and so near, close enough to touch, to kiss, to fall into step beside. And now he was gone and she was here without him, discovering feelings for someone else, as impossible as that felt, but realizing that someone wasn't who she'd hoped he'd be. She carried Kyle's shell in her pocket, her finger tracing the rough outline as she walked. What did it say about her that she was still tempted to go and hear Kyle out, even though she'd heard Claire's very compelling side of things?

And yet Kyle said he had a side too. One that no one knew. One that it sounded like no one had ever given him a chance to tell. He'd come back here, left Hollywood, faced the music in a sense. Didn't that count for something? What if Kyle missed Lily the way she missed Ryan? What if he was someone who could really understand the depth of her loss? Claire said that Kyle and Lily had been together their whole lives, practically. She knew that kind of loss had to have been substantial no matter what else — or who else — he had in his life.

She stood beside the house, her hand resting on the pilings stacked around it, someone's effort to keep it from washing away even more. Loss, she thought, as she surveyed the house, was inevitable. Erosion and tides and the declining condition of the world would take its toll on all of us. Whether it was mistakes made long ago or just last night, we would hurt ourselves and each other. She thought of one of the nights when Ryan had been in such agony, and instead of staying, she'd fled their house, leaving a hospice nurse to deal with him. She'd run away from their house, running as far and as fast as her legs would take her, reasoning as she ran how she could never set foot in that death house again. She'd run until she couldn't run another step and then she'd sat down on the sidewalk, uncertain of where she even was, as she put her head between her knees, focusing on nothing else but catching her breath. The world — and all its pain — had fallen away as she focused on the pattern in the cement, a little line of ants traveling along it, the ant hill beyond.

A woman pushing a baby in a stroller had stopped and asked if she was okay. She'd looked up, surprised to see another human being. "I'm fine. I'm . . . just resting." She gave the woman her bravest smile. "Leg cramp," she explained. Satisfied, the woman had gone on and left her alone to sob in private, crying so hard she later vomited into the bushes before getting up and, because she had nowhere else to go, limping home, her pace slowed not by her legs but by the ache in her heart. It was in that moment that she'd finally admitted that she was losing Ryan and that there was no stopping the future that awaited her. One of loneliness and aching isolation.

Maybe Kyle had just tried to stop it the best way he knew how. Maybe he thought that if he stayed away, he could stave off the inevitable. Maybe his running just took him farther and kept him longer than he could control. She would give him the chance to explain his side of things, because she wanted him to say what she needed him to say and because she was in no position to judge. She knew the feeling of wanting away from pain, of avoiding it. She'd avoided coming to Sunset even though Ryan had made it possible. And even when she'd come here, she'd still avoided this place that held so many tender memories. There was some reason Kyle had returned to Sunset, and Emily suspected she knew what it was. She'd let him tell her first.

She watched as the wind picked up the sea foam and blew it into the air, there one minute, gone the next. "We are but a vapor." She could hear the verse in her father's deep timbre, echoing in her heart.

"I will always miss you," she said aloud. "And I hope you can see that I'm okay. And that I love the house. Thank you. I will use it well."

She was walking down the beach in the direction of her house when she felt his answer return to her: *Use it to go on with your life.* She picked up her pace, a hopeful smile on her face as she walked toward her future.

TWENTY-SIX

July 20, 2007

It was fitting that she returned home to find Amber holding the plaque she'd brought with her, her fingertips tracing the words from Jeremiah 29:11. She looked up with a guilty expression when she heard Emily come in, nearly dropping the plaque back on the shelf where it had sat since she arrived.

"Sorry I was messing with your stuff," Amber said.

Emily shook her head. "No biggie. You didn't hurt it."

"Do you believe that? What that plaque says?" Amber followed her into the kitchen and watched as she pulled a bottle of water from the fridge and took a long drink before answering.

"Yes, of course. I'm a preacher's kid. Jeremiah 29:11 is one of the verses you have to have memorized by age ten." Amber's wide eyes told her she didn't realize she was just kidding. "Kidding! I'm kidding!" She held up her hand and laughed.

"I guess it's obvious I haven't spent much time in church." Amber gave a little forced laugh. "But I think it's cool you have. You know a lot about Bible stuff, huh?"

Emily nodded. "I do."

"And you think it helps? To know that stuff?"

Emily wondered how to respond. Did her Bible knowledge help her in life? Maybe if she relied on it like she should, reacting in truth instead of emotion, reciting scripture instead of running off at the mouth. She could do better at that stuff. Did it help in the face of loss? She wasn't someone who grieved without hope because she had the hope of salvation. She could pray whenever she felt uncertain or worried or just grateful. She had the confidence that came from knowing she was never truly alone. She grinned at Amber. "Yeah. It helps."

"Maybe you could teach me some of that stuff sometime."

"What if I found you a place to live until your baby is born? A place where you could learn that stuff while you're getting ready for him or her?"

A stricken look crossed Amber's face.

"You don't want me here?"

"No, it's not that. I just have to go back. This isn't my home. I'm just here for the summer. I've got a job and a life, parents, at home. I have to get back there and I can't just leave you here. I'm trying to get my father's church to help me find a home for girls . . . in your situation to live."

Amber slumped down in a chair at the kitchen table and dropped her head into her hands. "They won't let me in there. I'm not . . . like them."

Emily crossed over to stoop down in front of her. "You don't have to be like them. You just have to be your adorable self." Emily put her hands on Amber's knees and tried to get her to look at her, but it was no use.

"I thought about getting rid of it. Like really thought about it. Like —" She looked up at Emily. "I made an appointment and everything. Even after we saw that ultrasound. I knew it had a beating heart and I still dialed that number."

Emily refused to let on how shocked she was by Amber's admission. She'd thought the girl had been determined to have her child from the beginning. "But you didn't go through with it," she said evenly.

Amber shook her head and covered her face with her hands, rocking back and forth.

"But I knew if I got rid of it, I could hang on to him a little while longer. I was that stupid."

Emily grabbed Amber's hands and pulled them away from her face. Her heavily mascaraed eyes were starting to run because of her unspilled tears, giving her the raccoon effect. Her eyes were the color of a mountain stream she and Ryan had found on a weekend trip to Boone, the water reflecting the bright green algae below. "But you didn't. You did the right thing. And you're doing the right thing now. You care more for this baby than you care for yourself, and that is so very brave."

Amber glanced over at the plaque. "Do you believe that even I have a hope and a future? Even with this?" She gestured at her stomach.

Emily smiled and wrapped her arms around the girl. "Oh, honey," she said. "I believe we all do." She pulled back and looked at her. "And I'm going to make sure you find yours."

As she walked to the bridge that night she thought about hope and the future. She had known that verse all her life, had believed in it right up to the moment Ryan died. For a while it had seemed her future and her hope had died right along with him. It was really only as she'd been at Sunset — meeting Kyle, helping Amber, hanging out with Claire — that she'd started to feel hope and see a future without Ryan. She'd spent so much time convinced that Ryan had given her this house, but she hadn't been thinking big enough. She'd lost sight of the fact that God had made all of this happen. This new place and these new people she'd found in the midst of her grief had been put in her life for such a time as this. The perfect time. She didn't know how her conversation with Kyle would go, and yet it didn't matter. If she believed what she'd said to Amber, then she could count on more to come. God loved her enough — more than Ryan ever thought about loving her — to make sure of it.

She thought about her mother's phone call this evening. She'd been happy to hear she was coming home soon for a visit. And, thanks to Marta, she'd heard about Amber and was making calls to find a place she could get in. "Marta says she's just a lovely girl in a terrible circumstance," her mother said, tsk-tsking as only she could do. "You know, you do have a spare bedroom at your house."

"Mom, I'm not going to be fully responsible for this girl. She needs a lot more than I can give her." *In case you haven't noticed,* she refrained from saying, *I've only been hanging on by a very slim thread. Let's not put this girl at risk just in case.*

"I guess you're right. It was just an idea."

"I'm not running a maternity home for unwed teens," Emily quipped and her mother chuckled.

"Okay, I get it. I think I've got a lovely place she can go. It's not far. You could visit."

"That would be great, Mom. Thanks."

"You're welcome, honey. I'm always glad to help."

The time away from her parents had given her a fresh perspective on them too. When she got back she was going to thank them for standing by her the way they did, for being such wonderful, if imperfect, parents. She would tell her father some of what she'd learned about God during her summer at Sunset, share her insights about how He had been faithful even when she wasn't. She sensed that her dad needed to hear that.

She walked across the bridge to the tender house, hugging the side of the road as close as she could in case a car came across. It wasn't very wide and didn't leave much room for pedestrians. She paused at the door and whispered, "Here goes nothing," which was a type of prayer in itself. And then she knocked with a boldness and certainty she didn't possess. But she was learning that you didn't have to have it to begin with. You just had to make a move toward it.

"I'm glad you came," he said after he'd found her a seat in the tiny office area. The room was tidy and orderly.

"I'm glad you asked."

"You were? I didn't know how you'd feel. Claire certainly made her feelings known, and I didn't know if that would scare you off."

"Actually, Claire never told me about what happened before. After I got your note I made her tell me."

He nodded, his face pensive. "And even after hearing from Claire you still came? Impressive."

"It was what you said in your note. That you have a side too."

He nodded again. "I do. It's not a pretty side, but it's a side."

"So tell me."

"I was a stupid kid who believed people who know how to make promises. I never intended to stay. I was like a gambler who goes to Las Vegas to hit it big and then come home. The problem was I kept saying, 'Just one more hand.' "

"So you stayed longer."

"Much longer. There was always another print ad they wanted me to model for. And then they started sending me out on auditions. The movie one was just a lark. It wasn't ever supposed to be anything. And then one audition led to the next one, and the next one, and the next thing I knew I got the lead. Everyone called it a Cinderella story and — aside from the obvious feminine implications I didn't care for — it was true." He smiled and she smiled back.

"And what about Lily?" Emily couldn't be certain because the lighting was dim, but she thought she saw him wince at the sound of her name.

"I loved her," he said. "Yeah, sure, we were just kids and what did we know and all that. But I'm not a kid anymore. And I know how I felt about Lily. It was real. I know that now, more than ever." He gave a little ironic laugh.

"Then what happened?"

"Well, the movie offer was good. Way more money than I'd ever see back here tending this bridge like my father and grandfather before me. I honestly thought that I'd do this one last thing, cash out, and head home. It's why I changed my name, so I could come back here and just be Kyle again. That was always my plan, to come back. But then Lily got sick and I was under contract. They basically owned me. And I couldn't get back to be with her. I guess Claire will never forgive me for that. Not that I blame her."

Emily gave him a cryptic look. "You're leaving out Xandra."

He smiled and rolled his eyes. "Of course Claire had to include that. Not surprised."

Emily made a get-on-with-it motion with her hand and he laughed. "You're not going to believe this because no one ever does, but Xandra and I were always just friends. The press made a big deal out of us, and our publicists and agents thought it was a good idea to let them because it meant more attention for the movie. Xandra's very hands-on, shall we say, the touchy-feely type, but no one knew that about her yet. And it made it look like we were together, I guess. The press will go with anything. So when they started speculating on the nature of our relationship, we let them. We knew the truth. And I figured as long as I told Lily what was going on and was honest with her, it would be okay. And it might've been if she hadn't been sick. And had Claire constantly in her ear."

"Did she ever know the truth?"

He reached over to the desk and tugged open a drawer, pulling a small velvet box out. "I brought this up here tonight in hopes you'd come and I could show you. Prove to you I'm not the guy Claire says I am." He opened the box to reveal a huge diamond ring. Though Emily was not usually impressed by such things, she knew enough to inhale sharply at the sight of it. "All that time I was working, I was saving for this." He thought about it. "And putting aside enough money to set us up in life. I figured if I played my cards right, Lily and I could have a nice life and I could still tend this bridge I love." He looked at the ring for a moment and snapped the box shut. "I got it half right."

A lump formed in Emily's throat. "Did she ever get to see it?"

He nodded and closed his fingers around the velvet, the box nearly disappearing inside his large hand. "She did. I came as soon as I could. Asked her to marry me right there in the hospital." He paused and Emily knew he was remembering, as she was, standing beside a hospital bed, watching someone you love slip away to a place you cannot follow. He spoke again. "She was so sick by then, fighting to stay conscious." He chuckled. "She turned me down."

Emily twisted the ring on her left hand, around and around. "My husband died," she said.

He nodded. "I know. I've just been waiting for you to tell me. When you were ready. Then I thought that maybe I should go first."

She shifted in her chair, picked at a stray hangnail before looking back at him, a confession weighing on her in the midst of all his honesty. "Well, since we're confessing, I wrote a note on the state site saying that I thought the bridge was a danger, after that scare with Amber that night. I was upset and I wanted to complain to someone. I —"

He smiled. "I know. I saw it. You left your name."

She laughed. "And you don't hate me?"

He shrugged. "You had a point. And that was only further proved when that house burned down." He swept his arm to take in the room where they now sat. "It's over. I accept that. You didn't do that." He gave her a serious look. "You're not responsible."

"But you're out of a job."

"Maybe I'll go back to modeling." He flexed and posed, making her laugh.

"Do you know what you'll do? For real?"

He stood and held out his hand. "Let's not talk about real life tonight. Tonight I want to take you on the ride of your life. Something very few people get to do." He called down to the other guy who was working with him, Dan, and asked him to open the bridge.

"Now?" Dan called up the narrow winding metal staircase from the room below them where the equipment used to open the bridge was housed. He'd been politely making himself scarce while they talked. Kyle began pressing buttons on the control board and then ushered them outside. He instructed her where to stand and warned her to hang on. She obeyed, gripping the railing as the lights flashed, warning traffic that the bridge was about to open. But it was late and there was no traffic, and before she knew it the clanking, groaning metal indicated the bridge was opening. It moved slowly at first, then picked up speed as it began to swing outward, gliding across the water, making waves as the waters parted in the darkness. In the moonlight she could see his face as he stood beside her against the railing, see him smiling at her reaction. Together, they hung on tight.

"I'm absolutely not supposed to be doing

this." He laughed as they began to move.

"I don't want to get you in trouble!" she protested.

He put his arm around her for a moment. Then removed it so quickly she was uncertain that it had really happened. "What are they going to do, fire me?"

She laughed as she felt the night air whoosh across her cheeks and then a slight jolt when the bridge got to where it was going and stilled. They stood watching the dark water churn underneath them and inside her, she felt her heart lift, and open wide. But this time instead of sadness coming out, she felt joy flowing in. She looked in the direction of where her dock was, thinking of these lights she'd stared at in the distance so many nights, never even daring to dream that anything like this could happen.

She looked up at him, and thought of that moment on the dock when she'd told him she wasn't ready to kiss him. She didn't know his sad story and he didn't know hers, she'd said. And in a way, she'd been right to tell him that they needed to know each other better. Because their stories had shaped who they were. And she didn't want to be involved with anyone who didn't know about the love she'd had, and the love she'd lost. Ryan had changed her forever. And Lily had changed him. Later she would tell Kyle that when she and Ryan used to talk about children, the name Lily was at the top of the girl names' list. Somehow it just all fit together. She wouldn't try to make sense of it. She'd just enjoy the ride.

She felt his hands on either side of her face, interrupting her thoughts. She looked up at him, the moon bright in the sky above his head, glinting on the dark water. They blinked at each other in the darkness, silent for a moment before he leaned forward, his mouth close to hers as he whispered, "I'm not going to ask this time" just before he pressed his lips to hers, cautious and tentative. They stayed that way, frozen for a moment as her mind reeled. She was grateful that she wasn't the first to pull away.

"Was that okay?" he asked, sounding so uncertain she nearly laughed.

Instead she just smiled up at him. "It was very okay." He hugged her, swallowing her up in his strong arms, making her feel that she could disappear there, safe and protected. The fear of losing played at the edges of her mind, as she suspected it always would, but she pushed it away. She couldn't live in fear of losing. She just had to enjoy what she had without worrying about the future. She would cross that bridge if and when she came to it. She smiled to herself, there in Kyle's arms. Bridge. It all came back to that.

When she got home she would talk to her father about all she had learned about bridges this summer. She would share with him what she'd learned about God too. She'd discovered that people don't make good bridges. They were kind of like the old bridge — unsafe, unreliable, unstable. If you counted on other people to get you where you were going, you'd be disappointed. The only way you could safely get from one place to the other was to count on God to get you there. She would tell her father that losing Ryan had shown her where to put her trust, and to not be afraid of what waited on the other side. God had used this summer to link where she'd been to where she was going, as only a bridge can do. He'd given her a hope and a future, even when she'd given up on that ever happening.

Kyle spoke up. "You know I was thinking that it might be good to get rid of this old bridge."

"Oh, you do, do you?" She laughed, her nerves jangling and her heart thrumming. "And why do you think that?"

"Because. This old bridge is part of the

history of this place." He stepped back from her but held on to her hand, looking down at her as he spoke. "We both have history, but I think we're both ready to focus on the future. I mean," he faltered. "I'd like to stop holding on to the past."

She felt the breeze on her face as the bridge began to close. The ride was ending, but a new life was starting. She reached for his hand and held tight, looking up at him as the lights of the bridge flashed across his skin, red, yellow, green. He kissed her again, this kiss already more certain, more lingering and familiar. She leaned into the kiss, into him. She didn't worry about the bridge closing safely or anything going wrong. Instead she thought of the smell of his skin, the curve of his smile, the steady presence of him beside her. She sensed this was something she could count on, a bridge to take her somewhere she'd never been before, but couldn't wait to see.

EPILOGUE

January 7, 2011

Emily stood near the water, stamping her feet to keep warm, her eyes on the cluster of state officials and workers who were down on the bridge, officiating its dismantling. Over to the side, arcing across the sky above them, was the new bridge, an impressive and expensive structure that had been open a few months. She looked over at the new bridge and back to the old one, catching Kyle's eye and winking as she did. He winked back and turned to finish the conversation he was having.

Emily turned to the other ladies who had fought hard to save the bridge, making sure everything was on go for the old bridge to be salvaged. They had orchestrated a last-minute coup to save the structure, including the tender house, with big plans for it to be placed on a piece of land nearby. The idea was for the bridge to become a community gathering place. There was talk of future festivals and holiday celebrations for the residents and tourists. She had thrown herself into preserving the old bridge, working tirelessly to garner donations and solicit the needed help to physically move the structure to its new home when the state retired it today. It was good to honor the past, and Emily knew that.

Behind her she heard a cry that had become as familiar to her as her own voice. She turned around to find Claire carrying a crying child toward her. "There's Mommy," Claire was saying, pointing Emily out in the crowd. "There she is. See? I told you we'd find her."

Claire handed the little girl to Emily, who snuggled her daughter and covered her little cheek with kisses, then ruffled her red hair, which was no longer in the little ponytails she'd spent time on this morning. She didn't bother asking Claire what had happened.

"I swear," Claire said, leaning against a railing. "This is taking forever. Don't these guys know how cold it is out here? This child is cold. And so am I!"

Emily sighed and cast about for a solution. "Maybe you should just take her home with you and I could come get her later?"

"No way! You promised Amber a photo of her on that bridge."

"Amber and her obsession with history. I'm so glad she's majoring in it. Though who knows what she'll do besides teach. Bless her heart." She looked into her little girl's emerald green eyes, who studied her silently and intensely. She was past due for a nap and Emily hoped this wouldn't drag on much longer.

"Thanks again for being here today," she commented to Claire. "Where are Rick and the kids? Did they have enough of the cold and decide to go home?"

Claire waved her arm, indicating the area behind them where people were milling around. "They're around here somewhere. Trust me, they'll surface soon."

"Thanks so much for coming out."

"That's what friends are for. I knew you'd need my support. That big jerk down there is no help at all." She pointed at Kyle and giggled. Claire had forgiven Kyle gradually once Emily told her the rest of the story, the part that Kyle had never been able to share with her. She still loved to tease him but it was all in jest. The truth was, Claire and Kyle had finally bonded over their mutual loss, each one looking to the other to help them remember the remarkable girl who once graced their lives.

Kyle saw them looking at him and gesturing and walked over to make sure things were okay. "Are you sure we shouldn't get her out of this weather?" he asked, stooping down to kiss the little red-headed girl. "I'd hate for her to get sick."

He scooped his daughter out of Emily's arms. "Lily, Lily, Lily, you are Daddy's girl, aren't you?" he crooned, balancing her on his hip with the confidence and ease of an experienced dad. He put his arm around Emily and together they watched for a moment as the engineers scurried around, making the necessary notations and adjustments as they prepared to open the bridge one final time and then take it out of commission forever. Many of the former bridge tenders had gathered for one last ride, a sentimental occasion that had brought tears to more than one eye.

After that, the bridge would be pushed up the intracoastal by a barge and beached until the construction company they had hired could move it piece by piece to its new home. But as she watched, all Emily could think of was her late-night ride with this man who now stood by her side, this man she had fallen in love with, the man who had suggested they get married so Amber's little girl could be adopted by a mother and a father. It had all been so fast, and yet not once did it feel wrong. As the three of them stood there together, it felt very right indeed.

"You want to get the picture for Amber now?" Kyle whispered, interrupting her thoughts. "We better do it soon or we might not get it at all."

"Yeah," Emily said, feeling weepy and sentimental. She summoned Claire over to snap the photo, wishing Marta and Phil could be there, but Marta was on bed rest for her first child, a child, she had said often in the last few weeks, who would most certainly be an only child.

"I've heard that just because it happens with one doesn't mean it will happen again," Emily offered the last time she visited her friend, bearing her chicken salad and stacks of mindless magazines.

"Look, just because the baby fairy showed up at your house and dropped a gorgeous child on your doorstep doesn't mean you're in any position to be doling out helpful advice, Missy," Marta said, rolling over in bed. "We can't all be so blessed," she groaned as she positioned her girth.

Blessed. Once she had been blessed, then she wasn't. Then for so long she felt anything but. And now when someone used that word to describe her life it took her breath away. Not because she was surprised, but because it was true.

She took her place beside Kyle on the bridge and together they coaxed Lily to look at the camera, waving their arms and acting silly to get her to smile, generally looking like fools, but happy fools. Fools who had taken a chance on love again and found more than they bargained for. Though they couldn't have known what waited on the other side, they'd trusted the bridge to take them there.

RECIPES

"Meaning of Life" Chicken Salad

6 chicken breasts, cooked and shredded
1 1/2 cups mayonnaise
Salt
1 cup toasted pecans
1 1/2 cups red seedless grapes, cut in half

Combine mayonnaise and salt (to taste). Add shredded chicken with enough of the mayonnaise to cover, then add pecans and grapes. Serve at room temperature on a bed of lettuce or croissants.

"MIRACLE" CHOCOLATE CHIP MUFFINS

2 large eggs
2 cups sour cream
1 cup milk
3 1/2 cups all-purpose flour
4 Tbsp. sugar
2 tsp. baking powder
1 tsp. baking soda
1 tsp. salt
2 cups (1 12-ounce bag) chocolate chips

In a bowl, beat eggs. Stir in sour cream and milk. In a large bowl, combine flour, sugar, baking powder, baking soda, and salt. Pour egg mixture into flour mixture and stir just until moistened. Fold in chocolate chips. Spoon batter into greased muffin tin, filling cups three-quarters full. Bake in 400-degree oven for 20 to 25 minutes.

"COMFORT FOOD" CUSTARD PIE

1 unbaked pie shell
3 large eggs
1/2 cup sugar
1/2 tsp. salt
1/2 tsp. nutmeg
2 2/3 cup milk
1 tsp. pure vanilla extract

Preheat the oven to 350 degrees. Beat eggs slightly, then add sugar, salt, nutmeg, vanilla, and milk. Beat well and pour into the unbaked pie shell. Bake for 35 to 40 minutes. Remove from oven and cool. Sprinkle the top of pie with nutmeg and serve.

AUTHOR INTERVIEW

Marybeth, where did you get the idea for this book?

This book came from being a regular visitor to Sunset Beach, North Carolina, and being aware of the debate within the community about the pros and cons of a new bridge. I wanted to write about that debate and someone who gets sucked into it but is not really part of it. I also thought that the symbolism of the bridge would be so great to delve into.

Why have several of your books been set in Sunset Beach?

I just love it there. I say it's where my heart lives. While I'm not a resident, I am like Emily in that I fell in love with the place on a trip years ago. I still dream of owning a home there someday so I can spend more time there. In the meantime, I venture there in my mind each time I set a book there —

409

a mental vacation I take full advantage of!

Was there really a fight over replacing the bridge in Sunset Beach?

It was more a debate than a fight, but for the sake of the story I dramatized it a bit. People within the community definitely had views on whether or not the bridge should be replaced. There was, for the record, never a fire that couldn't be put out by fire trucks, but it could've happened. Some residents I interviewed were actually the ones who gave me the idea of a fire that happened at high tide so the fire trucks couldn't reach the island to put it out. That was always a danger and safety concern when the old bridge was in operation. I just made it happen in this story.

Where did the character of Kyle Baker/ Brady Rutledge come from?

He came from my love of old John Hughes movies. Every girl who saw *Sixteen Candles* was affected by the perfection that was Jake Ryan. And yet the actor who played him opted for an anonymous life away from Hollywood after making just a few films. When I read that about him I thought, *What would it be like for a girl who had idealized him as a teen to run across him years later in this com-*

410

pletely different setting where he's just trying to be a normal guy? And, thus, the character of Brady/Kyle was born in answer to that question. To put Emily in that rather surreal place was great fun for me and — I hope — for readers.

While Sunset Beach is a real setting, your books are fiction. Do you ever take liberties with the place?

Funny you should ask! I'm pretty meticulous about staying true to place and pointing to real landmarks that visitors can actually go and find should they want to. This is the first book that I took some creative license with the setting though. In the story, Emily and Ryan, and then Emily alone, visit a house that is falling into the ocean. That house is actually one beach over, at Ocean Isle Beach, North Carolina. But as I wrote this story I just couldn't shake the image of Ryan and Emily visiting this house, and how symbolic it was. There they are starting their marriage even as they're standing beside this collapsing house. Ultimately it is this house that is a touchstone for Emily and a place where she comes to understand her own journey. I had to leave the house in the story and alter the setting a bit. I hope the citizens of Sunset Beach and Ocean Isle will forgive me for playing with their geography. You can see the actual house — you just have to go one beach over to find it!

What happened to the old bridge? Is it really preserved for visitors?

The Old Bridge Preservation Society has created a park-like atmosphere near where the old bridge used to sit. You can walk on the bridge and go inside the tender house. They offer many special events and volunteers are there to share history and details about the bridge. For more information, visit www.oldbridgepreservationsociety.org.

What's next for you?

I've got a few more Sunset Beach ideas I'd love to write. Plus a lot more women's fiction up my sleeve. I hope to just keep telling stories!

DISCUSSION QUESTIONS

1. Why do you think Emily didn't immediately buy the house at Sunset Beach? Would you have waited or rushed out to fulfill your husband's wish?
2. Did you have a teenage film star crush? What would it be like to find him living an anonymous life in a small coastal North Carolina town?
3. How did Jeremiah 29:11 fit into Emily's life? Kyle's? Marta's? Amber's? How does it fit into yours?
4. Was Emily's involvement in Amber's life a risk? Why do you think she was drawn to the girl? Have you ever been compelled to reach out to someone in need of help, even though you barely knew her or him? Did you?
5. Was Emily right to leave the comment about the bridge on the state site?
6. How was Marta a good friend to Emily? If you have someone in your life like

Marta, send a handwritten note or card thanking them for being a good friend.

7. As you read the story, why did you think that Claire didn't like Kyle?

8. How did Ryan and Lily shape who Emily and Kyle became? Have you had a significant loss that shaped your life?

9. The bridge is symbolic for both holding on to the past and moving toward new beginnings. How is God at work in both?

10. In the end, Emily decides she's going to share with her father what she's learned about God — how He is the bridge we can rely on in our lives. How will this help her father? How has it helped her? How will seeing Him in this way help you?

ACKNOWLEDGMENTS

My thanks go out to . . .

My husband, Curt, and children, Jack, Ashleigh, Matthew, Rebekah, Bradley, and Annaliese. You all are my hope and future and I thank God for your love and support as I chase this dream of writing novels.

To my mom, who never fails to encourage me with her unwavering belief in me.

To the team at HarperCollins Christian, who made this book possible in so many ways.

To Nicci Jordan Hubert, who served as both editor and cheerleader. I don't think I'll ever forget our initial discussion about this book.

To the lovely folks from the Old Bridge Preservation Society who shared their information and experiences. You welcomed me into your home (Ann) and your cause. I am so glad you worked tirelessly to save the old bridge the way you did so we will all have it to enjoy and remember. I hope this book honors what you've done in some small way.

To Ariel Lawhon and Kimberly Brock, my She Reads team and dear friends, for aiding and abetting my particular brand of crazy. My life wouldn't be nearly as much fun without you in it.

To the book mavens of the Pelican Bookstore: Pat, Ann, and Suzanne. Your support is a mainstay and touchstone for me.

To my friends IRL (in real life), thank you for the long lunches and long phone conversations, and short messages and texts. It all serves to bolster me in this sometimes lonely occupation. Without you all, I'd be a hermit. I'm not even going to try and name names, but you know who you are.

And finally, to The Bridge, who takes me out of where I've been and shows me amazing new places waiting on the other side. Thank You for faithfully getting me where I need to go, and teaching me I can trust what's waiting on the other side. Because You are already there.

ABOUT THE AUTHOR

Marybeth Whalen is the wife of Curt and mom of six children. She is the cofounder of She Reads, an online book club focused on spotlighting the best in women's fiction. Marybeth is the author of *The Mailbox, She Makes It Look Easy, The Guest Book,* and *The Wishing Tree.* Marybeth spends most of her time in the grocery store but occasionally escapes long enough to scribble some words. She's always at work on her next novel. Marybeth and her family live in North Carolina. You can find her online at www.marybethwhalen.com.